There's No More Room in Hell

A Story of Survival

David Wilson

ISBN: 979-8-218-26325-6

DEDICATION

To all the readers who enjoy the subgenre of horror that is of the 'undead', and to the man who started it and created fans out of all of us, Mr. George A. Romero.

CONTENTS

ACKNOWLEDGMENTS

In 1968 John A. Russo, Russell Streiner, and George A. Romero introduced us to a new subgenre of horror. Without ever calling them 'zombies', George Romero created a huge fanbase to what would later be referred to as the 'Zombie Apocalypse'. His work would spur countless screenplays, comic books, graphic novels, and movies, all undoubtedly inspired by his work. Mixing horror with political and social topics of the day, something which I try to do in some of my books as well, George first brought us *Night of the Living Dead*. Several more in the series would follow in the years ahead, with my personal favorite in the series being 1985's *Day of the Dead*, not at all intending to downplay the masterpiece that was to become the 2nd in the series, *Dawn of the Dead*.

Many people have been inspired by the works of George Romero, however, there will forever only be one master of the horror genre, and I wish to give him the credit that he so deserves.

PREFACE

It only took twenty short years for everything to turn into absolute chaos. In actuality, it was much shorter when you consider the sequence of events, only to ultimately arrive where I am now, and how the world looks today.

It was inevitable when you think about it. We didn't take my generation's "first global pandemic" seriously, treating it as a political battle instead of what it truly was. So, when the next one came along, only two short years after the last was declared over and done with, there was just no hope at all for humanity, or civilization.

It's really quite sad. We had the chance to step up our game during SARS-CoV-2, affectionately known as COVID-19, and take it seriously, or at least respect each other's opinions in dealing with it. But we were too stupid and pig-headed. Instead of listening to the health community, we each chose a political side and stood our ground. Some believing in the vaccines, and others that didn't. Instead of treating it as a war against an invisible enemy, we treated it as a war against each other. Before we'd conquered it, we lost interest and patience, and in turn we left 'bodies' on the battlefield in the form of those who succumbed to the virus, along with our health care officials and first responders. We should have been smart enough to put politics aside and fought the war together. But we didn't.

And from all that, we should have learned.

There were no surprises that when SARs-CfR-5 broke out and overtook the nations around the globe, we were completely screwed. Nobody took it seriously, nor did we use any precautions whatsoever. We were still reeling from the three-plus years that we had endured COVID. It was all simply too soon. And, again, we hadn't learned anything. Additionally, when this one hit, it hit hard. We just weren't prepared for another serious upper-respiratory illness coupled with the gastrointestinal problems that it caused.

Not to mention there was the problem of where this one had originated. A chemically generated parasite that attacked the wheat fields in all of Eastern Europe. You can probably guess how that occurred with the war that had been taking place there during that time, and which side decided to use the chemicals.

Eastern Europe was the major wheat supplier to most countries, so anything organically created from the wheat that was growing in that area ended up infecting millions. Pasta lovers were dropping like dead flies. The parasite was tough, too. No amount of processing, cooking, or boiling could kill it. Nobody was immune. It hit hard and fast all around the world.

The first symptoms were the typical, flu-like stuff. That, along with the severe stomach cramping. A fever followed, and this is where it caught everyone by surprise. The experts believed that once the patient's core temperature reached 106 degrees Fahrenheit, and the sustained hyperpyrexia occurred, that the person was basically a goner. Only, that didn't turn out to be the case. This was simply the turning point where the infected only appeared to have died. And, in most if not every case, the individual fell into a temporary coma. Many were buried prematurely when the physicians could no longer detect a pulse, and all body functions had essentially appeared to cease.

It wasn't until after the bodies were piling up so high inside of the mortuaries and crypts that the first person regained consciousness. The crypt keepers must have shit themselves when the first ones got up and pounded on the door to be let out. Their body temperatures were now above 110 degrees and holding. No amount of treatment, or ice, would bring them back down. They were there to stay. At least, stay until the body entirely broke down, which took time. A lot of time.

Plus, they weren't exactly "zombies" in the true sense of the word. I mean, they were technically still alive, they just weren't able to function. The fever was destroying their brains. By the time they regained consciousness, most about a week after being declared 'dead', they'd lost many of their motor functions. They could no longer talk, let alone have any power of thought or deliberation. They couldn't relay their thoughts or most feelings, although, they did seem to recognize those who they were closest to in 'life'. Either that, or they were simply seeking attention from anyone.

And, basically, that was their purpose at that point and until the end. They were like pets, the same as dogs and cats that required attention. It wasn't like it was in the movies. The "zombie apocalypse" didn't necessarily create violent creatures. They did not need to feed, nor did they display any symptoms of hunger. They weren't fast, either. They lumbered clumsily. More like George Romero's creatures from 'Night of the Living Dead', they bumped into things while following you around, only seemingly seeking to still be 'loved'. The obvious problem with this was that they were still sick with the infection. And a highly contagious infection at that.

A nickname was given to the infected, "walkers." Because that's all they could do, walk, and really nothing else.

Also, unlike most movies, they didn't necessarily 'bite'. Although, by the same token, again much like a hyperactive dog or cat at play, they did nip. So, now you had two problems. Not only could they transmit their disease through close contact by airborne means, but they also could transmit the sickness by 'nipping' you if they broke the skin.

About the only thing the creatures retained from their normal existence was their basic tendencies. Meaning, if you'd been a timid or polite person, you became a zombie that was easier to handle. If you were a dickhead in life, you were most likely a dickhead zombie, and a bit harder to deal with.

Zombies with attitudes. Go figure.

So, as you can imagine, in the beginning, this all led to many issues. Because they didn't do what we'd been taught they would through film and comic books, society didn't know how to deal with them. They didn't intentionally try to kill us, so in turn we decided that we couldn't just kill them, either. Plus, for all technical purposes, they weren't 'dead', so their families still wanted their loved ones around. So, they kept them.

By the way, this was a truly bad idea.

First off, because people hadn't dealt with our newest pandemic correctly this led to quick, and terrible results. Nobody was masking or social distancing from the creatures, so people were becoming ill at accelerated rates. Entire households were becoming infected and required to be locked down. People weren't even putting masks on the creatures themselves in the most basic of precautions. Plus, those right-wing fanatical idiots that were telling people not to take precautions at all, and still believed that the infection was some sort of government lie, weren't helping matters a bit.

It wasn't until about a year had gone by that people stopped listening to both the radicals and the politicians and began using some common sense. And, at first, it appeared to level off the situation. People finally figured out on their own that the only way to keep a creature was to segregate them and use basic precautions, meaning wearing masks in the home if they wanted to keep them around, and muzzling the infected so they couldn't nip. But, by that time half of the neighborhoods across America had already been wiped out.

And this time around it wasn't a shortage of toilet paper or canned food, it was a shortage of caution tape to keep people away from the residences that refused to use any precautions in dealing with their infected family members.

This all led to the next issue; how to deal with households that were infected. I mean, it was easy to dispose of them after they died 'naturally'. On average, it took around two years for the fever to cause the body to decay to the point that it simply dropped. And by then they smelled pretty awful. As a result, there was also a shortage of household air fresheners before too long.

When an entire household was infected, there was the need to deal with disposing of all of them, and quickly before they 'wandered' outside and became someone else's problem.

This steamrolled to the next big headache; the protestors. Just like with any other issue that people had no business sticking their noses into, there were the groups that wanted to fight for the 'creature's rights'. Simply dispatching a loved one on your own, or by somebody else, became an illegal act, written and enacted into law as a result of public pressure. Although, that didn't stop everyone as you can well imagine.

But legally, there were problems. Again, the politicians showed no signs of a backbone to the protestors. So, as you can surmise 'other' ideas quickly evolved. "Exterminators" is what they were called. Companies sprung up like head shops, each promising to humanely dispatch your infected loved one. That is, if you chose that route rather than wait for nature to take its course.

The legal businesses required you to bring your 'zombie' to one of their locations. Their establishments very much resembled the little convenient medical centers that you found on every street corner. They were relatively clean places with trained medical staff who would euthanize the creature and dispose of the body in an incinerator. Of course, these were very expensive, and insurance companies obviously fought to avoid having to foot the bills.

So, as a result, there were also the 'questionable' companies that popped up. You know, like "Triple-A Dispatch Service." Named so they'd be listed first in the phonebooks, that kind of thing. These were the greaseballs that would offer to show up at your home and deal with your problem on-site. They were messy, as well as highly illegal. Most of the time they'd simply build a bonfire in your backyard or pile them up in an unmarked box truck and dump them at the local landfill way after dark. These companies were hard to catch, too. They'd advertise on social media and once the cops were onto them, they'd just change their company name, create a new magnetic sign for their vehicles and get a new IP address, all the while keeping their business up and running.

To make matters worse, the punishment for these scumbags after being caught was no more than a slap on the wrist. So, there wasn't any deterrent for the ones who were getting away with it. And they cost nearly as much as the legal businesses did. Unless you had an internet coupon code or a connection that would hook you up, you were out some serious cash.

So, the cost to keep and dispose of the creatures, not to mention the shady companies ultimately brought up another issue, the illegal zombie trade. A lot of these exterminators would simply promise to dispose of your loved one, only to trade them off. And, for what you might ask? These things certainly had no skills to speak of. No practical use whatsoever. Oh, I suppose there were those 'dickhead' ones that could be prodded into fighting, so there were the underground and highly illegal "zombie fighting" clubs. Plus, we won't even go into what the street brothels attempted to do in Vegas. That was just disgusting. Disease transmission was very high in both arenas. So, the slave trade, which insanely enough was more popular than

Bitcoin at the time, was dealt with fairly stringently and came with significant penalties.

Still, with all the disease-carrying creatures and high rates of transmission, the protestors still attempted to fight for more rights for the infected. Licensed "daycare" centers popped up, which were highly unregulated I might add, but still paid for by the government. Families with creatures could get state and federal aid for each one they kept. More food stamps and other welfare-related relief programs were created for families of the infected. Although, for the life of me I don't know why seeing that these things didn't eat anything. More stimulus checks got sent out to households and were being passed out like candy. Just some real, crazy shit.

One creature was even elected to Congress in Georgia as the write-in favorite. Although, this really didn't surprise anyone.

With these things 'living' longer and longer, there didn't seem to be an end to their growing numbers. And how you might ask, did these things manage to hang on? Well, that's another interesting little tidbit. You see, again, we learned nothing from COVID. Of course, by the time the vaccination for SARs-CfR-5 was approved by the FDA sometime in the second year, we were right back to our same old habits. There were those who believed it was a cure, versus those that felt it would kill us. Either that or they believed it would eventually cause the growth of a third arm or an extra testicle.

Well, as usual, both sides were wrong. The truth was the vaccination did neither. What it did do, though, was prolonged the length of time it took for the decay to destroy the body and brain cells. Instead of two years, they could go on for several before they dropped over. It ended up slowing the necrosis and permanently lowered their temperatures by just a degree or two. This allowed the blood to flow freely, as the heart muscle function was also affected, and it slowed the inevitable coagulation that would occur naturally as the heart slowed over time. With the vaccine it was no longer an issue surrounding the fever, it was the eventual decay of the other organs from the illness that ultimately caused their 'final' death.

So, the conundrum then became; how long did you want these creatures to last? Did you want the exterminators to rid you of the problem expeditiously, or did you want them to 'die' naturally over the course of two years? Or did you want to provide them a vaccine that would keep them upright for several years while you prepared your final "goodbyes," and collected as much as you could in welfare benefits along the way?

Oh, and just an FYI; the zombie traders all voted for the latter choice so that they could collect the illegal welfare benefits themselves. Another perk of the trade industry, when they could get away with it.

Of course, the battle remained highly political over which choice was the correct one, rather than common sense prevailing in any way. Hence why we were ultimately doomed rather than having the brains to put a quick end to the situation as we should have. Instead of just dealing with the issue at the onset, we caved to all the politicians and protestors, and ultimately, we lost the battles entirely.

So, to continue, spotting one that was wandering among us during the gestation period was pretty simple. There was the flushing of the skin, the perspiring as their fever worsened, and the whites of their eyes were turning blood-red. Not to mention, it did affect their intestines too, so there was the rushing to the restrooms quite often. If somebody suddenly bolted in public, you took warning. Thank goodness that after waking from the coma they didn't still have that particular symptom.

From the onset of the fever, they had about two-to-three weeks before they dropped over into their brief coma. And, if that occurred in the public's eye, then the panic would follow. The cops, firefighters, and EMS attendants didn't want to touch them, and the hospitals were full beyond capacity.

The smarter individuals who caught the disease knew enough to stay at home once their symptoms began. This is also when decisions had to be made. Ride it out for the short term and let your family decide or get a shot and last a little longer. Or simply call the exterminator right away. Suicide rates were fairly high, too, as you can well imagine.

Oh yeah, and, of course, the 'gun control' issue sparked up again during all this. The protestors wanted more gun control and fewer suicides, along with the welfare benefits. Not to mention there were those family members who felt that assisted suicide was the way to go. Gun sales soared, along with certain drugs that could be obtained on the black market to assist you with a quick death. The little black pill was popular, and also very hard to come by.

So, just a bit more on the silly laws that were created. In the beginning, it became illegal to take your zombie out into the public. If you were caught leading one around for any reason you were quickly jailed, and your family member was dispatched at an extermination center. As you can probably imagine, the protestors had issues with this too. And, around year four, they won their court battle. You could then bring your 'pet' everywhere with you as long as you were both masked, they had on a designer muzzle, and you socially distanced yourself from others. Your zombie had to be under the owner's control at all times, either by voice or leash. Although, the protestors fought against the leash laws, too. Luckily, they lost that battle.

Businesses did have the ability to refuse service if you tried to bring your zombie inside one of their establishments. Most restaurants wouldn't allow them, citing the fact that the creatures didn't eat anyway. Some simply caved to the public pressure and went back to outside seating, and special areas designated for your zombie. Airlines didn't like them at all. It was when they tried to tout them as 'service zombies' that most finally had enough of them wandering around in public. It was around year seven that the laws were finally rescinded, and you had to keep your zombie at home at all times, or in one of the licensed daycare centers. But you had to make certain that you picked them up by 5:00 p.m. or face penalties.

America wasn't the only country with issues. Canada had outlawed the keeping of the creatures entirely. Because of this, they obviously had the better extermination centers, paid for by the government. If you were caught attempting to cross the border into Canada with a creature, you were immediately arrested and deported while your loved one was seized and destroyed right there at the border station by a mobile unit. This obviously caused increased tensions between the two countries, and the border was eventually closed entirely.

East and West Germany also conflicted on how to handle the problem, and the wall was built back into place during years nine and ten.

It was rumored that smaller countries like Cuba and Jamaica, and all others, simply couldn't deal with the infection. With their rather small populations to begin with, they eventually all became infected and 'died' off. This was also rumored to have occurred in every South American country, as well as everything from Mexico south, which killed the American drug trade with virtually nothing coming across the borders anymore. All of the chronic, hardcore drug users that didn't end up killing themselves each learned how to grow marijuana fairly quickly because that's truly all they had left and knew how to grow.

It was difficult to determine just what occurred in most other countries, as everyone had their own ideas on how to handle the situation. And nobody was talking to each other. Communications failed globally with everyone believing they had the answer, and 'your' answer wasn't as good as 'theirs'. Country leaders battled, and summits were canceled. Finally, everyone stopped answering their telephones altogether.

It was ultimately the Russians that screwed it up for

everybody.

Whereas the chemicals that had caused the parasite had been generated in their labs and given the fact that it was discovered that they'd been playing with more than just the one variety in their test tubes, the Soviet Union ended up having more problems than most. It seemed they'd been mixing some 'other' ingredients together and had been using their own people as guinea pigs. They'd actually concocted some pretty nasty stuff, worse than what drifted into the wheat fields when it had initially been released into the wind.

You see, rebels had attempted to seize one of the larger laboratories in Moscow, and during the fighting, the sealed containers with the virus had been damaged. As the story goes, a certain sect of their own population had grown weary of their government over the years, and tired of their lies and propaganda. In return, the rebels had invaded the laboratory and released not only the SARs-CfR-5 virus but also had taken anything else they'd discovered and held onto it for a while. After the initial wave of the virus had wafted into the wheat fields and had taken effect, meaning that once the wheat had been distributed internationally and infected many populations around the world, the rebels then decided to let the rest go and dumped it into their own drinking water. The results obviously weren't good.

Eastern Europe had already been through some hard times, seeing that Russian vodka had a primary ingredient of wheat. As a result, most of their population had already been infected, but now they had even nastier stuff in the life liquid that they were drinking instead of the vodka. Of course, their government then saw this as an opportunity rather than a problem.

The Russian government, as a result of all the wars they'd caused and countries they'd invaded, was losing ground fast. Their disregard for their own soldiers, not to mention the virus itself, had depleted their numbers significantly. Other nations like Belarus, who had formerly provided soldiers to the Russian army, had given up on that idea, having had their own issues to deal with. So, the Russians ultimately came up with the terrible idea to attempt to genetically enhance the creatures into fighting machines, encouraged by the problems the rebels had caused. The result being that their creatures did, in fact, turn out to be nastier than everyone else's. Unfortunately, this only encouraged their government to play around even more with the formula inside the existing labs.

What they ended up with were creatures that attacked, bit, clawed, and ate their victims. But they still couldn't be taught how to use weapons effectively, and very much couldn't be controlled, let alone answer to simple orders. They didn't see an 'enemy', they just went after whatever, and whomever they encountered. At first, this was fine with the Russians, as they felt they had created Kamikaze suicide squads. That is until the creatures became so chaotic that they began attacking their own 'masters', and then things spiraled completely out of control.

It didn't take long before the Russians decided that rather than admit defeat, they needed to eradicate the problem entirely. Not only for themselves but also for the rest of the world too. Fearing that if not, and in their continued state of paranoia, other countries would take advantage and modify their creatures, and then point them in the direction of the Soviet Union's border.

So, nearly 17 years after it all began, and out of severe paranoia the Russians decided to launch everything they had. And, with no real hard target, they pointed their weaponry literally in all directions. Luckily, though, their munition supplies had severely dwindled, but they still caused catastrophic damage. Not to mention the nukes they'd kept for themselves and detonated over their own land after launching them in an effort to eradicate the problem, while the ones in power planned to retreat underground for the next thousand-or-so years waiting for the air to clear.

America, and a few other countries, did what they could

in the form of countermeasures. Although, with everyone being distracted with their own problems, and not having prepared for what the Russians had planned to do, they had little effect other than to deflect the nukes, which was the primary objective. Nothing was left for the regular mid-to-long-range series of missiles that were landing everywhere. The Russians were firing them off randomly like someone pointing fireworks into the air to see where they'd land. The short-range stuff took out most of Central, Northern, Southeastern and Western Europe. The morons even destroyed their best friends in China, while the prevailing south winds allowed the nuclear fallout to do the rest. The mid-range stuff took its toll on Africa, Australia, and surrounding smaller countries.

America was hit hard, too. Most of New England and Alaska became large craters when the Russians aimed both east and west, and there was random large-scale damage throughout the central part of the country as well. All-in-all it was fairly devastating, and social societies were either eliminated or collapsed during the ensuing anarchy and chaos. We were in bad enough shape as it was, but this certainly did us in. As electric grids failed and all forms of media had no way of getting information out, the masses experienced an uprising and complete civil unrest. As societies often do; rioting, looting, and crime became rampant. Supply chains were attacked and ultimately non-existent as all forms of transportation ceased to function. The economy collapsed and governments dissolved, martial law failed, and it truly became every man, woman, and child for themselves.

In the aftermath, the doomsday preppers obviously became the ones that managed to hold out the longest and had some of the skills needed to survive. Some maintained their individuality, holding their own, while others grouped and created new mini-societies. Regardless, everyone was protective of their own, and it became too risky to associate with anyone that you were not familiar with. With mass communications down and only short-wave still in existence it became hard to determine where, if any, safe areas were located. Groups began using the airwaves to lure in those who may have something that they wanted, as it became difficult to find an area that hadn't already been scavenged. Plus, it simply wasn't safe to be out there searching for stuff. As you could well imagine, it became the 'living' that was far more dangerous than the infected were, and are now.

Of course, everything is all just rumors now. Speculation as to who, and what is still alive and functioning. One of the stories that had circulated while the remaining cities were falling apart, and the airspace was in threat of being closed entirely to travel, was that several organized flights to the north and south poles had been arranged. Many were believed to be fleeing to the coldest areas, believing that the dead and diseased couldn't survive in those climates. The problem was, nothing could survive there, and nobody was offering to continually bring supplies to those areas. Living and surviving there would've been hard, if not entirely impossible.

The other problem with that idea was that as far as the infected were concerned, the 'survivors' were fundamentally wrong in their assumptions that if the infected were to wander to the Poles, they'd simply freeze to 'death'. But, because the infection elevated the victim's body temperature, this ultimately allowed the creatures to not only survive but also thrive in the cold. So, it only took one person who had the virus to ruin it all for everybody. As the story was told to me, all 'life' ended shortly thereafter in the colonies that attempted to establish themselves in the Poles.

So, you might ask, where did I ultimately end up? Well, my friends, my theory, right or wrong, was that I needed to go someplace where the infected couldn't follow, and other people were scarce too. Someplace off the mainland.

So, that's what I did.

There's No More Room in Hell

A Story of Survival

David Wilson

Chapter 1
FLOATING ON THE OCEAN

At first, it wasn't difficult to find a sailing vessel to fit his needs. Even after the tsunamis struck, following the bombings, there were still plenty of boats perched in the dockyards that had survived. Not so much in the water, as many had been thrown ashore, battered, and torn apart. If not during the first wave, then in the weather that followed in the short term. Violent storms battered the coastlines far into the mainland for months. But still, as long as you could find the equipment needed to manhandle the vessels that had been stored and survived, some even still encased in shrink-wrap, then you ended up with a pretty good boat. In fact, Kirk was on his third vessel over the same number of years now, each time having found something larger and more suitable, yet fairly easy to handle by himself.

Of course, in the years since the bombings, boats have become harder to find with most by now having been scavenged. Anything that had been in the water that may have remained afloat had now been taken, or simply weathered and sunk. Either that or, as mentioned, destroyed right away when the big waves came. Parts still remain fairly simple to locate. That is if it's safe to dock where the parts can be found and you're willing to dive into unsafe waters to scrounge for them on boats that are sitting on the bottom.

Kirk's boat now was a 35-foot, full-keel cutter. With a center cockpit and aft berth below deck, it surely had been quite the expensive sailboat for someone during its time. Kirk kept it clean and neat, too. Storing as much as he could, he did his best to keep it stuffed full of necessities such as food, weapons, fishing, and navigational equipment. The vessel has a 110-horsepower diesel engine for backup. However, it's nearly impossible to find fuel now. For this reason, Kirk keeps extra sails stored in the stern just in case his deployed sails are damaged, and he always has plenty of extra rope.

The only real problem was with the name of the boat. The "Rotten Banana." A terrible name for a seaworthy vessel. It wasn't even yellow, or brown. It was tan and white.

Kirk's original theory was that possibly the infected couldn't handle the warmer climates, just the opposite of what everyone else had been thinking. He theorized that if the infected's body temperatures were forced above the limit of the fever, potentially they couldn't *survive* in the scorching tropic temperatures. He also had theorized that now, at 42 years of age, and a good-looking and fit 42 at that, he was going to find an island somewhere in the south pacific and *retire*. That idea, he came to realize quickly, was far too grandiose. Not to mention, he hadn't been alone in his thought process. Plus, he'd been incorrect in his theory. Others were seeking the tropical life too, not realizing that the infected could also continue to exist in that climate as well, just as good as they could in the cold. The virus was tough, and the infected ones were virtually tougher.

Another concern for Kirk was that there were ocean pirates lurking everywhere, the same as the street gangs on the mainland. All seeking to pillage whatever didn't belong to them and kill the ones they stole it from. Hunkering down in one location would potentially make Kirk an easy target for them. So now, he simply remained on the move.

Going up and down from the Florida Keys to as far north on the Atlantic as he could. Although, with much of New England having been made into a crater by the bombs, he typically didn't venture beyond Massachusetts. He was far more careful when he neared the Florida coast, especially during the hurricane seasons, which had altered in their time of year since the bombings. The devastation had resulted in major climate changes around the globe. Nothing was as it had been anymore.

Very often he was forced to hunker down in a bay or marina when the weather was foul. Although, it was difficult to hide his upright vessel among other half-sunken wrecks. And, with this now being nearly his fourth year of traveling up and down the eastern coastline, he knew all the safe, and not-so-safe marinas and yacht clubs to tuck into. Although, that was subject to changes too.

Kirk only docked when it was absolutely necessary, though. On most of his supply runs he anchored out and used a small, pontoon dinghy to motor into the mainland. The tiny craft having both a gas and a separate electric motor. But he never stepped on land before putting a drone up and scanning the area. First, the area surrounding his sailboat to make certain that no others were lurking. The drone was very useful in that his radar and other electronic gadgets mounted in the cockpit and below decks don't always paint a true and accurate picture. The pirates had simply become too sneaky.

Once he was satisfied that the location where he'd anchored was relatively safe, he'd scan the mainland. His electric drone had the ability to send back a signal as far away as 12 kilometers. And, with Kirk having equipped his vessel with various electric generating sources that included a small solar, wind, and hydro setup, battery charging typically wasn't an issue.

Once on the mainland, he'd always be required to limit himself to what was close by and easily accessible on foot. Operational motor vehicles were no longer just parked and waiting to be used. If they weren't being driven by the land gangs, they'd long since been scavenged for the gas or other parts necessary to keep other junkers running. And, unless Kirk was truly desperate to find something in particular, he didn't remain on the mainland for more than a few hours at a time, and never overnight. If he thought he was in a productive area, he might remain anchored and go back and forth for a day or two, but for no more than that out of fear of being spotted on the mainland, or his sailboat being discovered parked on the ocean.

He also didn't necessarily use the drone to scan the mainland for good supply spots. That was always hit or miss. And no matter how many times he went up and down the coast there was always something to be found, or not. The drone was used primarily to locate unfriendlies. That, and packs of the infected. Which, slow or not, it wasn't a good idea to be somewhere where they could wander up and overtake you. They were highly contagious, and if two or three got a hold of you while you were reaching for something, you were most likely in a lot of trouble. You didn't need to be in their personal space for too long before catching something you didn't want or being nipped if they managed to get a grip on you.

Of the two choices, walking dead or living people, he'd rather encounter one of the infected. Generally, you could see or hear them coming and avoid them. Whereas, with the living, you were always in jeopardy of being ambushed or overpowered. Kirk had experienced too many 'close encounters' and had nearly lost everything more than once, including his life.

When the coast was clear, so to speak, obviously food was at the top of his list. And it was becoming very scarce. But you had to keep looking, as seafood typically requires something to go with it. Although Kirk did eat quite well on the various and unlimited sources of fish in the ocean. Swordfish was his favorite as long as it came with some sort of seasoning, a side dish, and a good bottle of wine. With this combination, he was happy. Although, there had been many times when these weren't available, and the meal was bland. Plus, he absolutely hated sushi. Right now, he had a limited supply of stuff on board to make the meals tasty. Not to mention, you pretty much had to settle for seafood to achieve any form of protein. Nothing of the sort on land was available anymore. In fact, animals of any kind were basically extinct, as Kirk hadn't seen any in quite a while, except for maybe birds. But he wasn't certain that they weren't infected too, and he didn't feel like taking a chance on the seagulls that very often circled his sailboat or hitched a ride.

The fact that he couldn't even trust a bird obviously added to the loneliness Kirk felt at times, being on the ocean by himself in a relatively small space. There simply wasn't anyone left, or anyone that could be trusted, to take on as a passenger or mate. Infected people were dangerous. Live people were scarce, and even more dangerous.

Kirk did have an electronic, robotic dog for a while. He'd found one inside of a university campus he'd searched at the Myrtle Beach Center off the coast of South Carolina. It didn't quite resemble a dog, only in that it had four robotic 'legs'. Otherwise, it looked like something built from an erector set. Not to mention it looked quite expensive. It only lasted a couple of months before the salty ocean air corroded the electrodes, and one afternoon it launched itself off the bow and sunk. It was too bad, really. Kirk had even named the little metal guy 'spot'.

It was for this same reason that Kirk hadn't pointed himself towards Japan and braved the open ocean to see if he could locate one of the fabled 'AI' robotic women that he'd seen on YouTube before the internet had crashed permanently. It was rumored that they'd created an entirely electronic, synthetic, latex, and frighteningly lifelike female sexbot. Complete with the power of independent speech, thought, and the ability to learn. Not to mention the lifelike features and hauntingly accurate sexual organs. What a shame that would have been if he'd had the ability to locate one just to have her jump overboard once the salty air corroded her computerized brain. He wouldn't even have had the ability to keep a fake woman on board! Kirk chuckled to himself at the thought as he stood at the helm of the wheel mounted on deck, enjoying the warm breeze and smelling the ocean air.

Not to mention, as far as Japan, the trip wouldn't have been worth it. He knew that if anyone was left in Japan, which was unlikely after the bombings, they'd probably already scoffed up all the available models in exchange for the real women who'd most likely only been complaining about the inconvenience of the nuclear winter they'd most likely been experiencing. Kirk chuckled again to his own thoughts as he navigated the seas that were calm this day.

YouTube had also been the resource in which Kirk had learned all about sailing, not having been a sailor before everything had turned to shit. In fact, he never owned a boat before it all happened.

Before the internet finally crashed for the final time, he spent hours learning the necessities, knowing well he'd probably be spending the remainder of his life on the high seas. Hours and hours of watching professional videos and amateur how-to shorts on sailing, navigation, deep sea fishing, and weather charting. Not that any of it made him an expert. However, that, and just getting on the ocean and doing it had made him fairly good at it. Possibly even an expert.

The cockpit on his sailboat resembled a room at the Kennedy Space Center with all the electronics, radar, and navigational equipment he'd scavenged. That, along with a compass, the second interior steering wheel to his rudder, and all the radio equipment. With modern communications now gone, he'd resorted to the ham system and short-wave citizen band radios that the living were all using again. He scanned and monitored frequencies to pick up on the local conversations, and to help warn him against going on shore whenever he overheard chatter. When he heard voices on the short wave that he suspected were other scavengers, land gangs, or ocean pirates close by, he'd avoid them.

He also monitored AM radio channels and scanned both AM and FM for anything. Although, if and when anything was heard, it was usually untrustworthy gibberish and only seeking to achieve in luring suckers in, only to be ambushed and robbed, if not outright killed.

Kirk had become quite cunning and cautious. If not, he surely would have been murdered long ago. Plus, he knew he was sitting on a bounty with his sailing vessel and cashé. Among all of the navigational equipment and storage of food products, he also had a good supply of various weaponry that he wasn't about to part with. He had several handguns and rifles that he either had owned in his past life or managed to find with some luck when searching private residences along the coastline. He'd also scored a re-load kit and materials he'd found in a gun shop in Virginia. Most looters and scavengers didn't think or put the energy into reloading. They were only looking for the bullets that were ready to fire. Once again, he had to thank the internet for teaching him how to reload his own ammunition, as he'd nearly lost a couple of fingers in his first few attempts on his own.

His favorite weapons, though, were his crossbow and longbow. Nothing on the internet had taught him the skills he now had with them; aiming at colorful party balloons bobbing up and down on the waves of the water had. With both the target and the boat moving, he'd taught himself to be a very good archer, which also led to him being an excellent shot with a firearm. And, with many brands of arrows having the ability to float on the water, this had become an excellent time-consuming hobby of his. He'd even become good enough that when his patience was cooperating, and the seas were calm, he could spear any fish that swam near the surface or jumped out of the ocean. And voila! Dinner!

Life had become a combination of sailing, cautiously scavenging, and passing the time listening to the airwaves and fishing. Not to mention, his DVD collection and never-ending selection of movies that he enjoyed during long nights spent in his water-bound prison cell.

Which is how Kirk felt at times.

Chapter 2
PLOTTING A COURSE

Unfortunately, YouTube hadn't taught Kirk how to avoid seasickness. And today the seas were choppy, and his stomach was reminding him of that fact. One would have thought by now that his guts would be accustomed to any less-than-desirable weather. But the truth was, he was just prone to having a queasy stomach. It had stormed during the overnight and his guts were taking a beating. Even though daybreak had brought the sunshine back, he'd avoided breakfast until he felt a little better.

According to his charts, he was once again nearing Chesapeake Bay traveling south, having come from what was left of the New England area. He contemplated whether or not to enter the bay and head toward Baltimore. A risky venture, no doubt, whereas if he were to encounter unfriendlies in the waters between the Bay and the Inner Harbor area nearer Baltimore City, he'd have a difficult time escaping. Especially if some type of ambush were waiting somewhere in between. He'd been chased out of the bay before, and going underneath the Bay Bridge, which was still partially intact, was tricky. An ambush was almost certainly imminent if you didn't choose the right route. But the risk could oftentimes be worth the reward. The problem being these waters weren't navigated by those who weren't seaworthy. Those with little to no experience didn't often make it out alive. He'd have to think about this one for a while before deciding to brave the Bay or not.

Kirk generally tried to keep land in his view as he navigated the East Coast. Today, he was in his little wheelhouse and noticed by the use of his charts that he was passing just off of from Assateague Island when his radio picked up a broadcast from the mainland. The AM station was staticky.

"(static)…Safety awaits you…We're a group of survivors that have set up an encampment in Snow Hill…(static)…Our walls are guarded, and the virus doesn't exist here…Food and fresh water…(static)…"

He smirked and shook his head, forgetting about his seasickness for a moment. Kirk had heard this broadcast before. He knew it was a ruse. A trick to get innocent, naïve sailors to fall for it, if there were still any left. He knew what was waiting for them as he'd managed a couple of years back to get in close enough to put the drone over their compound. He'd caught a glimpse of the savages before they noticed the little flying machine overhead and began throwing stones and taking potshots with their primitive weaponry. Kirk had seen inside the walls that were constructed of telephone poles and metal roofing material that spanned about a half-block or so. Inside was the street gang of cannibals. Many of whom were infected, no doubt. He'd also noticed a good deal of dead bodies. Not entirely intact bodies, either.

They were a group of maybe twenty-five to thirty men, women, and unfortunately, children who'd already ravaged whatever they'd managed to find in their immediate area. They'd been utilizing the airwaves to attempt to bring in more victims that they could attack and take whatever wasn't theirs. Kirk assumed that this particular group hadn't any working vehicles or fuel, and most likely no modern projectile weapons. Just a few junk black powder rifles that shot pebbles and close-contact weapons like knives and clubs.

And, again, he'd assumed cannibalism because, along with the bodies, he'd spied something on the drone's camera. In the corner of one of the metal walls was quite a pile of bones. Either that or they were the bones of their own that had either been killed, eaten, or just eventually rotted away after being infected. Still, most likely cannibalism whereas they were *hiding* the bones and bodies inside the walls rather than scattering them outside where anyone approaching might take caution. Or at least taken them further away whereas the smell had to be entirely unbearable. Another indication that the ones still walking upright were probably infected and they just didn't care.

As Kirk caught another gust of wind in his sails, he thought about the depravity of the radio broadcast. He also thought about the fact that no matter how lonely he may be feeling at times, being out on the open ocean was still far better than anything that awaited him on dry land now. Or, at least as far as he knew there was nothing better to be found anymore.

At least the broadcast let him know exactly where he was. He glanced down at his compass and then checked the paper charts he'd laid out. He was right at the mouth of the bay now. It wouldn't be long before he'd be rounding the horn and find himself at the Bay Bridge.

He glanced up at the clear skies, it was nearing noon. He decided to slow up and wait it out here while he made his decision. Either to go under, or more appropriately find a way through the bridge, or continue south towards Florida. He could just simply spend the day getting just a bit closer and monitoring the airwaves. Or possibly he should anchor off Fisherman's Island near Cape Charles, motor in with the dinghy, and put the drone up. He could also fly the drone over the bridge and see where the safest spot to cross would be during this trip, as circumstances could have changed since he was last in the area. And then, he could continue on. Too many thoughts, too many possibilities. There were places along the bay that he really wanted to check out. Places that he could easily hide the sailing vessel and see what there was to see, and possibly scavenge.

Kirk thought to himself that maybe he could go up the Potomac River a distance before encountering another bridge that was showing on the map and see what may still be there. He hadn't done that yet. He knew that he didn't want to go anywhere near Baltimore again. Not after last time, and the savages he barely escaped from there. Baltimore was still a rough city, even today.

Kirk squinted while looking at his charts and he noticed an area near Tangier Sound called the Hooper Straight. He spied Hoopersville on the map near Hooper's Island. He chuckled and thought of the movie *Jaws*. "Hooper drives the boat, chief," he said out loud and laughed again. He also decided that *Jaws* would be the movie tonight on the DVR from the collection he'd amassed over time. So many that for purposes of space, he only had room for just his favorite movies in his berth, and many more below the cabin decks in storage.

A decent dinner, a good movie, and possibly a strong drink, and then decide in the morning where he wanted to go.

Chapter 3
DUPED

Kirk wiped the phlegm from his chin and onto his shirt as he gazed up at the morning sunlight. He spit the last of the vomit from his mouth out into the ocean. Another bad morning. Although typically his stomach would settle after a good, morning puke. Hopefully, that would be the case today.

He'd made an effort to catch a few delicious blue crabs that he'd pulled in from his traps just after daybreak this morning, having set the traps the evening before, and he couldn't resist boiling a handful for the morning meal. He wasn't happy that the sunrise had brought waves which caused him to return the delicacy to the ocean in the manner that he had.

During a breakfast, which he now truly wished he hadn't eaten, he'd made the decision to go under the Bay Bridge and up into the bay to check out a new location. He was still quite a way out, but now the choice had been made and he could set a course for the mouth of Chesapeake Bay.

Grimacing, he squinted and looked ahead, shading the bright sunlight with his hand after wiping it again on his short-sleeved shirt. *Mouthwash would be good to find,* he thought to himself as he created his grocery list in his mind. All of the things he wanted to try and find while on his next trip ashore.

Kirk squinted in the bright sunlight, catching a glimpse of something on the horizon. As he peered into the distance, he thought he could see it. Grabbing his binoculars, he confirmed it. He spied an old wooden cabin cruiser pointing in his direction. As he gazed, he wasn't overly concerned…yet. Although he did prepare for a quick turn-a-round if need be to avoid a confrontation just in case.

Kirk wasn't' worried about other vessels that he deemed 'safe' approaching him or even having their crew viewing his deck. He didn't keep anything within view as far as provisions or weapons, as he didn't want to advertise. Weapons were well hidden and easily accessible if need be. He did, though, keep a 9mm semi-auto tucked in the back of his pants with his shirt covering his waistline to hide it. This was for any close encounters. His other weaponry was never far from reach, either, with a crossbow mounted just under the top of the bulkhead that goes down to the interior cabins, and several other weapons tucked under ropes and other nooks and crannies on the deck. There were also plenty of additional weapons in the interior below deck where he could run and grab them quickly if it was absolutely necessary.

As the other vessel drew closer, and he continued to gaze through the binoculars, Kirk saw the mound of junk rounded so high that it was causing the vintage 20-foot vessel to list to one side.

It was a *junk boat*. Quite typical for this, and many areas along the coastline. All local sailors whose primary purpose was trade. A floating flea market. Kirk lowered his binoculars and could see the vessel with his own eyes now. He grimaced, as junk traders were primarily just a pain in the ass. And some worked for the pirates. Scouts, if you will. Allowed to peddle their crappy wares in exchange for information. Some of the pirates even stocked the junk boats with a few good items just to lure others in, and then receive reports from the scavengers on what they'd encountered, and where. Just so they could chase the other boats down and ambush them.

He raised the glasses back up and admired the boat itself. It must have been something in its day, Kirk thought. The red and white wood design must have made this a boat to covet when it was new. Now, it was just a floating tinker's cart full of useless pots, pans, knives, and other crap. All hanging from ropes and mounts that were clanking into each other, and that he had no need for. Chances were this guy had nothing of interest. But avoiding these leeches was far more effort than simply stopping and bullshitting with them for a few minutes. Running from one, especially one who was working for the pirates, sent the wrong signal that you had something of value to hide. No, Kirk would stop and provide the usual lies in an effort to get on his way without any trouble.

As the junk boat closed in Kirk heard a strange noise. He'd seen the smoke billowing as it was coming towards him and thought the guy simply had an engine that was seriously in need of maintenance, or that he was burning old motor oil and shitty diesel. But it appeared as it was something else. Something that truly impressed Kirk as it arrived within a rope's throw.

The boat was making a "Chug, chug, chugging" noise. Kirk smiled at the ingenuity. This guy had apparently found an old, very old, wood-fired steam engine and had mounted it to the boat. Or at least somebody had. It reminded him of a movie he'd watched recently on his DVD player. An old Humphrey Bogart flick, *the African Queen.* A movie Kirk had thoroughly enjoyed. There was certainly no speed to the vessel approaching him now, but it was about as reliable as you could get, and this guy probably had plenty of fuel to keep this old boat moving forward.

Kirk's smile turned down as the clunker floated up next to his sailboat, and Kirk spied something else. Seated on deck at the front of the cabin cruiser was a woman. She had long, dirty, stringy hair dangling over her head and shoulders. Her clothes were tattered and barely covered her sun-scorched and filthy skin. Her shirt sleeves were ripped and torn at the elbows, and the same for her jean pants near her knees. Her head was down, allowing her hair to conceal her face. Extending from her neck was a short chain that connected a choker collar to an O-ring mounted to the deck, preventing her from moving anywhere on the boat. Kirk shook his head at the sight of her.

As the boat bumped against Kirk's, all the metal on the junk boat swung and clanked as an old man emerged from his tiny wheelhouse and smiled a mostly toothless grin, waiving a skinny arm.

"Howdy, friend!"

Oh boy, Kirk thought, *this should be interesting.* The scrawny, old junk dealer had a long, reddish-gray beard growing down below his chest. His bony arms extended out of his short sleeves, his dark wrinkled skin hugging his bones tight. He picked up a rope and tossed it to Kirk, who caught it and tied the two boats together.

The old man began to climb out of his boat to gain access to Kirk's, placing a foot up on the gunwales. Kirk held up a hand, "That's close enough, old man. We can do business from right where you are." Not only did Kirk not want this guy to see what he had to hide, only to possibly report to the pirates, but he also didn't want to catch anything this guy may be carrying.

The old sailor displayed a gaping smile and stepped back down, waving a hand in the air. "Okay, no problem. I understand. I get it. Can't be too careful."

Kirk looked over the mound of salt-rusting junk hanging from the boat. "You got anything of use there, old timer?" He pointed and waved a hand, "No offense, but I got no need for any of this crap."

The salty old man smiled again and motioned with his head beyond his wheelhouse to the front of his boat. "I got plenty of useful things." He belted out a crusty, scratchy laugh.

Kirk, whose sailboat sat higher in the water, looked down at the old man as the two bobbed in their respective vessels. He then glanced at the girl up front, who hadn't moved from her seated position. Her head remained down, and she sat with her back to Kirk. He looked at the old man and motioned his head, speaking nonchalantly, "What's the deal with the friend of yours?"

The old man giggled again. "Oh, she's friendly alright. For the right price, she's very friendly." He cackled again.

Kirk cocked his head and said with disdain, "Old man, you're disgusting."

The old salt threw Kirk a look of surprise. "What! Why?! She ain't got nuthin'!"

"The hell she hasn't."

The old man held up a hand, "Honest! She's clean!"

Sarcastically, "And how would you know this, old man? Have you had a taste?"

Another surprised look crossed the old sailor's bearded face. "Who? Me?" He let out another crusty laugh, "Hell, I'm too old to dip into that. I couldn't get this old dick up with an entire tub of Viagra." He turned his head and soured his demeanor, sternly yelling past the wheelhouse to the girl. "Show him whatcha got!"

Kirk looked over to see the woman turn her body from where she sat. Her dirty hair fell from her head, revealing her face. She was maybe in her late 20s or early 30s. As she turned, with her tattered shirt and buttons open, she provided Kirk a peek at her naturally, well-endowed chest. The woman looked up at Kirk with no expression and he felt a bit of compassion. She'd obviously been an attractive woman at one time. The fact that she'd responded to the old man's voice command proved nothing, though. She was certainly infected, beyond the gestation phase, and probably into full zombie mode now. Kirk felt that she wasn't too far into the infection, though, from the looks of things. She'd probably been some pirate's squeeze until she caught the virus and was given to the old salesman to use as bait once she turned.

"What's your name, honey?"

The woman didn't respond. She just continued to stare blankly at Kirk.

"You're name, sweety. I'm just asking your name."

Still no response. Kirk annoyingly glanced back to the old man, his eyebrows raised.

"She's deaf."

"And I'm dumb, right? How'd she respond to you if she can't hear? She can't even see you from there."

"Instinct!" The old man blurted back.

"Instinct, my ass! I got your instinct right here. And my instinct tells me that something's up! What's the deal with the choker collar?!"

"Well, you know. Not everyone is happy about their situation. I don't need her jumping overboard and drowning."

"Bullshit. She's infected and both you and I know it!"

"She ain't! I swear!"

"Okay old man, then how about you hop to the front of this tub and give Miss America a nice, big kiss? Show me a little tongue action and then I'll consider it."

A nervous expression came across the old man's sunburnt and leathery face. He glanced to the front of his boat before looking back and flashing Kirk another toothless grin. "Who? Me? *Ahhh*....she ain't my type."

"No doubt. Forget it, old man. I ain't buying what you're selling! She's infected! Maybe not long into it, but she's got it!" As he said the words, Kirk looked back over at the woman, who turned away from him, quite possibly still understanding what had been said.

Kirk began to turn away himself as the old man held his hands out. "No problem, no problem. It was just a thought! I got plenty of other good stuff! Don't run away yet!"

When Kirk turned back, he sighed heavily as he drew his 9mm from his waistband. The old man's eyes grew as Kirk hesitated only a moment before he extended his arm straight, aimed, and fired the weapon. The woman's head shot forward as the bullet entered the back of her skull and exited her forehead, causing her hair to fly away from her face as a chunk of flesh followed the path of the bullet into the ocean. Brain matter and small pieces of bone struck the bow's gunwales and splashed into the ocean like buckshot, peppering the surface of the water.

Kirk noticed a great deal of blood splatter as well. Another sign that she'd been a 'fresh' one, probably infected recently as her blood hadn't coagulated yet, as the more rotten ones tend to do. The blood stained the boat's wooden rails and dripped into the sea. The woman's body fell forward and she slumped to the deck, causing more of her blood to stain the already sun and salt-worn deck boards underneath her body. When her head hit the deck, the chains around her neck clanked against the wood.

Almost immediately a school of sandbar sharks swarmed and jumped out of the water just off the bow, taking advantage of the woman's blood and small pieces of brain that were now chumming the ocean. Kirk gave a puzzled glance at the aquatic life, determining quickly that fishing the immediate area was out of the question for the day. Not that there were any scientific studies that the flesh of the creatures affected sea life, but he wasn't about to take any chances.

"What'dcha go and do that for?!"

As Kirk bent down to pick up the spent shell that luckily had landed on his deck and not in the water, he replied directly, "Preserving the lives of others! Yours included!"

The old man blurted out as he stretched his neck out to see past his wheelhouse over to the woman's body, "She weren't yours to kill!"

"She wasn't yours to keep, either! Don't you know it's illegal to keep the infected?!"

The old man looked angrily towards Kirk, "Whatdya mean?! There ain't no laws no more!"

Kirk pointed and spoke sternly, "Look here, old man! Unless you have some Dramamine somewhere on that old tub, we're done dealing here!"

"Drama-what?!"

"Never mind!" Kirk's stern expression turned puzzling, "Just what is it that you think I have on my boat that you want in trade, anyway?!"

The old man ignored the question and hobbled to the bow, looking at the blood and flesh now staining his boat. He groaned to himself, *"Ohhh, they're gonna be so mad."*

And there it was, Kirk thought, as he overheard the old man mumbling to himself. "Working for the pirates, eh, old man?" Kirk then had a thought, and he gazed out at his ocean surroundings, noticing that no land was in sight. "You're pretty far out here. Very far, in fact, for someone running an old steam engine-powered junk boat! How'd you know that I was out here, to begin with?!"

"Huh, what?! I...*ahhh*...saw you out here. I got a telescope."

"Bullshit!" Kirk was pointing again, "You know damn well that you hug the shoreline with that old steamer! You knew I was out here!" He pointed to the boat's deck, "What do you have down there? What kind of electronics are you hiding?!"

"Nuthin! I ain't got nuthin'!"

Kirk now realized his mistake. He looked to the western horizon. *"Fuck!"* He squinted to see if he could see them. Luckily, he didn't immediately spot anything. He gazed in anger back down to the old sailor. "Where is it?! Where's your beacon?! You're sending signals all over the place! You're telling them where I am right now, aren't you?!"

"No, I swear!" The old salt yelled, his voice cracking as Kirk lifted his binoculars from around his neck with his free hand and scanned the waters. "Where are they?! How far away are they parked, you old *asshole?!*"

"I didn't.....!"

Kirk whipped his right hand back up and pointed the

gun straight at the old man's head. "Quit stalling! You're nothing but an old liar that's working for the pirates! Start telling the truth or I'll reunite you with your girlfriend!"

The old man put his hands up to defend himself. "Okay, *okay!* Let's not be hasty! No need to get violent." He let out a crackly, nervous laugh.

"There's plenty of need to get violent! Now answer me!"

The old man slumped his shoulders and sighed heavily as he turned to gaze into the distance and particular direction. "About thirty nautical miles over that way."

Kirk gazed intently in the direction the old man was pointing. "Dammit! What are they driving? How long until they get here?!"

"They've got a cutter. A big one. They won't come in that, though. They'll send out a couple of skiffs." He continued to stare at the horizon. "Their engines ain't that good, and they can't fix things for shit. The gas they're running is pretty stale, too. From where they are I'd say it'll take them another hour…hour and a half or so."

"How do they know when to come?"

"They track me. When they see my boat stop for more than a half hour on their radar, that's when they send out the ambush. They keep their AIS off, so you won't see them. It's too late now, they're on their way for sure."

"You old piece of crap! How many have you helped them take?!"

In a defeated tone, "I dunno. A few."

"Anyone make it out alive?!"

"No…not that I've seen. They can be pretty cruel, too. It doesn't take much to amuse them." The old man looked back up at Kirk and began to plead, "Look, mister. Please. Let me go. I didn't mean nuthin'. *Please?*"

Kirk now felt disdain for the man's begging. He also put no confidence in his sincerity. "Doesn't it bother you, old man, to know you help those scumbags steal from others and kill whoever they want?"

"I don't do nuthin'. Please! *Please!*" Then the old man

perked up, "You know something? You can run! If you go now, you can outrun them! They ain't got shit to chase you with! I can just say that you didn't want nuthin' and left quickly! I'll stall them for you!"

"Uh, huh." Kirk pointed, "And how are you going to explain her?!"

"I'll just…I'll just…I'll think of something! Please! Just let me go!"

A slight gale blew up and caused the two boats to bob up and down in the water. Kirk dropped the binocs and they slapped against his chest. He wiped his face with his hand as a wave of nausea struck his guts, and he sighed again as he rubbed his eyes. "I tell you what, old man. I'm going to let you get out of this pretty easily."

The old salt smiled his rotten-toothed grin. "You are?"

Kirk reached down under a pile of rope at his feet and pulled out a sawed-off 12-guage double barrel while tucking the 9mm back into his waistband. "Yup, I'm going to kill you quickly instead of jumping down there and beating the piss out of you first!"

The old man's eyes bulged as he stared straight up at the two barrels that were now pointing at him. He had no time to duck or jump before Kirk unloaded one barrel into his chest. The old man's body somersaulted backward as the blood and entrails flew from the gaping hole that the double-ought-buck created in his chest. The impact to his old frail body drove the round straight through his thin frame, and splintered the wooden gunwale behind as his body flipped over the now blood-soaked rail, and he landed in a bellyflop into the ocean.

Just moments after his body hit the salt water and the blood began to mix with it, a great white came straight up, taking the old man in its jaws. The fifteen-footer breached the surface completely before twisting mid-air and splashing back down, taking the old man's body into the depths with it. A red plume stained the saltwater for a few seconds before dissipating in the waves.

"Well, there's something you don't see every day," Kirk mumbled. "So long, Quint." He scanned the horizon again, still not seeing anything yet. Kirk jumped across into the old man's boat and he peeked into the wheelhouse. Nothing special was to be found there, so he descended the stairs below the bulkhead and wasn't surprised to discover just what he had assumed. Below the deck was a setup that looked like the bridge of a police patrol. Radio equipment, long wave and short. Radar, sonar, and GPS navigation. It was loaded. Hell, Kirk thought, the old man could have located the Titanic if he wanted to with all the equipment that he had on board. He had everything except usable supplies to trade. It was obvious this guy had been set up for some time to simply be a scout for the ambush boats. This guy literally had nothing to trade other than life itself.

Kirk took a quick look around, finding nothing that didn't compare with the equipment he already had onboard his sailing vessel. And, he knew he didn't have a lot of time before trouble arrived. He snatched a tote of canned food and some fresh water that was in view and threw it onto his deck before going back down below deck and unloading the other barrel of the shotgun into the electronic tracking equipment. Sparks flew and Kirk determined that he'd hit the spot when every little flickering light on the equipment in the cabin went out. No more power, no more signals being sent. He knew it was too late, though. The pirates most certainly had a lock on him by now. But he still wasn't about to make it easy for them.

Just before leaving, he spied an unopened bottle of Scotch Whiskey peeking out from underneath an old blanket. When he lifted it, he also discovered several fine cigars, obviously a few more luxury items the old man probably used to haggle over and keep unsuspecting sailors talking until the pirates arrived. He grabbed the bounty up in the blanket.

Climbing back out on deck he opened the shotgun's breach and pocketed the empty shells. After jumping back over to his own boat, he went below to his reloading station and dropped all the shells that he'd collected, and the booze and smokes. He dug into a drawer and took out two more high-powered slugs and pocketed them. He then grabbed two additional specially crafted exploding shells and loaded them into the shotgun. Lastly, he grabbed a set of ear protection and made his way back to the deck.

After putting the muffs on, he aimed one load for the bow of the old cabin cruiser well below the water line, and he pulled the trigger. *"Ka-Boom!"* The wave rocked both boats as Kirk was able to see that he'd left a nice-sized hole in wooden construction that was almost certain to quickly start sucking in the salt water. He aimed for the stern and just before pulling the trigger, he gently shook his head. It was a shame, he thought, to lose that antique steam engine to the depths of the sea. But he knew the vessel would sink quickly under the weight of the old, cast-iron engine. He aimed and unloaded the second round, blowing a hole straight through the boat's deck and through the lower stern, shattering the rudder on its way out.

◆ ◆ ◆

Kirk was well out of the area before the two skiffs arrived. The grimy little group of sea scallywags, four in each boat, were making circles where the old man's boat had shown on their radar and was supposed to be. The greasy, dirty, long-haired, short-tempered, and heavily armed group argued with each other as to who had messed up the reading of the navigational equipment and managed to get them lost on their way to where the junk boat should have been. Kirk would be long gone before one of them would ultimately discover the first of the floating debris and they'd finally figure out what truly happened.

◆ ◆ ◆

Later that evening Kirk drifted south, having decided against entering the Chesapeake Bay area in fear of what else might be waiting for him. Instead, he decided to set a course towards the Florida Keys and try another, possibly safer location along the way to do his scavenging.

Kirk lounged in his cabin below decks sipping on some good Scotch Whiskey and enjoying a Cuban. He glanced over to the S-band radar, one of two that he had onboard, with the other being located in his cockpit. He saw no activity that he needed to be concerned with. He then turned his attention back to his small flat screen and smiled.

It was the beginning of the *'SS Indianapolis'* scene in the movie. Quint and Hooper were comparing their legs.

Chapter 4
GOING ASHORE

"Never get out of the Goddam boat." A line from another of
Kirk's favorite DVD movies, Apocalypse Now. A line he
thought about every time he needed to go ashore. Sort of
a warning to himself to never become complacent. But the
truth was that Kirk had to leave the boat every so often
for supplies. There was no avoiding it. Not to mention,
sometimes he just needed to get off the boat and stretch
his sea legs.

For the next few days, Kirk sailed south. The seas were
calm, and the weather cooperated for the most part. At
one point while he was in the area of the southern Virginia
coastline he did anchor out and motor in on the pontoon
to check out a small seaside village. He did it primarily to
exercise his bones, rather than hope to find something
useful. As usual, he used the drone first to get a bird's eye
view of the area before going ashore. It appeared safe.

He didn't remain on the mainland long during his
excursion. Just time enough to pick up a few treasures and
encounter more of the walking dead than he'd preferred to
while doing it. He'd packed his 9mm, an M-16 slung over

his shoulder, and a longbow with a few arrows in a quiver. Enough to protect himself, but not enough to overweigh or slow him down.

In the tiny seacoast village, he managed to scrounge through a few dilapidated trinket and souvenir shops to see if anything was left. He scored a few bottles of spices that he'd been seeking to liven up his seafood meals, and also a case of suntan oil, something he never had enough of. He found a couple of T-shirts to replace his fading and sea-worn ones and a new pair of boat shoes. Luckily, in his size.

He'd been surprised to discover that in one little shop, the owner was apparently still working. Probably out of some sort of instinct or memory, however, behind the front counter was the infected entrepreneur. He'd smelled as bad as he looked, and one side of him was severely burnt where the sun had reflected through the shop's broken windows each day and cooked him to a point that he was quite well done. The remainder of his unburnt skin was more of a deep, leathery hide rather than anything still resembling human flesh. Dried blood covered his face from his eyes where they'd bled terribly, oozed, and encrusted. This was another side effect of the late stages of the disease, severe bleeding from all orifices as the blood boiled out from the fever before thickening from the slowing of the heart. When it finally exited the victim's body it was more of a syrupy substance.

The creature's eyeballs were a veiny, deep maroon color. His pupils were severely dilated and jet black. The man appeared to have been in his 40s and he was still wearing a tattered shirt that displayed the shop's name and logo across the chest. The fingers on his right hand were all broken and the nails missing where he'd instinctively been pushing buttons on the cash register continually, over and over again.

With the owner stuck behind the counter, Kirk continued his shopping. He kept a close eye, and he startled each time the virus-ridden shop owner grunted as if to tell Kirk in which aisle to look for various souvenirs that he may be seeking to purchase.

Before Kirk left the tiny store, he stopped to stare at the shop's owner, and he reflected for a moment. The creature continued to press the buttons on the long-broken cash register, and he also tried to reach out and get to Kirk, only to continually bump against the waist-high counter that held him back. Kirk wondered to himself just how much of what happened to this guy was the virus, or a combination of infection and whatever radiation that might be floating through the air now. And what was to become of himself? Was there a promised land somewhere that he hadn't yet discovered where he'd ultimately spend his days, and possibly find a mate? Or was he destined to catch the disease and become just like Mr. Shop Owner here? Maybe there was radiation in the air, and he was going to die a slow death from it anyway instead of the virus, or from both. Who knew?

Before leaving, Kirk pondered on whether to finally put Mr. Shop Owner out of his misery or leave him to continue to overlook his business and rot away like all the others that do over the course of time. He also wondered at what point do the infected lose their power of deliberation. When does the brain decay to the point of not knowing anything? This guy was still here trying to run his store, so does he realize what he's doing? Or is it just pure motorized instinct?

Ultimately, Kirk simply left the store and the shop's owner. The shop's door, mostly broken off its hinges, rang the tiny little bell that was mounted to the top one more time as Kirk left the shop's owner to tend to his business.

Before making his way back to the shoreline where he'd left the dinghy, he managed to locate a small amount of drinkable water in the basement of another little store, and he managed to siphon a couple of gallons of fuel from a few of the boats that were strewn on the shoreline and in the marina. He'd take the fuel back to his own vessel and add a bit of stabilizer and octane booster before using it in his own equipment.

"*Man*," Kirk thought, "*I'm tired of cleaning stale gas and gunk out of the carburetors.*"

He was tired of a lot of other things, too.

Chapter 5
DANGER ISLAND

The following night a squall blew up and Kirk spent a good deal of time at the rail, praying to the sea Gods. The following morning, he woke up feeling a little better and he studied his ocean charts. He decided that his next stop would be an estuary off the coast of North Carolina called the Albemarle Sound. He hadn't explored this area before. He'd read that the waters in the Sound were fresh due to the rivers that drained into it from the mainland. He also felt he could catch a nice meal of herring, or maybe striped bass, which the Sound was noted as being popular for according to magazine articles of the past that he had on board.

Of course, having no history of the area he didn't know what dangers that he may be in for. But as they say, no risk, no reward. In looking over the maps he decided he'd first stop at Kitty Hawk and put the drone up for a look around before rounding the bend near a spot called Nag's Head and entering the Albemarle Sound. If he spotted anything suspicious with the drone, he'd re-evaluate his decision to go any further.

And, speaking of meals, Kirk's stomach was empty, and the waters were calm and clear today. He was feeling the hunger as he rubbed his belly, and it made a growling sound.

He also hadn't anything fresh to eat onboard, so it was time to do some fishing. Kirk looked out past the wheel from his cockpit and checked his bearings, making certain he was pointed toward the Sound. After taking a compass reading, he activated the Turner pilot. The 'autopilot' for sailing vessels, and he went out on deck. Next, he planned to put out a couple of steel lines and see what he could catch. He had plenty of bait that consisted of a cooler full of rotting fish guts that he could use for chum and bait, so success on this day came with better-than-average odds.

Kirk gazed out over the waters. The waves were visible but calm enough that his stomach was fairly settled, and he was ready for a decent brunch. He grabbed a deep-sea pole in one hand as he looked out over the bow. He noticed something bobbing on the waves out ahead, and he squinted through his sunglasses. He lifted them and shaded his eyes with his hand. Something was definitely in the water.

Lifting his binoculars from around his neck he saw several of what he believed were various-colored buoys floating in the water ahead of the boat a few hundred yards away. Kirk quickly ducked back into the cockpit and checked his radar. He saw no other vessels or anomalies in the area. He glassed the area again and counted at least a dozen of the buoys that he could see, and probably more in the distance that he couldn't.

Crab or lobster pots, maybe?

He wasn't certain. But he was curious. Probably a bad trait, as we know what being curious does to a cat, he thought. However, seeing no other boats in the area, if they were to be crab pots this would be a quick and easy meal.

Not that Kirk was into stealing food from another, but he was hungry. He felt that he could just pull one up and, if there were to be a bounty within it, he could replace the live seafood with some canned goods in trade. Any gesture to let the rightful owners know that the intention wasn't to simply steal their catch. Taking only what he required for a decent meal, he'd leave something behind in good faith, and move on to other fishing grounds where he could take his time. It seemed like a reasonable idea to Kirk.

His mouth began to water, and not from nausea this time, but from the thought that there may be a few delicious red or blue crabs within his reach if these were to, in fact, be crab pots below the buoys, which was a fairly good assumption. There's no other reason for these to be out here bobbing in the ocean, he thought. Kirk used his binoculars again and still didn't see any other vessels in the area, so this wasn't an ambush situation as far as he could tell.

Kirk cautiously drifted up beside the first buoy. Land was just in sight now, a little less than a nautical mile away he determined, so he waited a few minutes before taking any action. Scanning the shoreline and glancing at his radar again, he was making certain no boats would come flying his way. While he waited, he bagged up several extra cans of food. He had some extra veggies and fruit that he could spare. He even added a tin of fancy candy mints. He made certain to use a clear bag, so the rightful owners could see what was inside when they pulled the pot later on. He chose not to add the tuna fish, believing that would be a bit insulting. Trading cheap, canned tuna fish for expensive red crab would simply send the wrong message.

When he was done and satisfied that he was alone, he placed the buoy line in a small winch he had mounted to the starboard side, and he began to raise whatever was below.

He continued to watch his surroundings as the winch slowly brought the saturated rope into the boat and Kirk coiled it on the deck. Several minutes went by before his attention was called to the port side when Kirk heard a "whoosh" and his sailboat rocked a little harder than just from the ocean waves, which were still fairly calm. Puzzled, he didn't immediately see anything as he glanced back. When he returned to focus on the rope, he startled and jumped back from the rail.

"Jeesus!"

On the gunwale of his vessel an arm had appeared. The hand attached had grabbed hold of the rail, and then the creature's head appeared. It appeared to be male, its skin white and bloated, and its eyes entirely missing. From the sockets, ears, nose, and mouth the seawater flushed back out of its head as it rose above the gunwale. The face of the infected man was pockmarked where sea life had obviously been nibbling. Below the rail where Kirk couldn't see was where a large part of the man's lower torso had gone missing. The entrails of his stomach and intestines were dangling from what was left where a shark had recently clamped its jaws and had torn a section away from its stomach area. The same would be discovered below its knees, where it no longer had lower legs or feet. It was primarily just bloated, dangling flesh floating in the water as it held its grip on the boat. It had been attached to the trap line with a collar, and another line on a belt that was holding its tattered pants to its waist, the only bit of clothing it still had on its body.

"What the…?!"

Kirk's aim was dead on when he took his 9mm from his waist and performed three quick hip shots, hitting the waterlogged creature in the arm and shoulder before striking it square in the forehead. Chunks of rotten flesh flew from the body along with the little bit of uncirculated blood that was left. Pieces of humerus, scapula, and cranium flew backward after exploding from the rotted, soft flesh that had been containing it inside its body. Parts of its decomposing brain also exited its skull with full force, splashing into the ocean. The thick, coagulated clots were staining the water reddish as small fish quickly began to school around the area and feed.

The creature's body slumped back into the water just as a bull shark sped by, gaping its mouth and clamping its razor-sharp teeth down on what was left of the creature's torso. More flesh littered the waters as the shark trailed away along the surface with its prize in its jaws, leaving a string of intestines in its wake. The rope that Kirk had coiled was now exiting back out of his boat, along with the buoy bouncing back past Kirk and out onto the sea as the shark darted away with its catch.

Kirk simply stared. "Goddam sharks are hungry today," he quipped.

"I'd appreciate if you don't shoot my trap guards! Them things ain't easy to wrangle and secure on them lines!"

Kirk's eyes closed and he whispered, *"Awwwe, shit."*

The male voice had a deep, southern drawl to it, "I'd also appreciate it if you'd drop that pistol in your hand and turn around slowly."

Kirk knew damn well that he had a gun pointed at his backside. He dropped his head and let the 9mm fall to the deck before raising his hands. With a disgusted, defeated expression he turned around. Gently bobbing up and down just off his starboard side, from the lower torso up, Kirk saw a rather large, muscular man. His sleeveless button-down shirt exposed his hairy shoulders. His hands tightly held onto a rifle that was pointed straight at Kirk's chest. The man had long, stringy black hair on his head, and facial hair to match.

Puffing on a blunt stogey cigar, the man continued, "Although, they don't tend to last long anyway. Less than a week or so before we have to put new ones on the line when the sharks are done having their way with them. Of course, up until now, I wasn't certain they were going to work. That is until your stupid ass came along and tried to steal our dinner! Looks to me from your reaction like it worked out really good, too! Even if we hadn't been in the area, you weren't getting nuthin'!"

"Ingenious idea," Kirk remarked sarcastically. "I wasn't going to steal your stuff. Not exactly, anyway. I was going to leave you something in return." Kirk began to bend down to show the man the bag full of goodies.

"Get your hands back up!"

"Fine." Kirk did as he was commanded and slowly stood back up with his hands high. "Don't believe me."

"Excuses are like your dirty arsehole! You were stealing! There's nothing else to it!"

Kirk quickly assessed the situation he currently found himself in. Pointed at him was a piddly .22-caliber, lever-action single-shooter. A crap gun, but one that could do some damage, especially where it was pointed. Even with the guy bobbing up and down in the waves, it wasn't worth the risk to duck and dive for another one of his own weapons that he had hidden on deck. It was time to try and talk his way out of it…and possibly buy some time.

"I know that you aren't the almighty and didn't come walking on that water. And, by the looks of your lit cigar, you didn't swim here either. So, what do you have down below your waist there?"

A dirty-toothed smile emerged from beneath his thick mustache. "Not that it's any of your business, but I got me one of them fancy electric submarines! Found it mounted on one of them cruise-type ships! You didn't see me coming, did ya?!"

Kirk had heard about these things. They were primarily once used for tourism and ocean exploration. If what he figured was true, this guy was standing on a little ladder at the top porthole of a six-or-seven-person submersible. They had a range of about twenty hours before needing to be charged back up again. This guy probably had a solar setup nearby where he recharges the batteries. Kirk had learned this all from magazines he had on the boat at one time or another, recalling the article. He had a lot of time to read seeing that he had nothing to do for the rest of his life other than sailing up and down the east coast.

And, no. Kirk hadn't seen this thing coming, he thought to himself. He'd also never thought to check the sonar. He probably would've assumed it to be a whale or something anyway if he had.

"Junior! Get up here and board this boat!"

A younger boy, possibly in his late teens, squeezed his tall and thin body up past his father, and he began to board Kirk's vessel.

Kirk couldn't help his thoughts, *"Junior. That figures. Nice name. Couldn't come up with anything more original?"*

The skinny lad landed on deck, tripping on his own feet before standing nearly face-to-face with Kirk. He smiled a dorky smile and pleasantly encountered the captive. "Howdy."

Kirk flashed a sarcastic grin with his hands still in the air, "Howdy."

"Don't talk to him! He ain't got nothin' to say! Just see what he's got!"

The kid had on a sleeveless, red flannel shirt, much the same as his father. Plus, his jean shorts that went just below his knobby knees. On his feet were blue, torn canvas boat shoes. He turned his torso awkwardly and glanced around. "Ain't much on deck. Just ropes and stuff."

"I can see what's on deck, numb nuts! Go down below and see what he's got!"

The boy hopped down the stairs to the cabin space below and only moments later he popped his head back up from the bulkhead. He had the same southern accent as his father as he blurted, "Holy shoot. He got lots of stuff down here, Daddy! It's a gold mine!" He tripped on himself again as he exited the stairwell and landed back on deck. "Canned food, clothing, electronic gadgets up the whazoo…and movies!"

As he passed by Kirk, the boat's rightful owner couldn't help himself. "You call your father, daddy? How old are you kid?"

Junior looked back to Kirk as he kept walking nearly straight into the center mast. "I'm twenty-three. And he is my daddy, so what am I supposed to call him?"

Kirk shook his head and whispered to himself, *"Jeesus."*

The young man threw a confused look back, "You want

me to call him Jesus? Why?"

Kirk sighed, "I don't want you to…never mind!" He turned his attention back to the man with the gun, "Hey, Daddy! Can I put my arms down now? I told you I wasn't taking something without leaving something. I got no beef with you. No harm, no foul. Let's call it a day!"

"Shut up! And keep them hands up!" The man motioned with the gun before yelling to his son again, "Take some of them ropes and tie this arsehole up good!" He turned his attention, looking over the boat, "Do you think you can sail this thing back or do you want to take the sub?"

The lanky young man responded as he fumbled around for a rope that wasn't too long or too short to tie up their captive, "I can sail it, Daddy!"

"There's a short rope down there," Kirk said, motioning with his head and not wanting the boy to root around too much and discover any hidden weapons.

"Shut up! The boy can find one himself! Now, sit your ass down at the base of that center mast!" He motioned with the barrel, "And, no funny stuff while my boy ties you up or I'll put a hole in you and tie you off to one of the trap lines!"

Kirk stepped up on top of the captain's cockpit and over to the forward deck to the mast and sat down with the boy right behind him, rope in hand. Junior began tying Kirk to the wooden pole. And, unfortunately for Kirk, he was pretty good at tying knots.

"What? No handcuffs? Nice glass of wine maybe?" Kirk called back to the kid's father, "Dinner and flowers? Or maybe you're getting a bit jealous of your boy here having the honor of tying me up! Did he learn by doing the same things to you late at night?!"

"Shut up! Shut your face or I'll kill you sooner rather than later!"

Junior tightened the rope around Kirk's wrists, snapping the rope taught before adding another knot.

"Hey, take it easy kid. I ain't going anywhere."

"Sorry."

"Don't talk to him! Just get him secured and get on that wheel in the cockpit! Follow me back to the island. And don't run over me getting there! Stay back behind me!"

"Yes, Daddy."

"Hey! Don't you need to change out the bait on your line before we go?! Or are you all out of zombies?! I hope you wear a mask and gloves when you're baiting those traps!"

Kirk had turned his head to watch Junior jump down into the tiny wheelhouse when he felt a sharp pain in his left shoulder and at the same time, he heard the *"Crack!"* Small chunks of wood ricocheted off the mast where the small-caliber bullet lodged, along with a piece of Kirk's flesh that had been carried along with it. Kirk looked down and saw the blood beginning to stain his shirt, then looked up to see 'Daddy' lower the gun from his sight.

"Jeesus! You shot me! What the hell did you shoot me for?!"

"I told you to shut up! The next one will really hurt if you don't mind me! My aim will be a lot better, straight into your skull!"

Kirk moved his shoulder around. It hurt like hell, but it was still functional. He was just glad this guy was a decent shot, or he may have just ended up with a hole in his face. He was also glad the bullet had gone straight through his upper bicep, as a .22 doesn't have a lot of force, and he didn't feel like having to perform surgery on himself later on once he figured out how to get himself out of this mess.

Shit, this hurts! Kirk kept his thoughts to himself, looking down and watching the dark red liquid begin to stream down his arm.

"Pick up his piece!" Pointing towards the deck where the 9mm lay. "And keep it on him! If he squirms out of them ropes, feed him to the fish!"

"Yes, Daddy."

It was apparent to Kirk that the .22 lever-action they brought with them was probably their only decent weapon.

Otherwise, they'd have brought better firepower to deal with potential encounters. Now, they had the .22 and his 9mm. Kirk didn't want them snooping around his boat anymore and finding bigger and better firepower, so he needed to think quickly. He figured that their submarine probably didn't have a very long range, so their base of operations had to be close by somewhere.

'Daddy' threw the rope he'd used to tie off to Kirk's sailboat and his head disappeared as he descended back into his submersible. Once Junior spotted the wake of the sub trailing away just below the surface, he swung the wheel, picked up the wind, and began to follow in a general direction toward the mainland.

Kirk looked around at his situation as the young man sailed his vessel. His shoulder pain was getting worse by the minute even though it appeared the bleeding had slowed. Good, he needed it to clot. He couldn't afford to pass out cold from blood loss and not have the ability to see where they were going. He also needed to remain sharp. He looked through the open window into the captain's cockpit and figured he better start talking to the boy who was watching the ocean intently and being careful to keep the sailboat behind 'daddy'.

"Where'd you learn to sail, kid?"

Junior continued to gaze out ahead while responding, "We got a sailboat hidden on the mainland. We go get it and use it to bring out the dead ones and tie them up to the crab pot ropes when they need replacing. Sometimes we use it to go exploring on the coast for supplies. Mostly Daddy likes to keep it hidden away from the island."

It didn't seem to Kirk that Gilligan here was going to hold back much. In fact, he felt that the kid, without his father present, might just be in a chatty mood.

"What do you fish for, kid? Crab?"

"Yup. Blues and reds. Sometimes we get lucky and find a lobster." The boy still didn't look away, he kept his eyes straight on the wake of the submarine. He appeared to know what he was doing and was handling the sailboat fairly well.

Kirk looked around before rotating his shoulder again and grimacing. "I could use a band-aid, kid."

"Don't worry, Ma will fix you right up when we get there."

Great, now there are three of them. "Get where kid? Where are you taking me? What did you mean when you said that you hide the boat? What island?"

"We got an island. But Daddy doesn't want anyone to know that we're living on it, so we keep the boat on the mainland. It ain't nuthin', really. Just an old sailboat we use to get the dead ones out here and go looking for stuff."

"Yeah, you said that already. An island, huh? How many more of you are there on this island?"

"Just the three of us. That's it." This time the boy looked straight at Kirk, "I shouldn't be tellin' you all this."

"Don't worry, my lips are sealed." Kirk looked around again. "What's your father planning on doing to me?"

The boy glanced over and sighed. "Most likely kill you. Especially if you keep mouthing off. He don't like that. If you keep quiet, you might last longer."

Kirk could tell by the look on the kid's face that "lasting longer" didn't seem to be much of an improvement over a quick death.

"How many others have you ambushed and killed, kid?"

Another sigh, "Two that were killed straight away. There were others on them boats, but two of them couldn't keep their mouths shut, neither. That's not counting the ones we keep in the pen." He perked up and said with enthusiasm, "We ambushed them others with the sub on the open water! We used the sailboat and anchored it. We made it look like something that somebody would want to check out. When they'd stop, we raised right up underneath them, same as we did with you. You're the first to get caught checking on our traps, though."

"Lucky me. Whose idea was it to tie the dead ones to the lines?"

"Not mine." Junior looked sheepishly at the console. "I don't like them things. It wasn't my idea to kill the others, either." The boy perked up again, "They would've lived if they hadn't been mouthy, too! Well, lived to be put in the pen, anyway!"

"The pen?"

The young man flashed another pathetic expression and turned his attention out over the ocean again.

"What's your mother think of all this?"

Another sheepish look crossed the boy's face and he looked at Kirk before answering. "She's worse than Daddy. She's mean. Getting worse, too, all the time."

"Then why in hell would she want to fix me up? Just so one of them can kill me."

"I shouldn't be tellin' you all this."

"C'mon, kid! You don't seem that bad and I'm in a tight spot here! I wasn't trying to steal your stuff! What are they going to do to me…I mean, if I keep my mouth shut and all?"

"Well, she…" Junior hesitated, and his tone turned sour. "And she ain't my real mother by the way! My momma died a long time ago!" He turned somber again as he guided the boat, being careful not to pass the submersible. "She likes to play with things."

"Play with things? What do you mean, play with things? What's the deal, kid? Your daddy can't get it up anymore?"

Junior thought about the comment for a moment with a puzzled look on his face before understanding its relevance, changing his expression to one of surprise. "No, not that! They do that all the time. What I meant was. Well…she likes knives."

Kirk's eyes widened, "Oh, *terrific!* You mean she's into torture!"

"She likes knives. She's kinda' weird that way." Junior looked straight at Kirk, whispering loudly as if someone else might overhear, "She did things with them others from the boats…the ones that Daddy didn't kill. She also likes to go out hunting on the mainland for zombies. She gets the dead ones ready to put on the trap lines, too. She's into that kinda' stuff. That one that you saw that crawled onto your boat? It wasn't the fish that took its eyes. They were dangling from the sockets when we put that one in the water. She did that. I guess the fish ate them after that."

"You've got to be kidding?!"

Junior simply shook his head in response. "She'll play with you for a while and then put you in the pen with the others…until you're dead too and then they'll use you to put on the trap lines. Either that or Daddy will just kill you after she's done." Junior stretched his neck out and whispered loudly again, "Try not to scream too much when she's *playing* with you. Daddy don't like screamers."

Kirk's eyes were wide. He was quickly arriving at the realization that he was up shit creek, literally, if he didn't think of something soon.

"What do you think of all this, kid? Are you into their game, too?"

"Me? No. I don't like it. I don't like treating people bad. I don't have much choice, though. I try not to watch or listen. I just do what I'm told."

"You're an adult, kid. Don't you have a mind of your own? You obviously have skills. Why don't you take off and build a life for yourself somewhere?" Kirk adjusted his shoulder again. It was throbbing. The waves had picked up a bit too and Kirk was feeling the action way down in his stomach. It was certainly much different with someone else driving his boat.

"Ain't nuthin' for me out here. Besides, we have it pretty good on the island. Food, shelter, people don't bother us. I just do what I'm told."

The young man took another wave and the sailboat rose and dropped hard, forcing Kirk's backside to jar against the mast. *"Goddammit!"*

"Sorry." Junior perked up and pointed, "Hey! There it is!"

Kirk turned his head and wriggled around to see out over the bow. They were approaching a small island, part of a cluster as far as he could make out. It wasn't far off the mainland, as Kirk could see that too off the starboard side. He also spotted the wake of the submersible, still out ahead of the sailboat. The kid had done what he was told and kept behind it the entire way. He certainly had skills in sailing. Well, with Frankenstein and his girlfriend busy playing with dead things when they weren't playing with each other, Kirk was pretty sure that operating their boat was this kid's primary function, and everything else that had to do with basic needs was his secondary responsibility.

Kirk hadn't noticed the little walkie-talkie that Junior had hiding under his shirt until it squawked. *"Anchor that sailboat where you are! I don't want it too close to the island! We'll bring him in on his own dinghy and come back out for the bounty once we have him secured!"*

Junior grabbed the two-way from his waistband, "Yes, Daddy!"

"Stop calling him daddy! Why don't you help me out of this deep shit instead of feeding me up to be someone's sick medical experiment?! Your *daddy* and his girlfriend are obviously twisted individuals. You seem like a pretty straightforward kid!"

Junior answered as he was fumbling on deck and preparing to get the anchor out, "I can't. I'm sorry, mister. I just do what I'm told."

This time Kirk heard the submersible as it surfaced and both vessels bumped against each other on the waves. Big Daddy emerged again and climbed aboard Kirk's boat, and the two captors loaded their hostage into his own lifeboat. Kirk continued to verbalize his discontent as he was roughly escorted from the deck to his dinghy, causing more intense pain in his shoulder. His wrists remained tied tightly together behind his back.

"We'll take him in and give him to your mother!" The man blurted to his offspring as he manhandled Kirk into the dinghy, "Later we'll come back out, take what we want off this tub and scuttle it here, so nobody sees it parked near the island!"

"Yes, Daddy."

"Watch the arm!"

"Shut up! Your shoulder is the least of your worries now, you thief!" As he shoved Kirk onto a seat, he spoke into his walkie, "Do you see anything around us?!"

A female's voice squawked back, *"Nope, nothing moving nearby that I can see on the radar!"*

"Ten-four! We're coming in on a small pontoon! Be ready and meet us at the rock!" Turning to his son, "We'll leave the submarine tied off here! We'll get it later! I want to get this guy into shore before he becomes a problem!"

Junior pull-started the pontoon's engine and steered the craft through the waters. This was something that also annoyed Kirk in knowing that his precious gasoline was being burned to take him into this island of terror, rather than on one of his own mainland expeditions for supplies.

As they motored towards the islands, Kirk kept rotating his shoulder. The blood had well-stained his shirt and arm. He needed to make certain that no matter how badly it hurt that it was still functional. He was going to need it when he determined the right time to make a move. He'd thought about trying to take out the big guy while they were boarding the dinghy but with his wrists tied, he was afraid that he would've gone right over the side along with the gorilla, and they both might have drowned. Or, at least he would've as it was certain that the boy would only have attempted to save his father. Not to mention, he still wasn't certain about this kid and what his intentions were. His simple demeanor could be a ruse.

As they drew nearer the islands Kirk looked over the area. It appeared that there were several small islands in all. The one they were pointed to looked to be only a couple of acres in size. It was well-wooded and certainly didn't have anything surrounding it that gave the appearance of being occupied. No wharf and no other vessels that he could see.

Junior motored around the side of the small land mass. In between this and the immediate adjacent island was a narrow tributary that they were navigating towards. Junior motored up the narrow river. As soon as the pontoon was out of sight of the open ocean, Kirk spotted Mrs. Frankenstein. She was standing on a rock outcropping with a rope ready to throw. Next to the rock was another small boat, a Boston Whaler, just slightly larger than Kirk's pontoon. Kirk also spotted the charging station for the submersible mounted just on the bank of the island. Everything was well-hidden from the open water in the little river between the two islands.

As they neared, Kirk could see that the woman was maybe in her mid to late 40s. Not unattractive by any means. Brunette, tall and well built. In fact, just a bit muscular and certainly qualified to handle the creatures that she apparently enjoyed playing with. Her fit arms and legs extended out of the raggedy clothing she was wearing. Like her hubby, she was wearing a button-down shirt with no sleeves, or bra, and jean shorts that she fit into nicely. He could tell from her scowl and pointy eyebrows that she had that insane, mean streak that Junior had mentioned.

"He's a good-looking one, Billy Bob!" She called out in a voice that sounded rather cigarette damaged as they bumped the pontoon against the rock.

Billy-Bob. That figures.

"He'll be all yours in a few minutes. We gotta' head back out and deal with his boat! It's gonna' take a bit. Lotsa' shit to bring back!"

As Kirk was *assisted* off the boat and onto the rock, using his bad arm, the woman reached over and grabbed his face cheeks. "You're a cutie! We're gonna' have some fun together!"

With his lips pinched, he managed to squeak, "I'd prefer it if you didn't touch me."

The woman cackled and slapped Kirk hard across the

face, and then she placed a choker collar and short chain around his neck. He also felt the barrel of the .22 poke into his back, prompting him to walk.

Kirk was led up a rather long, winding trail to the center of the island. It seemed as if they'd walked forever, but it was mostly due to Kirk's shoulder hurting and the thoughts racing through his brain that made it seem like a hike. As they walked through the wooded area Kirk could make out wiring strung high in the trees above and determined there must be cameras along the path, as he believed he'd spotted a few. There were also wires running along the ground, most likely to power the battery charger that lay on the shore.

Ultimately, up ahead of them, the foliage opened up to a decent-sized compound. At the mouth of the path, Kirk noticed something unique that solidified his belief that this group didn't have a lot of modern weaponry available. As they emerged from the trailhead, they passed by what looked like a folding gun-rest table once used for sighting long guns. Mounted to it was a pair of vice grips, and within the teeth of the grips was a shotgun shell pointed down the trail. A hammer sat on the table. Kirk knew this was a primitive, hammer-operated shotgun. When a nail that was pointed at the primer on the shell was tapped with the hammer, it would set it off. It appeared the nail was on a trigger mechanism using rubber elastics to make certain that when tapped, it would strike the primer hard, and the shell would hopefully fire. The only problem was that the shooter took a chance that when tapped, the shell didn't explode back in their face. Kirk had heard of this archaic form of projectile weapon but had never seen one. This was a one-and-done deal unless you could get the grips open fast enough to mount another shell between the teeth before your prey caught up to you or shot you first. He wondered how many more of these devices they'd set up nearby to protect their compound.

A two-story log cabin sat in the center of the clearing and another of Kirk's suspicions was confirmed as he looked around. There were solar panels mounted to the top of the cabin, and the trees surrounding the main house had been trimmed back to expose the sunlight to the rooftop. A shed just off the house had cables and colorful extension cords running from it to everywhere, and a humming noise could be heard coming from the outbuilding. Kirk knew the batteries and other solar equipment were housed within the shed. There were several other small outbuildings, along with various boat parts, junk, and garbage scattered about.

There was also another larger barn-like building off to one side and attached to it was a fenced-in area with their playthings wandering around inside of it. The fence was heavily secured in barbed wire. There looked to be at least a dozen creatures inside the fence, both male and female, each experiencing various stages of the infection. In fact, one woman in particular that was sitting up against the fence and gazing out appeared to Kirk as only being in the early stages of the illness and hadn't 'died' yet. Everyone in the pen had similar collars around their necks, but without the chains attached. Several chains were hanging near the fence's door, along with a couple of wooden poles with hooks on the ends, ready for use.

The infected ones didn't stir when the foursome emerged from the woods. A couple of them straddled up to the fencing and reached through, but for the most part, the majority meandered inside the pen, barely acknowledging the existence of others.

As Kirk looked around, he recognized that it wasn't a bad setup with solar power and natural canopy for cover. The island was small enough, and the setup was well hidden in the interior. It would most likely be ignored by most of the vessels passing by that were looking for other treasures and necessities. Not a bad idea, other than the obvious fact that this group was a trio of whackjobs. The one thing that did stand out was the stench from the infected and other piles of garbage. The ones that were still walking, plus, the pile of truly dead ones stacked up in one corner of the pen caused a smell that brought a new wave of nausea to Kirk. Several beyond-dead bodies in as many stages of decay, right down to one that was mostly only bone, enhanced the already sickening odor wafting through the air.

Good housekeepers, they obviously weren't.

As they emerged from the wooded area into the open compound Kirk also noticed, almost immediately, that the scantily clad creatures inside the fenced area did, in fact, have other abnormalities. More than just the disease itself. Many were cut, scarred, and stitched back up. All had sundried blood and puss extending from their wounds, as well as from the orifices that the infection naturally caused them to bleed from. Some were without fingers, and even missing entire hands. The one seated at the fence was missing an eye and had a long, sutured cut on her left forearm that was actively seeping blood and other gelatinous fluids caused by severe infection.

Junior had told the truth; this bitch did enjoy playing with knives, and apparently her sewing kit too. *Nice hobby.* Kirk noticed that from the location of dried blood on their raggedy pant wear, a few of the male creatures were most likely missing their man parts as well. Or at least they'd been removed and re-attached.

Kirk also noticed that off to the side of the fence's gate door, nearer where the woman was sitting, was a wooden pole mounted into the ground. It was about the circumference of a telephone pole and standing tall about eight feet high. The faded wood was stained reddish, as was the ground below it. The pole had a large O-ring mounted up high and another chain extending from it.

Next to the pole was a long folding table covered in a sheet that was dried deep maroon from the blood of her victims. Next to the table was a small, metal rolling cart with what appeared to be dried blood staining its once shiny surface.

Kirk thought to himself; what was this woman aspiring to be, some type of Saturday night, self-taught surgeon?!

Was life really so boring on this island that they had to stoop to creating their own live-action horror-gore live theater? The woman was most definitely mad. These three were all the walking definition of a severely dysfunctional family!

The woman, walking ahead of Kirk and pulling on his chain, turned around and winked at him, "Welcome home, lover boy."

Kirk flashed a dirty grin, "Thanks, Mom."

"The name's Maggie. And you and I are going to get to know each other *really* well. Intimately well." As she walked backward and tugged on Kirk's chain, she laughed, winked, and blew him a kiss. Kirk could hear her other half cackle behind him.

Kirk also noticed that for a summer's day with temperatures only in the low 70s, this woman was perspiring pretty badly. Her button-down was stained with sweat at her breast line and under her armpits. Plus, beads of sweat on her brow under her long, brown hair was dripping down her face. Kirk squinted and looked closer at her eyes as the chain connecting the two put them only about six feet apart from each other. He saw that her eyes were bloodshot, and her pupils were far too dilated in the bright daylight.

This bitch has the fever! He thought to himself before stopping, causing the chain to tighten as well as the gun barrel to dig into his back. *Well, how could she not? Playing with dead things like she does!* He finally turned and said out loud, "Get this infected bitch away from me! She's got the virus!"

Billy Bob threw a puzzled look past Kirk, tilting his body to see his woman while holding tight to the .22 now pointed at Kirk's side. "No, she ain't!"

"The hell she hasn't! Look at her! She's sweating like a pig and her eyes are blown out!" Junior was now looking past his father, who was still looking past Kirk to his makeshift wife. "Tell me! Who sweats like that in seventy-degree weather?! Look at her eyes! For *Chrissake*, think about it! She plays with infected bodies! What do you think is going to happen when you play with fire like that?! Look at her!"

They had all ceased walking. Billy Bob hesitated a moment, glaring at both Kirk and then his woman. For a moment, Kirk thought he might just believe him until he glared back at Kirk and raised the gun higher. "You're just trying to get outta' this! Now, shut up before I put another hole in you!"

Maggie tugged the chain hard, spinning Kirk around and he tripped towards her. He turned his head and held his breath as they came face-to-cheek with each other, the woman smiling wide, and she cooed, "Don't worry, honey. I ain't got nothin' that you ain't gonna' catch sooner or later in that pen."

Kirk backed himself up, feeling the barrel of the gun against his spine again. "Bullshit! You've got the infection, lady! And, you know it! I'll bet anything that your guts are turning and you're having trouble staying off the toilet, too! Am I right? Tell me you haven't got the shits right now!"

A worried expression was soon exchanged for an angry one from Maggie as her stomach growled. "Shut up!" She looked over to the other two. "Chain this *asshole* to the pole! I'm going to cut out his tongue and sew his lips together!" Maggie held out the chain as Junior scooted up and grabbed it from her. He led Kirk to the pole and hooked the chain that was around his neck to the O-ring. He then used another short rope to secure his arms to the pole without untying his wrists. He was, though, truly attempting to be careful not to hurt Kirk's shoulder any further.

"Sorry for this, mister," he whispered as he secured the ropes.

"It's okay, kid. I get it."

The happy couple were talking off to the side while Kirk was being secured to the pole. Maggie assured her man that she wasn't infected and in return, he asked if she were all set while he and the boy returned the sailboat and collected items before planning to cause it to sink to the bottom of the ocean. Once she made it clear that she was not only all set but that she planned to have 'fun' with her newest toy, the two lovebirds planted an infected kiss on each other. Along with a bit of groping that caused Kirk to wince as he watched the grotesque displays of affection between the two.

He turned back to Junior, who was finishing up on the ropes. "Hey, kid. I'm telling you, stay away from that chick! She has the virus. Most likely your dad does too."

Junior gave a cautious glance to them and avoided eye contact with Kirk, as if not wanting to hear the bad news, but also believing it at the same time. He said nothing as he left with his father to begin their journey back to Kirk's pontoon.

Kirk knew that time was running out as Maggie sauntered up in front of him, cocking her head and smirking.

"How was your day, honey?" Kirk's tone was snarky.

Maggie didn't respond other than to chuckle with her mouth closed and flash her eyebrows up and down before wandering away in the direction of the cabin and disappearing for a few minutes.

Kirk struggled against his chains and ropes, his shoulder throbbing in pain in return for the effort. He looked around before finally glancing down at the woman sitting on the ground in front of him about eight feet away. From the other side of the fence, the woman was staring up at Kirk with her one eye that was left on her blood and puss-encrusted face. She appeared in her 20s and was wearing a dirty, one-piece bathing suit that she'd probably been sunbathing in when her boat was ambushed by the Manson family. The only other clothing was a sun cover poncho, mostly torn, tattered, and stained. She was expressionless and still.

He glanced back to the cabin to make certain Maggie wasn't returning yet before speaking softly to the woman. "Can you hear me?"

The lifeless face nodded slightly in response.

"Can you speak?"

The woman opened her mouth to reveal that her tongue was mostly missing. The stub that was left after being ripped out had swelled inside her mouth. Several maggots fell from her lower jaw which she seemingly didn't realize had been nesting within her mouth. Either that or she was beyond caring. When she closed her mouth again the thick stump forced clotted blood, mucous, and the writhing insects to trickle down her chin. She coughed and spit a glob of deep red onto the ground, the life within it squirming in the congealed substance that was left in the dirt.

Kirk felt as if he were going to vomit. "Okay, okay! Just take it easy. Don't choke yourself out." Kirk also felt compassion. He knew that this woman had endured unimaginable, painful torture. Not having turned full zombie before Maggie had cut her body up and left her to 'die' inside this cage with the other fully infected creatures. Some of whom had most likely also been tortured before the virus took their pain receptors away.

"Can you stand up? Are you able to move?"

The woman slowly reached up, grabbing the fence to help drag herself as she wobbled to her feet. Luckily, of which she still had both, along with her hands and fingers too. The strain caused the wound on her arm to seep, as well as from her ears, nose, eye, and eye socket. It was obvious she didn't have much time left before the fever would cause her to slip into the coma, and she would eventually wake back up as a living dead person the same as the others inside the pen.

"Can you find something sharp? Is there anything in there that you could use as a weapon? Maybe a sharp stick or something that you could point outward? Anything?"

The infected girl turned from side to side, searching with her only good eye. Infected, jelly-like greenish-red fluid continued to ooze from the socket where her other eye once was.

"Anything! Hurry!"

The woman scanned the ground again, looked up to the others wandering around, and then over to the corner of the pen. She wandered away as Kirk glanced back again to make certain the coast was clear. The woman stopped at the pile of bodies lying on the ground and she reached down to the one that was mostly bones, with only little bits of flesh and muscle remaining. After coughing up more maggots and red mucous onto the pile of bones, she reached down and took hold of a fibula. With strength that she didn't really have anymore, she tugged and tugged until it broke free of the remainder of the leg, leaving in her hands a ten-inch tool. It was complete with one end blunt, and one splintered, plus a little flesh dangling from it which she used her hand to clean off. Expressionless, she walked back over in front of Kirk with her newfound weapon.

"Good! Now hide it. Hold it down to your side and don't let her see it!"

The woman did as she was told, holding the bone close to her body, and using her own arm to conceal it against her tattered, encrusted, and stained sundress.

Maggie emerged from the cabin carrying a small plastic container. She swaggered over and plopped it on the metal cart. The contents clanked, revealing that it was full of stainless-steel knives, both household and surgical, and other sharp, pointy objects. After dropping the container, she noticed the woman standing and swaying at the fence, gazing out at them. She didn't notice the fragment of bone the girl was holding to her side that was pointed away from the two.

"Make a friend?" Maggie smirked with sarcasm.

"I thought I'd try for a date. Maybe dinner and a movie, see where it goes."

"Don't be cheating on me, lover boy. We're just getting started."

"You know that you're infected, don't you? Why don't you just come clean before you take the other two down with you? At least send the kid away while he's still got a chance. Before you and your boyfriend end up wandering around here like all these ones in your little playpen."

Maggie grabbed a scalpel that didn't exactly appear clean, the same as all the other items in the container. She held it up and turned to face Kirk. "I think it's time to take care of that tongue. I'm tired of hearing you talk. Besides, once it's gone, you'll match up with your girlfriend there." Motioning behind herself with the scalpel towards the woman. Maggie turned her head to look at her again, "Well, once I take an eye too, then you'll be a complete match. There won't be much tongue action between the two of you, but I'm sure you'll find something else in common before too long. You can gaze into each other's eye." She cackled loudly in response to her own brand of humor.

After she quieted, Kirk responded, "*Hmmph.* I thought you and I were going to get it on first. A little adult action while the boys are away." He smirked and raised an eyebrow.

Maggie smirked back. "Well now. That might just be arranged." She swung her hips up to Kirk. Too close as he held his breath again and she reached with her free hand to his midsection and grabbed it tight, giving it a good squeeze. She glanced down, and then back up at Kirk. "Oh, my. You do have something down there. Would that make you happy before I start cutting, lover boy? One last dip in my hot, wet ocean?"

Kirk's stomach reacted again, and he held his breath tighter. She released her grip and just before Maggie took another step closer, he said through his teeth, "Nothing would make me happier!"

Kirk pushed his back hard against the pole in an effort to get any additional height that he could gain against the ropes and chains, and then he lifted both legs from the ground. "Now!" He called out to the woman as he planted both of his feet against Maggie's stomach and thrust his legs forward with all the might he could muster. He aimed for the spot between the steel cart and the folding table.

As Maggie's eyes bulged and her body flew backward, the woman raised the piece of bone and kept the blunt end in her palm while shoving the splintered end through the fencing. She braced the weapon with her other hand, planted her feet, and used the last of her dying strength to hold tight. Maggie's back impaled on the bone, driving it deep into her lower lumbar and straight through her spine. She let out a quick, loud yelp before the woman let go of the weapon and Maggie slumped to the ground, the bone catching on the fence as she dropped. It clicked against the links as she fell, working the fragmented end up and down, ripping into her spinal column further as she dropped to the ground. When she landed, she was frozen in place, feet out and arms dangling at her sides, unable to move any part of her body and gasping for air from the pain.

"Check her pockets for a key!" Kirk yelled softly, hoping that the boys hadn't heard Maggie cry out. He now had his feet planted back on the ground again. His shoulder was pounding from the beating of his heart, however; his adrenaline was running too high to notice.

Maggie's eyes were wide, staring straight up and she gurgled up blood and it trickled down her chin while the woman reached through the fence and fished through her pockets, ultimately locating a small keychain. She pulled herself up as quickly as she could, which wasn't quick at all, and she made her way to the gate and unlocked it.

"Don't let the others out!"

The woman closed the gate again before limping over and working on the chains and ropes that held Kirk to the pole. Once again, he kept his head away and held his breath each time that he turned to check her progress. As he wiggled, he looked down again to see a pool of blood beneath Maggie's body. Her gasping had ceased, and he was fairly certain that she was dead. At least for the moment. He wasn't exactly certain what happened when an affected person dies from an injury, or whether they'll regain consciousness. But he was certain that with her spine severed, she wasn't getting back up either way.

When he finally wriggled free, he removed the collar from over his head and threw it to the ground. He also took a few steps away from the woman before facing her.

"Thank you! You did great!" In response, there was no visible emotion from her. She was too far gone, Kirk thought. "I need to move fast before the other two leave the island! You wait here, I'll be back!"

He grabbed a butterfly knife that was in the plastic container, flipped it open, and ran for a clothesline that was attached to the cabin. Several tattered, but seemingly clean articles of clothing hung there. He grabbed a shirt and wiped the handle of the blade, dropped the garment, and grabbed another. He ripped this one into strips with the knife and finally tied off his wound, wrapping the strips around his upper bicep. He removed a third garment and shoved part of it into his back pocket. As he was about to start down the trail toward the water he heard voices.

"Shit!" The boys were on their way back for something. The voices didn't sound frantic, and he didn't hear running, so they probably hadn't heard Maggie scream. They've forgotten something, though, Kirk thought. He looked back behind, there was no time to hide the mess now, they were too close. He ducked into the woods just off the trail and crouched down, deciding quickly that he'd jump out and take Billy Bob during that brief moment of surprise when he sees his woman lying dead on the ground and one of their creatures wandering around outside the fence.

The two were approaching quickly. Kirk could hear the man belittling Junior. "…Hurry up and go get the gas can! …I can't believe you let our boat sit down there on empty without taking care of it sooner! What if we needed to get away fast?!…You're an idiot!"

"…Sorry, Daddy…"

Kirk waited in the underbrush and watched. The two came into view of the compound and passed by Kirk without spotting him, and halted. Billy Bob reached across with his arm to stop Junior from moving once he saw Maggie on the ground. "What in the hell happened here?!"

Kirk took advantage of his opportunity and leaped from the brush, landing just behind the big man. He drove the blade of the butterfly knife deep into Billy Bob's jugular while holding tight to his neck with his other hand. Billy Bob's scream was cut off as the twisting of the blade located his larynx. Blood shot straight out from the wound covering Junior's face and down the front of his shirt. It startled the young lad to the point that he froze in place, his arms up in defense as the blood of his father continued to squirt from the pumping vein and all over the young man.

Kirk, with his grip still tight on the man's throat, thrust forward and sliced the blade clean through Billy Bob's neck and out into the open air, cutting at least a quarter of the man's head off. More blood flew from the blade and gushed down from the gaping wound.

"Daddy!"

Kirk was quick to lower the hand that had hold of Billy Bob's neck, catching the rifle as the man's limp body slumped to the ground. He quickly raised the gun and pointed it at Junior. It wasn't until Kirk was breathing again that he felt the pain return to his shoulder as the adrenaline began to wash away. He noticed his own panting and forced himself to get his breathing under control. With one hand on the gun, he reached back and took the clean garment from his pocket and began to wipe the blood from himself where it had squirted from Billy Bob's neck and covered his hand.

"Sorry, kid, but the old man had to go!"

The boy, with his arms still outstretched and body saturated in the blood that was dripping from his nose and chin, was in shock. He looked down at his father and then over to Maggie's body. With his mouth wide open, he turned back to Kirk. "What do I do now? You killed them both! Why did you do that?!"

Still slightly panting, "I said I was sorry, Kid. Sooner or

later, it was going to happen. If not by me, then someone else! But, holy crap, you're better off without either of them! It's time to grow up and do something for yourself!" These probably weren't the right words, but Kirk didn't have time to discuss life and the whole good versus evil thing right now. Kirk stood straight, let out a huge sigh, and lowered the rifle. "Why don't you just go get yourself cleaned up, kid."

Junior dropped to his knees at his father's body and began to weep. Fairly satisfied that the boy wasn't going to be an issue, however, still not letting his guard down Kirk started walking towards the pen while holding his aching shoulder with his free hand. He stopped briefly at a barrel underneath the eaves of the cabin whose purpose was to catch the rainwater. He quickly washed his hands, grabbed another garment off the clothesline and wiped, and then approached the woman who'd helped him. He stood several feet away and looked her in the eye.

"Again, thank you. I wish there was something that I could do for you in return. Is there anything…anything that I can do to…"

He saw a tear form and it streamed pink down her face as the salty eye-water mixed with her own blood. As she stared at Kirk, her mouth formed a brief smile. Not having the ability to verbalize what she wanted him to do, and after a minute or two of silence between them, she simply closed her eye and tilted her head forward.

She didn't need to say it. Kirk knew what she wanted, and needed. He sighed again, raised the rifle, and with one hand squeezed the trigger, lodging a .22 caliber bullet in her skull. The woman dropped to the ground, entirely dead, and free at last.

He stood for a moment, staring at the body. Junior's voice finally startled Kirk from behind and returned his focus. "Take me with you!"

"*What?!*" Kirk spun around.

As the young man began to pick himself back up from

the ground, dripping from blood that wasn't his, "Take me with you! I don't want to be here anymore!"

"Kid, I can't. I really can't."

"I won't be any trouble! I promise!"

"It's not that…"

The young man began to weep again, burying his bloody face in his hands again. "I have nothing left here. You took it all. Please, take me! You have to take me..!"

"Awwwe, shit!" Kirk let out another huge sigh, his problems having grown larger again. He shook his head in disgust and attempted to refocus the bereaved young lad. "I don't suppose you have any aspirin in that cabin?"

Junior perked up as if to be excited about an ice cream cone rather than being surrounded by, and mourning, his dead *family* members. "Aspirin?! Yeah, I think so!" He darted towards the house.

"Hey!"

Junior stopped and turned around.

"How about you give me back the piece first?"

A look of bewilderment came over Junior's face and then it dawned on him. He reached into his beltline and produced Kirk's 9mm, handing it off before bolting towards the cabin again. Kirk accepted it in the cloth he'd been using to wipe his hands.

Kirk yelled to the kid's backside as he disappeared into the rustic house, "Clean yourself up while you're in there, too!"

As he wiped his gun, Kirk looked around, finding nothing useful that he wanted to drag back to the boat. He just wanted to get out of there. There was already a good chance he'd caught something. He looked at the infected ones wandering around in the pen and shook his head again. He looked at the cabin and determined he didn't need to go inside it regardless of what treasures it may hold.

He also had made the decision not to take the kid. Not just because he may be infected with the virus, which was a good bet, but because he was too much trouble. Skilled at sailing or not this kid would be a handful, and Kirk was no babysitter. And the simple act could be a cover for something far more evil. Not likely, though.

Junior's lanky body came bouncing back out of the cabin, nearly tripping on the front steps. He'd splashed some water on his face but hadn't changed his clothes. He was still a clumsy mess. In his hands was a wad of tissue paper.

"Here!" He ran up and extended his bloodied arms. "I found these. I think they're aspirin! I put them in the tissue so I wouldn't get blood on them."

"Thanks, kid." Kirk accepted the gift and downed several painkillers, swallowing them dry.

"I'm going to go get cleaned up and get my stuff! Oh, and Fido, too!"

"Fido? What's a Fido?"

"My dog! He's okay! He's not mean or nuthin'. We found a pack of dogs on the mainland about a year ago. He was the only one that wasn't mean, or feral, or nuthin'. I'll go get him!"

Oh great, a boy and his dog. This was becoming worse by the minute. "Wait!" Junior stopped and turned around to Kirk. "Look, kid. I don't mean to be…well, mean. But I fly solo. I can't take you…" Kirk could see the hope wash from the boy's face. "I mean, I just don't have it in me to take on a deckhand right now. But look, you got it really good, right here. You're all set up. Not to mention, you were certainly the brains behind this operation. You have skills. And, hell, before I came along, nobody was really bothering you guys. If you clean this place up…"

Junior looked as if he were about to cry again with his eyes welling back up, and he lowered his head.

"Look, kid" Kirk already regretted what he was about to say. "I'll help you get the place cleaned up, okay? We'll take the ones in the pen and lead them down to the water and feed them to the fish. Then, we'll bury the other three right here. After that, I have to leave you to the place. I need to be gone before dark and get back to my boat. You'll be fine, really."

Kirk didn't want to give the young man a chance to complain, whine, or cry, so he turned away to check the outbuildings. He was in hopes to discover the boat gas that Billy Bob had been complaining about when they'd returned. He peeked into a storage shed and located a few 5-gallon gas cans and figured he'd take two of them. To keep from damaging his arm any more he figured that he'd shove a pole under each handle and carry them on his one good shoulder back to the boat. For the time being, he purposely ignored Junior and left him to his own thoughts while he located a rake. He bent down in the shed and shoved the handle between two of the gas cans and braced himself to lift.

"Are you sure you can't take me?!" Junior's voice echoed from the other side of the compound.

Kirk never looked out when he yelled back, "No, kid! I really can't! I'm sorry! You'll be fine!"

The young man's distant voice sounded pathetic and weak, "Okay."

Kirk was startled when he heard the shot and stuck his head from the outbuilding just in time to see Junior's body slump to the ground beneath the rifle stand at the trail's head. He stood up and ran over to the boy, who now had only half of his head left attached to his neck. Bloody brain matter and pieces of skull littered the earth and peppered the trees and brush behind where the remainder had flown upon impact.

Junior, in his defeated state of mind, had knelt down and stuck his face in front of the shotgun shell that was clamped between the vice grip's teeth, and he'd reached around and tapped the nail to the primer with the hammer. The contraption had done its job in that Junior's face was now missing. Deep red liquid and brain fluid oozed from the crater the blast had caused. A bit of smoke was still rising from the empty shell that continued to be locked in the bite of the vice grips.

"Goddammit! Stupid kid!"

Kirk slowly shook his head and then turned to retrieve the gas when he heard a noise and he turned toward the cabin. It wasn't the barking that he'd expected when the kid had mentioned a dog. He'd thought to himself that when Junior had mentioned a 'pack' of dogs, he'd pictured a wolf-hybrid or something. What he spotted in the window, featuring a pathetically weak bark, was a little Benji mutt dog yapping at the vision of its master lying dead on the ground.

"What in the hell is that?" Kirk wandered over and up the front stairs. The dog jumped down and waited at the cabin's badly torn screen door. When Kirk opened it, the scraggly, little pooch ran out, ran in a circle, and parked its butt right in front of Kirk, pathetically looking up and panting.

"*Jeesus.* You're not a real dog. You're just a chew toy for something bigger."

Kirk returned to the shed and tied the two cans to either end of the rake handle. He hoisted up the cans of gas, straddling them on his good shoulder. When he came out of the shed, he noticed the mutt still waiting patiently on the porch and watching his every move. Kirk walked over to the pen's gate and unlocked the latch. "Find your own way out," he called to the creatures that were wandering aimlessly inside.

With the empty rifle in one hand, gas cans and pole in the other and mounted on his good shoulder, and his 9mm tucked back into his waistband, he started towards the trail. When he got to the wood line, he heard the whimpering. Looking back, he called out, "Well, c'mon! Daylight's fading!"

The little dog trotted down the stairs and never stopped at the bodies as it kept right on Kirk's heels all the way back to the pontoon. It followed right beside Kirk as if it was following the Tin Man down the yellow brick road. At the landing, it hopped from the big rock without any prompting and found the front bench-style seat as Kirk loaded up the cans and started the engine.

The conversation was brief as Kirk made his way back to his boat, speaking only once to his new friend. "Listen! The first time you steal scraps off my plate, I'm tossing you overboard!"

It was well into dusk when they boarded the sailboat, now heavy by one little dog. The scraggly mutt wasted no time in locating Kirk's berth and making a place for himself on the bunk while the owner re-secured his pontoon. He located the buoy to the crab pot that he'd originally tried to rob bobbing in the waves nearby. He decided, seeing that there was most likely no longer a dead body attached to it, he'd take a chance and haul it up while leaving all the others to the depths of the ocean.

Kirk cut the submersible loose. It was nothing he was interested in or had the ability to drag around, even if it did have value. He did take the rope and buoy from the crab pot and attached it to the little electric submarine. Somebody may find it in time and keep as a treasure, or use it in trade, he thought.

He spent a bit of time cleaning up, and later he used a mirror to suture his wounds. From a collection he kept on the boat, he gave himself a SARs-Crf-5 home test. The kits were all long since expired, but he still felt good about himself when the test returned a negative result.

He and the mutt enjoyed a good, boiled red crab dinner that evening. He'd also scored an extra crab pot for his small collection for future use.

Chapter 6
THE LEATHERHEADS

Kirk spent the next several days primarily drifting south towards the Albemarle Sound, rather than the several hours it would have normally taken under full sail. He wanted to give his shoulder time to heal.

While recouping he'd enjoyed a few hours of fishing. He now had a few fresh catches in the chest freezer. Additionally, he'd discovered that his new friend knew a few tricks that the young redneck had apparently taught him. He knew to sit, lie down, and shake. The dog seemed happy taking up space on Kirk's bunk and feeling the warm breeze on his fur from the top of the bulkhead on deck.

On the third day, Kirk was feeling better, and the shoulder looked and felt pretty good. In fact, on this bright and sunny day, there were calm seas and a stomach to match. Kirk was on deck, blaring the speakers from his CD player and dancing like a goofball to Paul Simon's, *You Can Call Me Al.* Well, why not, he thought. It wasn't like there was anyone other than the dog that could see him. The mutt was cocking its head sideways to the display, not seeming to mind too much.

On the evening of day four he encountered a decent-sized storm approaching from the southwest. He was forced to take refuge in Mobjack Bay near Gloucester, Virginia. A spot he'd searched before, and, had taken safety in the calmer waters at the mouth of the bay during other trips.

He held up to wait out the storm, although he still spent an amount of time at the rail while the storm passed overhead during the next several hours. He dropped the crab pots while waiting it out, hoping to keep filling the ice chest, while involuntarily chumming the waters frequently with his own stomach contents.

By the late afternoon on the fifth day, the skies had cleared again. Kirk felt this was a good time to take an inventory of what he intended to search for on his next stop ashore, supposedly in the Albemarle Sound if the coast were to be clear. Although, nowadays, any find was a potential good find, with basic necessities being scarce.

He also discovered on this day that his reverse osmosis saltwater purifier had crapped out when he attempted to take a shower. The 50-gallon-per-hour filtration system was essential for purifying saltwater into fresh, and something he couldn't live without onboard. This was also an item that couldn't wait. Kirk knew he was going to need to find a marina here in Mobjack Bay and scavenge any boats that he could locate if there were any left.

Kirk checked his charts. He noticed that in one of the bay's rivers there had been a yacht marina that he hadn't yet visited. There was a good chance he might scrounge one there if he could locate a vessel that was still above the water line. He set a course for the Severn River, located inside the bay, and waited until dark before entering the waters.

After dusk, utilizing his navigational equipment, he sailed up the calm waters while keeping an eye on the radar...and the sonar. Plus, he used the darkness to attempt to spot the glowing fires where groups of people may be located if they were close enough to the shores to spot them. At around midnight, he anchored just upriver of the marina, or at least where it was on his charts, and he laid down for a night of rest.

Daybreak brought sunshine and sporadic clouds. Kirk was up early, just after dawn. He never could sleep once the sun broke the horizon. Nor did he sleep well given where he was located. He felt most safe on the open seas, not so much sitting on a tight river.

There was just a bit of fog laying low this morning and he waited for it to lift before moving. Once the sun burned off the vapors, it revealed that he had actually anchored just outside of the marina itself. As it lifted, Kirk stood at the stern shading his eyes with the mutt sitting right beside him. The once high-class yacht club was certainly not what it used to be. Only two of the many long, wooden piers extended from shore with the remaining half-dozen or so badly deteriorated, or gone entirely. Any vessels that were once moored in the marina had sunk, with several of the taller masts still breaking the water's surface. The remainder of the boats were now sitting on the bottom in their watery graveyard.

Using his binoculars, he looked onshore to the boatyard. There were still several yachts laying around, all in various stages of decay and had been victims of scavenging and vandalism. Kirk spotted the fuel pumps, guaranteed to have nothing left, and also a maintenance and storage building. Behind it all, just up from the shore and sitting on a knoll was the clubhouse itself. A massive structure surrounded by decaying concrete decks and dilapidated patios, plus a golf course now overgrown with weeds and other vegetation. The layout all looked like a haunted mansion now.

Kirk put the drone up and watched his video monitor, scanning the area in every direction to the limits of the flying camera. The village where the yacht club was located was fairly spread out with one central downtown area. The land mass itself was made up of a large peninsula. The once rich community was now a literal ghost town. Kirk saw no organized movement or residency other than the usual infected inhabitants wandering about that he typically discovered in every town and village. He flew the drone up and down the shoreline, finding no other floating vessels, large or small, that he could make out.

He still didn't like the idea of having his sailboat sitting in the river. He was much more comfortable leaving it out on the open ocean where it was more difficult to see. In here, anyone passing by would spot it easily. He hoped it wouldn't take long to find what he was searching for. A couple of hours or so, but no more. The worst-case scenario would be that he doesn't locate anything in the boatyard, and he moves on. He still had a few bottles of water, and he could go without a proper, freshwater bath for a few days. Meals were no issue, as he could boil his seafood in saltwater.

Kirk also decided that rather than bothering to anchor and motor in on the dinghy for just the stones-throw to shore, he'd anchor off the end of one of the two wooden piers. He chose the one that looked like it would still hold his weight for the walking distance to the shore.

He maneuvered the vessel gracefully, not wanting to bump the pier and knock it into the water, and he dropped anchor. He supplied himself with a toolbelt containing a multi-tool and a couple of adjustable wrenches, plus a hammer for loosening any rusty parts. To keep his hands free, he took only the longbow and quiver containing arrows, his sawed-off, and a .45 caliber semi-auto handgun with seven in the magazine and one in the pipe. He also pocketed two extra magazines and a few extra shells in a pair of cargo short pants.

Before disembarking, Kirk knelt down to the dog. "You wait here. And, any signs of trouble, you start barking, okay?" He petted the mutt, stood, and peered up and down the channel before looking back down at the dog. "And try to be loud about it if you need to! Not that pathetic yapping like you did on the island!"

Kirk climbed over the rail and lowered himself to the pier. He was reminded of his shoulder injury while doing so. He gingerly stepped onto the woodwork and tested its strength before making his way to the shore. The old, sea-rotted wharf complained, but it still held his weight.

Onshore, he searched through the boats that were strewn around the yard. Oddly, there seemed to be a large number of junked-out jet skis lying about and a few more inside what appeared to be an old maintenance garage. Everything had been picked over and robbed. No outboards, electronics, or even usable parts were left on most of the boats that had been tossed ashore long ago from the storms. Finally, after more than an hour of searching, Kirk located a vessel that at one time, he thought, must have been worth about a million dollars. Now, it was just a shell. It had been shrink-wrapped, although most of that had weathered and torn away. It had also been mounted in storage up on posts but had since dropped to the ground and tilted to one side. The good news was that while rummaging through, it still had a purifier intact. And bonus, this one could produce 80 GPH as opposed to the one he'd had that only had the capacity for 50.

By the time he'd removed the treasure, he was over the two-hour limit that he'd given himself. Still, he wanted to check out the yacht club's main house. Kirk felt that he could use a new polo shirt, and maybe a windbreaker, if there were still any to be found.

The building was badly weathered, and all the windows had been broken or blown out. Seaweed and other dead sea life hung from the building and were strewn about the yard and golf course. Old, wooden, fancy patio chairs and tables were tossed and flipped over. All evidence of years of natural weather and storm damage. As Kirk traversed the crumbling cement stairs, a walker lumbered from around the side of the building. It was dressed in a tattered, cracked, and dirty old yellow rain slicker and rain hat to match. The creature resembled an old-time sailor. It was dragging a piece of braided rope behind it as if he was going to tie off his sailing vessel to the pier. Its recessed eyes were severely clouded like an old man with cataracts. Kirk wondered if it even still had the power of sight. Its skin was tight and wrinkled against the frail bones. It had obviously been 'dead' for a number of years and its thick, dirty gray facial hair was caked and stained in the dried blood and other body fluids from its eyes, nose, ears, and mouth.

The creature didn't seem to notice Kirk, who stepped aside and allowed it to pass, watching the creature limp its way down the stairs toward the pier.

"Don't worry, he won't hurt you. He's been wandering around here for years," an old, gravelly voice called down to Kirk.

Kirk turned to see at the building's front doors, an old man standing under the rotting frame. Appearing to be in his 70s, he was also wearing slicker pants, rubber boots, and a heavy woolen sweater. He had an old, dirty fisherman's hat on his head and just as much graying facial hair as the creature that had just walked by, but without the visible blood stains to match. In his mouth was a curved bowl pipe, but no smoke rising from it, as it appeared unlit and empty.

"I don't suppose you have any tobacco on your sailing ship there? I ran out about three years ago." Taking his pipe out of his mouth and motioning to Kirk's boat with it. "Maybe in trade for the water purifier you just took out of that boat?"

"You run this place, old man?" Kirk was courteous, however, cautious. The old salt didn't appear to have a weapon, at least nothing in his hands other than the pipe.

The old sailor stepped down from the door, the joints in his old legs reminding him of his age. "I used to. It's been a long time, though. Now, I just live here in the old clubhouse. The name's Chester." The old man limped to the nearest old patio chair and struggled to turn it upright. He groaned as he let his body drop down into it and leaned back. "I was once the maintenance manager here. Now, I'm just about as useless as that old boat captain that just wandered past you."

"How do you get by?"

"Oh, I sit and watch the harbor during the day. Nothing else to do. At night I have an oil lantern to get me around. Still have some kerosene left. Not a lot, but a little."

"No, I mean food. How do you feed yourself there, old man?"

"The Argonauts keep me fed."

"The what?"

"Argonauts. Those fellas that go up and down the river here on their jet skis and whatnot. Kind of like a street biker gang, only on the water. Stupid looking bunch, too. I tinker on their machines, and they leave me be, and bring me food from time to time." Chester chuckled, "Heh, heh. Sort of a dumb name they came up with for themselves, don't you think? They're too stupid to realize that it means 'tiny octopus'." The old man laughed again, sending himself into a coughing fit. When he regained his composure, he continued. "I don't even think they know how to spell it. Speaking of them idiots, what'd you have to give up in exchange for them to let you pass and come up the river?"

"Pass?" Kirk scowled, a bit puzzled by the question, "What do you mean, old man?"

"I mean, what'd you have to give them? A toll. That's their thing. They don't let anyone travel up the river without paying a toll. They think they own the damn thing."

"I didn't see anybody, old man. I came up the river after dark last night. There was nobody chasing me to collect any kind of toll. I don't pay anybody anything to be on the water."

"Hmph. Well…*heh, heh*…maybe that's why they're all parked down there by your boat." Motioning again with his pipe, "They must be waiting to collect from you."

Kirk tilted his head back and closed his eyes, emitting a sigh before turning around and seeing them. In the distance, floating in the water at the end of the pier and surrounding his vessel were a dozen or so bobbing in the water. Most were riding jet skis. Some only had one driver, and some had a driver and passenger. One craft appeared to be a mini jetboat with a helmeted driver. Kirk also spotted one of them standing on his vessel at the bow.

Defeated, and primarily mad at himself, Kirk began to walk back to the wharf. He passed by the old sailor-zombie who was still making its way toward the shoreline. Kirk kept his hands in sight of the wannabe gang as he walked back out onto the pier. As he strolled closer, he took a mental note of what he was up against. On the weather-faded and junk watercraft were, again, some single riders, both men and women. Some had men with their women, and some had women with their women. They all appeared fairly rough-looking. And, quite ridiculous, he thought. They were dressed in leather gear. Vests, jackets, chaps, the works. All trying to look as if they were a gang of one-percenters on their Harleys. They all had some type of firepower, most holding onto rifles and shotguns. He noticed that a couple of them had crossbows.

Kirk looked up at the one dude standing on the bow of his boat. He was holding a large crossbow with the butt resting on his hip. Kirk also noticed that sitting on top of the cockpit was the mutt, happily panting. As Kirk approached the group, the dog stood on all fours and yapped at him.

"Good job, fleabag! You were supposed to let me know before they got here!"

The one that appeared to be their leader was the guy standing on Kirk's bow. He jumped down to the pier directly in front of him as Kirk arrived with his hand, and weapons in the air, showing that he wasn't intending on fighting.

Kirk was surprised that the pier held up as the guy landed. He was fairly large, in a muscular sort of way. He had only a leather vest on top, unbuttoned, and leather chaps over a pair of black jeans. He wore biker boots on his feet and a leather Brando biker's hat on his head. All of the cowhide was faded, cracked, and scuffed. The upper and lower garments also displayed dangling biker chains that were fairly salt-rusted. The guy's thick and long facial hair matched his equally thick body hair. Protruding from the hair surrounding his lips was a lit nub of a cigar. Kirk nearly chuckled, however, he purposely held it back.

Kirk looked around and discovered that most of the remainder of the group were equally unattractive, including most of the women. Several were even larger and more muscular than the men appeared to be.

Kirk looked back at his host, a most unimpressed expression on his face. "Are you all just coming from the Blue Oyster Bar?"

The man's voice was gruff as he removed the cigar, spit a big gob of mucous into the water beside himself, and blurted, "The what?!"

"Never mind." *Apparently, these bozos have never seen the Police Academy movies*, Kirk thought to himself. He had the collection on DVD in his cabin. Possibly even tonight's movie if he made it out of this alive, and with his sailboat intact.

Kirk continued, "I suppose you want something."

"This here is our waters! How'd you get up through here without us seeing you?! Nobody gets through without paying a toll!"

Kirk's answers remained sarcastic, "I don't know. I came up through last night. You and your group must have been busy performing karaoke at the Oyster or something."

"Why does he keep saying the *Oyster*?!" One of the group's members called out.

Another one yelled out, "Let's take all his equipment!"

And yet another, "Let's take his entire boat!"

The leader, still glaring straight at Kirk, directed his comments to his ensemble. "Shut up! I'll do the negotiating!"

Kirk eased up a bit when he detected the sound of one of them racking a shell into their weapon and determined he probably shouldn't agitate them any more than he truly wanted to. "Look, I can see that you run the show around here. But I'm also assuming that you aren't an unreasonable bunch. Hell, you feed the old man back here for nothing, don't you?"

"He don't cause us no harm! He's been here for years. Plus, in return, he fixes up our machines and keeps them running! We don't have much food, there just ain't hardly nothing left! But we give him something when we do have it. Hell, half of the time he feeds us from the one lobster pot he's got soaking off this very pier! We've got a soft spot for him!" With the free hand that wasn't clutching the crossbow, their leader poked Kirk hard in the shoulder, "But, not for you, trespasser!" Luckily, it hadn't been the bad shoulder, but it still annoyed Kirk greatly.

Their gravelly-voiced leader continued, "You need to pay up if you feel like leaving our river alive! Maybe we should take your boat!" He turned his head and spoke through his teeth which were clenched on the smoking nub, "The Rotten Banana?"

"I didn't name it." Kirk spoke casually as he lowered his arms, "Look, pal, you're not getting my boat. Not without a fight, anyway, and neither of us wants that. Somebody on your team would get hurt or killed before you take me down, and you know it. What else is it that you want so we all can part company intact?"

As the group's leader glared at Kirk. A throat from underneath the helmeted jetboat operator could be heard loudly clearing itself, *"Ahem!"*

The cigar-smoker rolled his eyes and said softly, "Shit. Not again."

"Look, I've got some food. Some fresh stuff. It isn't much, but you can have it. Some canned stuff, too if that's what you need. How about ammo? There's some of that too."

"Uh-AHEM!"

"Oh, for *chrissake!*"

Kirk raised his eyebrows and asked in a snarky tone, "Is there a problem?"

The answer came in a low, almost sheepish tone, "It's Bertle."

"What's a Bertle?"

As the question was asked, the person in the mini jet boat, who was gargantuan and barely fit inside the cockpit, removed their helmet. This exposed an individual, most likely female, however, as butt ugly as nature could have created her. She flipped her long, auburn hair around and slammed the helmet onto the hood of the jet boat. Her massive, dirty, and horribly tattooed arms bloated from the crusty leather vest she was wearing. She looked up at Kirk, raising one-half of her thick unibrow, and smirked. Possibly blowing Kirk an air kiss, but it was hard to tell with her pudgy lips being permanently fixed in the pucker position.

"That's Bertle." The leader spoke low and casually while looking back at the woman along with Kirk, "We promised her a mate the next time we caught someone. I don't think she cared whether it was male or female." He turned back to Kirk, who simply stared wide-eyed at the sight and at what he was hearing. "I tell you what. If you take one for the team and throw one into her, we'll call it even."

Bertle smiled wide, exposing her mostly toothless kisser. An even wider-eyed Kirk responded softly, however, directly, "Not unless she shaves first!" He looked back to the man, "Are you nuts or something?! I mean, it's been a while, but I'm not sticking any part of my body into that! And she's not sticking her cock into me, either! Are you even certain that that's a woman?!"

The gang leader glanced back down to the jetboat operator and responded hesitantly, "Pretty sure."

"All of the raw oysters on the planet couldn't get me prepared to tackle that!" Kirk remarked. As he said this, he glanced to see one of the members on their jet boat directly ahead and just off the pier raise their rifle and point it in his direction. As Kirk ducked, he saw that the barrel appeared to be aimed behind him, not at him, and he turned around just as the leatherhead touched off a round.

Kirk watched as the rain jacket of the old sailor exploded outward from the back of his upper chest. Puss-filled blood followed and mushroomed in the air behind the creature as its body cocked sideways. The infected sailor had made its way out onto the pier and was shuffling along only twenty feet behind Kirk and the gang's leader, who smiled as another of his group took aim and fired, this time using an UZI automatic and firing a barrage of bullets.

The front of the zombie's slicker became peppered with holes, and deep fluid flew in all directions. The creature's arms involuntarily flew to its sides as the bullets trailed up the front and traveled through its body, exiting along with this liquid and chunks of flesh. The final bullet struck its neck and mangled its jugular. Infected fluids spurted out and down the front of his crusty raincoat. However, the creature continued to remain upright.

Kirk remained crouched and yelled up to the gang's leader, who was smiling as the gunplay apparently was entertaining him, "Could you please tell the Village People to quit doing that?!"

As Kirk yelled out, it would be Bertle that would raise a shotgun and deliver the 'kill' shot.

The dead, old salt's head exploded off its shoulders. The very top of his skull, along with its old rain hat, went straight up into the air as bone, brain matter, and body fluids flew in all directions. His legs bent and the remainder of the body slumped to the pier. Small pieces of bone and flesh rained back down, sounding like a quick hailstorm as it bounced off the rotting timbers of the wharf. The sailor's hat and contents also fell straight back down into the slimy mess on the creature's upper torso.

Bertle let out a deep, husky laugh and winked at Kirk.

A distant, old voice called out from the clubhouse, "Why'd you have to go and do that?! He wasn't hurting anyone!"

A voice echoed from one of the gang's members, "Shut up, old man, or you'll be next!"

Kirk stood back up, flashing a look to the leader as if to say, *"Really?"* He received back a smirk and chuckle in response to his expression.

Kirk was quickly growing weary of the situation, and more than a bit worried, as it was now apparent that this crew had itchy trigger fingers and didn't mind wasting bullets and shooting at things. In fact, they appeared to be quite amused to be doing so.

"May I have a word with you? Possibly out of earshot of the rest of your entourage?" Kirk motioned with his head and the man frowned, however, nodded in agreement. The two stepped away from the boat, being careful in walking around the old sailor's headless body and not slip and fall from the slippery blood and guts now staining the pier.

After several more steps, Kirk stopped and turned to face the man again. "Okay, how about I buy my way out of here with some information?"

"Information? What information?"

"Listen, I'm going to guess that your living situation isn't the most desirable and life is pretty rough on the river. Am I right?"

The burly man scratched the back of his own head, thinking about the question. His crossbow was still held tight in his other hand, the butt mounted to his hip. "Well, it ain't great. Like I said, very little left for anyone these days. Food is scarce and there's competition on the mainland everywhere you go. Dead ones are wandering all over, and they sneak up on you, especially at night when you can't see them coming. Hell, if you just bump into one, you might catch their disease. We've lost more than we have left to the virus."

"Time to retire, maybe?"

"Where are you going with all this?"

Kirk glanced over at his group, then explained, "There's a cluster of small islands, not far from here. In the middle of one, there's a compound, all set up with a house and outbuildings. There's a solar setup and even a steady food source."

"Okay, fine. Who do I have to kill?" His tone reflected skepticism and doubt.

"Nobody. I took care of that already. A few days ago, they ambushed me and tried to take me captive. It didn't work out too well for them. They're gone and the place is empty…well, except that you'll need to clean up a bit of a mess that I left behind. I'm telling you, your group would be set for life, or whatever's left of it. Hell, there's even an electric submarine floating around near a group of loaded crab pots, and a solar charging station on the shoreline. There's also a sailboat on the mainland somewhere in sight of the island. Cameras, water, power, tools, clothing, and a little gas too."

The leader flashed Kirk a look that let him know that he wasn't convinced. "You're full of shit! If this oasis does exist, then why didn't you just stay there and take advantage of it all?!"

"I decided long ago that I'm staying on the open water. That, and it's too much to take care of for one person. Your little group can learn something out there and thrive, instead of waiting here to collect a toll from the one or two boats that wander in every few months. Waiting for you to take whatever they don't have to give anyway. Whadya say?"

Kirk waited for an answer, noticing that the wheels were turning as the gruff leatherhead looked down, scratched his chin, and tried to make sense of the information in his feeble brain.

He glanced back up at Kirk. "How do I know you aren't feeding me a load of bullshit?"

"You don't!" Kirk set his weapon down and pulled his short sleeve up past his recent wound and displayed the fresh stitching. "Look! I got this for my efforts when they tried to keep me there!" He let his sleeve drop and pointed, "Think about it! Look at what you're all driving out there! I bet you're burning homemade sludge in those engines, plus anything else that has ethanol that you can scrounge and dump into those machines, aren't you? How long do you think that'll last? The old man's probably out of extra parts, not to mention time!" Kirk motioned his head to the yacht clubhouse, "Hell, take the old man with you. These clowns could learn something from that old salt! Learn how to be human again."

The leatherhead continued scratching his head and glanced up at the shoreline. He took the nub from his mouth and spit another gob onto the pier, responding softly, "He won't go. He's been here too long."

"It doesn't hurt to ask him. He looks like he's treated you guys pretty good. Look, you said it yourself. You're dying off from the infected ones that you're coming into contact with here on the mainland faster than you can handle. Go out there where they can't get to you and live whatever time you have left." Kirk waited a moment more to let the idea sink in and then he extended his hand.

The leatherhead glanced down at his gesture and thought for just a second or two more, then he offered his hand in return. A deal was struck. Kirk picked his weapon back up and the two turned back to Kirk's boat. They stopped short on the pier when they both looked down to see Bertle scowling up at them while her fat, ugly ass was bobbing on the waves in her tiny jetboat.

Kirk leaned into his host and whispered, "How many of you does it take to help get her out of that thing?"

"Are you sure you don't want to? Just once? She's getting awfully cranky with everyone. We can't handle her much longer if she don't get some."

"I'll pass." Kirk kept walking while the lead leatherhead hocked another goober onto the pier and shrugged his shoulders at Bertle, smirking with caution as if to say to her, *"Sorry."*

♦ ♦ ♦

After Kirk showed the gang's leader exactly where the

islands were located on his charts, and also where the crab pots were to be found in relation to the island, the group motored off to make plans to move to their new home, leaving Kirk alone. A deal was a deal, even in the aftermath of the virus. To some, and luckily for Kirk this time, there still remained a code to a parlay between seagoing parties.

After they disappeared, Kirk scolded the dog one more time for not warning him of their presence, and then he rummaged around in his cabin seeking something he believed was there. After digging through several cupboards and slamming their doors, he smiled. Emerging in his hand was a sealed tin, about the size of a coffee can. He shook it close to his ear to make certain the contents were still somewhat fresh before climbing back out on deck.

"Try to do better this time," he said to the mutt before jumping down and trotting back up to the yacht club. He found the old mechanic in the bar that was once located within the clubhouse. He was seated at one of the dusty tables and playing solitaire with a partial deck of worn-out cards, having trouble making out the symbols and numbers. The only light, other than the last of the sunset that was quickly approaching, was the flickering from a small fire in the club's decaying, yet massive stone fireplace in the center of the room.

The old man looked up with a dubious expression as Kirk approached. Kirk said nothing as he set the tin of pipe tobacco on the table and turned to walk back out.

The old salt reached over, picking up the treasure with both hands and holding it up to his eyes. A smile formed beneath the hair on his face. Through the empty pipe still in his mouth, he said, "Thank you!"

His words were uttered to Kirk's back as he exited the room, and Kirk replied softly as he walked out, "Don't mention it, old man. Good luck…"

Chapter 7
AND THEN, THERE'S MAUDE

The following day Kirk was traveling around 18 knots on calm seas, sailing past the outer banks of Albemarle Sound along the peninsula, with the land in sight off to his southwest. As he approached Kitty Hawk, he picked up something on his radar. It indicated a small target, and only one, so he hoped he wasn't in for any more trouble. He glassed the waters out ahead. Having traveled these waters before, he had a suspicion as to what it might be and was hoping that his assumption was correct.

In his sights, he confirmed his suspicions. About a mile out he spotted the multi-colored, wooden cabin cruiser with two faded and torn sails flying, one in the center and one nearer the bow. The old sailboat was twenty-five feet long. Tied all around it were various-sized old car tires. The center-cabin was tall and draped over the top was an old blue tarp. Several ropes were holding the rain cover down and they extended all over the boat, all tied to the gunwales. Hanging from the ropes and scattered all over the floor of the deck was miscellaneous junk, with only a path allowing the boat's captain to access the ropes that controlled the sails.

Kirk smiled and lowered his binoculars, pointing his

vessel towards the anomaly. He looked out of his cockpit window to the mutt who was sitting on the bow and enjoying the wind blowing through its fur. The dog turned his head to look back as Kirk remarked, "It's Maude."

'Maude' was another junk trader that frequented the waters of the North Carolina coast. Kirk had first encountered her three years ago in the same area. On his last trip through he hadn't seen her and was afraid that something had occurred, so he was relieved to see her boat approaching.

Kirk believed that the woman had to have been in her late 70s and she was certainly rough around the edges. Nobody messed with Maude. Even the pirates left her alone because, well just because. A crusty old soul, she could be quite rude, but that was also part of her charm.

Maude always keeps her boat close to the coastline and within sight of land, going up and down the 200 or so miles of the Barrier Peninsula. It's rumored that when she's not on the water, she considers the Bodie Island Lighthouse her home. And it's also rumored that her humble home is loaded with electronic monitoring equipment so that she can keep tabs on the area and know when it's safe to venture out on the land or the water. Most likely it was very well-guarded or possibly booby-trapped, too.

Similar to all the other traders and junk boats, Maude never has much to offer. In fact, Kirk believed that most others provide her with more basic necessities than she trades back to them. But sometimes you could score something from her if she's recently been on one of her scavenger hunts on the mainland peninsula. If nothing else on this day, Kirk was hoping to get information from the old woman on parts of the Albermarle Sound that he hadn't been to before. He knew that the estuary itself was, in places, more than 50 miles wide and many smaller rivers splintered off from it. Kirk hadn't been in that area yet and he was hoping he could get some good direction from the old junk dealer. Maude was good for information if nothing else. And, if Maude uses the term, "I hear tell," it means that she knows for certain. Just another indication that hidden in her lighthouse was plenty of nautical spying equipment.

Through his binoculars, Kirk could see the old woman in her wheelhouse looking back through her telescope. He wondered if she knew who he was. Not that it would matter, Maude didn't back down from anyone. She'd probably even tell the pirates to 'kiss her ass' if they were to make her mad enough.

The two vessels drifted together side-by-side. The old woman, short and stout, was dressed rather warmly for a hot day off the Carolinas. She was wearing a tattered, faded wool sweater and torn wool gloves with the fingers missing. She had on slicker pants and high-cut water boots. Her stringy, gray hair was all up in a messy bun. She waddled out to the starboard gunwale and didn't say her first words until the two boats were secured together, making certain that there was going to be some type of business taking place this day.

Ultimately, the cranky old woman never looked up as she said casually, "Hello, there dickhead." Not that she recognized Kirk. She just called everyone that.

Kirk chuckled, "Maude."

"Whatcha need? I got lots of stuff," Maude remarked as she waddled back into her wheelhouse and sat down. The windows of the cockpit had all long since been broken out and Kirk could detect the aroma of sweet tea brewing. He looked inside and saw Maude steeping the hot drink in a small pot that was being heated over a rusty camping stove. Underneath was a tin can of Sterno. Although, the chemical heat was all gone, and she was burning wood chips in the cup.

Kirk jumped down, being careful of his footing, while the mutt waited and watched from the roof of the cockpit, his nose checking the air too. Kirk ducked under the ropes and other junk and crawled into Maude's tiny wheelhouse. He sat down on an old wooden bench facing her.

"What goodies have you got today?"

"Shit, I got plenty! The mainland's been good to me lately. Found some coffee, this here tea, a couple cartons of smokes, and some bottles of whiskey. All the tin and real silverware you could ever want. Beef jerky and some old beer that'll probably both give you the shits too…"

"You're a regular grocery store, there Maude."

"Fuckin right! Whatcha need?" Maude finally looked up from her teacup, displaying her severe cataracts. It was amazing to Kirk that she could still navigate in the bright sunlight. She certainly didn't have the fever, though. Not the way she was dressed, so Kirk was at ease with her.

"You can have anything you see…except for the tea! That shit's mine!"

"Not a coffee drinker, huh?"

"If the mood hits me. Not today!"

"I tell you what, Maude. I'll give you something instead. In return, I'm looking for some information."

Kirk spoke as he looked around her wheelhouse admiring all the crap that was hanging on the walls. It was apparent that at one time old Maude had scavenged a toy or souvenir store. There were rubber snakes, alligators, and crocodiles dangling. Dirty, stuffed toy monkeys, teddy bears, and other various animals bounced against the woodwork on the gentle waves. "I'm looking to do some scavenging in the Sound…"

"What in the hell would you want to do that for?!"

"Just someplace that I've never been. Figured I'd look around."

"Well, you better know what you're doing." Maude took a sip of her tea and continued, "Lots of water in there. Goes way up into the land on the Chowan River. Lots of other rivers in there too. There's lots to look at. Lots of trouble to be found, too!"

"What do you mean?"

"Well, I don't go up in there. But, I've heard lots of stories." Maude stared into her cup as she spoke, holding it with both of her gloved hands. "The north side, up the Pasquotank, is said to be where the *Rumrunners* are said to base, near Elizabethtown." Maude looked up at Kirk, "Do you know who they are?"

"Pirates."

"Yep, a rough bunch, too. They're at war with the *Outriggers*. A stupid name if you ask me! But they both just happen to claim the Chowan River on the west end as their own." The old woman reclined back in her captain's chair that had long since lost all of its cushioning and was covered in dirty, torn blankets and filthy yarn-crochet Afghans. "It makes for some interesting boating when them two are going at it, which is pretty much all of the time."

"I'm sure."

"They both have a setup on the mainland. Little cities with walls all around them to keep the dead ones out and keep inside whatever it is they keep inside. Must be quite the hell hole in both of their little setups, I'd imagine. Wouldn't want to think about what they'd do to an outsider who was snooping around there."

"So, you're saying I should avoid the north side."

"I'd avoid it all, but I ain't the stupid one that wants to go in there. You want some tea?"

Kirk held up a hand, politely, "No, thanks." He continued, "I don't get it, Maude. Why are they out here playing around and bothering others if they each have a setup on the mainland and are at war with each other all the time?"

"Stupidity, that's why!" Maude nodded and winked, "That, and just for a show of power and control. That's what it's really about. Nuthin' left on dry land but walking dead people!" Maude pointed with her cup to the shoreline, "It's too dangerous to be in there anymore! Them things can keep on walking upright for years! It's almost as if they've learned how to live again! If you get too close and they breathe on you, you end up just like one of them! The air over the mainland is foul! It's the sea air that keeps people like you and me healthy!" Maude went into a slight coughing fit from raising her voice, slurping tea over the sides of her cup while trying to cover her mouth.

"Yeah, I can see that." Kirk was being sarcastic, "We're all just walking, talking posters for how to live a healthy life."

"I'm telling you! There's a time limit on anyone still living in there! At least out here there's somewhere for the air to go. In there, it's all stale. Not to mention that shit them damn Russians played around with! Who knows what they did while they were fuckin' around with their chemistry sets?! Plus, all the effin' radiation they dumped all over everyone!"

Maude leaned out from her chair and refilled her cup. As she leaned back and brought the hot, tin beverage to her lips she motioned to Kirk, "We're all going to die from something that we didn't plan on twenty years ago. It's just a matter of when." She winked her clouded eye at Kirk and sipped her tea.

Kirk couldn't argue with the old woman's logic. He wiped his hand across his stubbly face and looked towards the coastline, noticing that the breeze had picked up and both boats were rocking a bit and bumping against each other. "What's that leave for me to take a look at? The south side?"

Maude peered out the glassless windows as well, "Well, there's the Alligator River on that side. I ain't heard much tell of it. It's a big area. Lots of smaller rivers and swamps spurring off it. I ain't saying that there isn't trouble in there, mind you. In fact, lately, something weird has been going on over there."

"What do you mean?"

"Well, about a year and a half ago I started hearing things on the short-wave bands. I didn't pay much attention. It all sounded like the usual crap. You know, the whole 'safety awaits you' bullshit that them bastards keep puttin' over the airways. And then you end up getting your throat cut when you go to check it out. But then I heard tell that some type of settlement popped up way in there near Hyde County. It turns out that's where the transmission seemed to be coming from. I also hear tell that the pirates don't go near it for some strange reason."

Maude motioned to Kirk with her teacup again, "You might be better off avoiding it all and checking out Pamlico Sound just south of here instead!"

Kirk stood up and stretched, "I've been there, Maude. Checked it all over. I need to adventure someplace new and see what's left to be found. I think I'll check the Alligator River and see what's what." He looked around at all of the garbage and junk, "Thanks for the intel, I appreciate it. What'll it be, Maude? What do you have a need for?"

Maude glanced around at her treasures. She looked left, right, and up. "I dunno." She looked into her tin cup and thought, "Got any tea? I'm gonna' run out quick the way I'm drinking this stuff. It keeps me regular!"

Kirk chuckled, "Yeah, old woman. I think I got some tea. Be right back."

As he started to exit the wheelhouse, Maude called out, "What about gold?"

A puzzled Kirk turned his head back, "Gold? You want some gold, there, old woman? Like a bracelet or something?"

"Not me, you asshole!" Maude motioned with her cup again towards the coastline, "Them ones in there! Haven't you heard? Pirates are pirates! Gold, real silver, anything shiny! They may be stupid, but they still know the value of a commodity!" Maude rocked to her feet and looked out her window toward the mainland. "There's rumors are that there's still a couple of cities in operation further inland. I heard tell that the pirates are trading the shiny stuff for weapons, food, and ammunition! Hell, it could be that someone's making gasoline again! Who knows?! I hear tell that someone in there is looking to put actual treasure back into the trade. Shit, I hear tell that even Happy Hour was accepting the shiny stuff now." She turned to Kirk,

"Something's brewing on the horizon!"

Maude pointed straight at Kirk with a stubby finger this time, "And, you can bet if there's a group wanting gold and silver in there, and is willing to trade for weapons or gas, it's gotta' be a politician! Something's up in there!"

"I can't argue with that logic. What's your point?"

"My point is, if you got some of that stuff it may just get you out of a hot spot if you get chased down by them foolish wannabees! Not that they won't just cut your throat and take it anyway! I'm just saying!"

"I don't have anything shiny. I'll just be careful." Kirk left the wheelhouse to retrieve some tea for the old woman. Returning minutes later, he sat two boxes of Darjeeling next to her stove, along with a tin of real Sterno.

"Shit! The motherload!" Maude picked up one of the boxes, holding it close to her face. "I suppose I should say thanks! Even if you are an idiot!"

"Don't mention it. Safe travels, Maude. I'll catch you on the flip side."

Kirk began to exit the wheelhouse again when the old woman called out, "Hey!"

Kirk turned his head back and raised his eyebrows as Maude spoke in a softer tone, looking down at the gifts he'd just left her. "Look…I've seen a lot of people go in there…near where we talked about…that I didn't see come back out…I'm just saying. Try not to be one of them, okay?"

Kirk smiled wide and responded, "I'll try not. You really are a sentimental old bitch, aren't you?"

"Kiss my fat, old ass.

Chapter 8
THE COLONY

Kirk left Maude behind him on the waves and set his sights on Nag's Head, a spot on the map where he'd enter the Albemarle Sound and make his way to the Alligator River. He decided that he needed to check out the area near Hyde County, or at least get close enough to see what Maude had heard rumors of and had been talking about. That whole "no risk, no reward" thing was back in his head again and eating at him. Possibly it was ego, but Kirk felt that he could handle whatever he was to discover, or at least was smart enough to determine beforehand whether it was safe or not.

It seemed that with every passing year that he managed to remain alive and relatively safe and healthy, he was doing things that potentially brought him closer to death.

Later in the day, he anchored off the point at Nag's Head, not immediately noticing anything alarming on his nautical surveillance equipment and he waited there until morning to continue his journey. That evening he and the mutt enjoyed a meal of tuna. In actuality, the dog enjoyed it more. Kirk had become a bit quite spoiled in that anything still in the chest freezer that was over two days old didn't taste as good as "fresh from the ocean." The tuna was four days old.

Kirk woke at dawn the next morning to light rain and some chop on the water. He spent the first half-hour bent over the stern, returning the tuna to the sea. By 7:00 a.m. the brief storm had passed and the fog that came with it had lifted. He soon discovered that he'd anchored closer to the shoreline than he'd intended, and he could see the sand beaches of Nag's Head clearly through his binoculars. He spied several people wandering the shoreline. Kirk put the drone into the air to get a closer look and discovered that they were a small group of the infected. All were wearing tattered clothing and their skin had burned to a crisp in the sun-drenched salt air. He could tell that they were very much 'dead'. They appeared to be wandering the sand like beachcombers searching for seashells. Some sort of instinctive act or memory of something they did at one time when they were once healthy human beings, he thought to himself.

Kirk pulled anchor and began his journey into the Albemarle Sound. He kept a close eye on the equipment. Just as Maude had described, he only saw vessels off to the northern banks of the estuary when he checked his radar. He kept close to the southern side and the speed slow at around 15 knots, and three hours later he was nearing the mouth of the Alligator River, so far without incident. It was here that he first picked up the transmission on the A.M. band that Maude had spoken of;

"...Hope awaits you...(static)...We are a small group of...(static)...We have secured our walls on all sides...Fresh water...Fresh gardens...Medicine..."

Interesting, Kirk thought, but not unlike any other transmissions he'd picked up over the years while sailing up and down the coastline. With the origin seeming about twenty miles upriver, he decided to stay in the sailboat and continue to where a bridge crossed the mouth of the river. There, he'd put the drone up, possibly venturing the remainder by dinghy if it appeared relatively safe.

Continuing on, and just a short distance from the mouth of the river, he viewed the remains of the Alligator River Bridge. Which, had it still remained fully intact, would have been only just high enough for him to squeeze the sails underneath. However, now it was broken into sections and easily passable. Kirk checked his radar and sonar, finding nothing on or under the water. He then found a nice, wide section to sail through. He still didn't see anything moving on the radar in the waters as he passed through the bridge.

Just on the other side of the bridge, he heard a transmission on his VHF which he had programmed to scan the airwaves. "…*Ahoy, sailing vessel Rotten Banana! You are nearing the refuge colony. Please transmit your intentions. All who are peaceful are welcome…*"

"Dammit! How'd they spot me?" Kirk was puzzled as he spoke to the mutt, "They even know our boat's crappy name!" He gazed out over the deck, looked all around, and finally spotted it. He was disappointed in himself. His own ingenuity had caught up with him when he spied a drone hovering off his stern. Somewhere nearby, most likely on the dilapidated bridge, was a sentry who'd watched him pass through. Maybe there was a gate operator's station still standing and figured that most likely a small boat was moored underneath the bridge that hadn't shown on the radar.

Kirk wanted to shoot the drone out of the air but knew better. That would be a sign of aggression, and he didn't need that right now.

"…*You are welcome and encouraged to continue, but we need you to acknowledge and state your intentions…*"

Kirk grabbed the mike and locked in the channel, "My intentions are peaceful."

"*Excellent. How many aboard your vessel?*"

"Just me, only one."

"*Thank you. Please wait there for your escort.*"

Before Kirk could ask, he saw the two airboats

approaching off his bow. Riding on each were a driver seated high up and operating the boat, and a standing guard out in front, each armed with an automatic rifle. One airboat came to a halt at his bow and the other to his stern. The two holding the rifles, a man riding on one airboat and a woman on the other, were not pointing them at Kirk. Rather, they were both holding them at the ready. All four on the two boats were masked, wearing N95-type face masks, and everyone had sunglasses. Neither being an unwise thing, Kirk thought, with how things were nowadays. Not only can the hot sun kill you, but they also certainly had no idea if Kirk was free of infection or not.

The armed rider in the airboat at the stern called out, "Please exit your cockpit, hands in full view. Please."

"You go downstairs," Kirk said to the mutt, who did as he was told. Kirk then did as he was told as well, his only weapon within reach being his 9mm tucked into his belt with his shirt concealing it as he crawled out onto the deck.

"Welcome to the refuge colony! May I ask how you came to hear about us? Who told you about us?"

"I didn't…I mean, nobody. I'm a scavenger traveling up and down the east coast. I've never been on this river and thought I'd see what was here." Kirk used his thumb to motion behind him toward the bay, "I heard your transmission on my radio just a few miles out."

The gunman was pleasant, with an added bit of pompous, "Well, then. Lucky you! You've managed to discover our sanctuary. We call it the Refuge. You have the choice to turn around now if you didn't actually intend to stumble upon us, or if your true intentions are anything other than friendly. Or you are requested to anchor here, and we'll take you to the sanctuary on our watercraft. You're sailing vessel simply won't have the ability to maneuver through the swamps. Our colony is part of the former National Wildlife Refuge. Don't worry, your vessel will be safely guarded here. Nobody will touch it."

Kirk had to think about this offer. Leaving his vessel, all

of his belongings, and the mutt was a huge risk in itself. Attempting to turn and run also came with risks, as they had him cornered at the moment. Kirk felt that if they were lying about having the ability to leave peacefully, he'd be in for a fight that he'd probably lose.

Keeping his hands where they could see them, "What's in there? I mean, what's the colony all about?"

An arrogant smile came across the face of the man with the automatic weapon. "Salvation! And I'm certain that you'll understand that's all I can say until you make your decision. We can't have our secrets getting out before you experience what we have to offer. Your trust is something you must earn. Times are different now, my friend. And, we must be cautious. Once you see what we have, you'll know more about why we can't just explain it all here."

Another moment of silence and deep thought while Kirk looked over the situation before responding, "Okay. Let's check it out."

"Outstanding! My colleague, Sally, will even make certain your pet is cared for while you're gone. Unfortunately, I can't allow you to take him. It would be too much of a distraction, and, you have a lot to see once we arrive. Don't worry, she won't take him from your boat." He motioned his rifle to the airboat at the stern. Kirk looked back as the lady holding her weapon briefly lowered her mask to provide an equally arrogant smile, apparently an indication that she was willing to perform pet and boat-sitting duties.

"The Rotten Banana?"

"I didn't name it," Kirk responded casually to the woman before turning back to the man who'd addressed him first.

"I'm certain you'll understand that we need you to leave all weaponry here. And, again, your sailboat and all of your belongings will remain untouched and safe. As you've most likely figured out already, we watch any and all movement through the bridge. Nobody wanders in at any point without our knowledge."

"Yeah. I got that part. Loud and clear." Kirk motioned with a finger, pointing at his belt line. The man nodded and Kirk carefully removed his 9mm and laid it on the deck.

He then prepared his vessel, dropping the anchor. He called down to the mutt to "stay" in his cabin, and the dog obliged, finding his spot on the bunk. Kirk leaped down into the airboat, and his temporary host handed him a face mask. Kirk obliged and placed the protection over his mouth, and he took a seat in front. The airboat had obviously been designed to be a tourist-carrying watercraft. It had several bench seats lined front-to-back with an aisle through the center. The gunman remained standing directly behind Kirk as they began their travels further up the Alligator River.

They hydroplaned for what appeared to Kirk to be several more miles before turning southeast into a swampy forest, passing by several decaying, floating cabins and houseboats to either side of the winding tributary. The waterway continually grew thicker and tighter, and soon they entered a marsh. The gunman had told the truth in that Kirk's sailboat would never have made it this far, and only the airboats could maneuver the swampland, as the vegetation, both alive and dead, was dense. Tall cypress trees that were covered in hanging Spanish moss hovered above, and thick scrub underbrush consisting of mangroves and hibiscus was woven in between the trees on the murky water's surface.

Several more minutes went by before Kirk spotted an opening in the marsh ahead. As they drew nearer, he saw an old wharf that led up to a large building on dry land. At one time the building appeared to have served as a visitor center to the wildlife refuge itself, indicated by the weather and age-worn sign above the front double doors. Along the front of the building as far as could be seen in either direction was a fence. Not an original design, but rather something the 'colony' had constructed. It was made of various types and lengths of wood, whatever they'd managed to scrounge.

However, it was still well-built. It was only about six feet high, and certainly nothing that would keep people out. Kirk felt its purpose was more to keep out the wildlife, specifically the black alligators that Kirk had spied hiding in the dark, brackish waters of the swamp and sunbathing on the land nearby. The fence was lined along the top with barbed wiring, which didn't necessarily surprise Kirk. Any groups left who were attempting to remain safe from both the infected and the living would need something similar to keep people out.

He also noticed, further up the river beyond the wharf, was a land bridge once used for tourists and visitors. Now it appeared only to serve the colony, as he saw the tops of several vehicles parked inside the fencing through a gate at the end of the bridge.

The airboat docked at the wharf and the two, plus Kirk, dismounted, and he was escorted to the gate. It was open and ready for his arrival.

Standing at the gate were two additional gunmen to either side of a man and woman, both dressed in medical garb wearing white surgical coats and scrub pants. All were wearing face protection and sunglasses, the same as the guards who'd brought him here.

"Greetings, my friend! I am Doctor Frederick Alverez! And this is my partner, Frieda." His new host briefly lowered his mask to display a creepy smile, then returned it to cover his mouth. While down, Kirk recognized that the man, and most likely his 'partner', had some age on them. Maybe mid-60s. The gray hair helped confirm his suspicions. Both were stocky and overweight, with Frieda being the more 'manly' of the two. Kirk also noted that the woman was carrying a notebook.

"Doctors? Doctors of what?"

"We are both epidemiologists," Doctor Fred chortled. "Formerly…and by *formerly*, I mean before…well, you know…formerly. We both worked for the CDC in Georgia." Dr. Fred spoke with enthusiasm, with a bit of arrogance and air about him.

Frieda chimed in, speaking quite directly and without the same pleasant demeanor, "We can explain all that later. First, we have a few formalities."

"Formalities?"

"Ah, yes." Dr. Fred continued jovially, "I'm sure you understand and agree that we need to be very careful here. We have created a safe haven for our colonists. We need you to understand that we want to extend our courtesy. However, we need to make certain of a few things first."

"What kind of things? What's back there?" Kirk pointed through the gate and beyond the building. He also looked around, noticing that the vegetation that lined the fencing from the inside didn't allow Kirk to see anything beyond it to the right, although to the left he could see the vehicles parked at that end of the building.

"It's a well-functioning colony of individuals," Frieda responded. "And they expect us to protect them!" Again, she stated the fact quite directly.

Dr. Fred, with far more pleasantness in his voice, "Ah, yes. They certainly do. Now, ahhh…?"

"Kirk."

"Ah, yes, Kirk! Now, Kirk, we have many that wander upon us that decide to stay." Dr. Fred quickly followed with an additional comment after receiving a look of caution from Frieda, "Or simply visit long enough to take advantage of what we have to offer."

Kirk's question was spoken with a cautious tone, "And what would that be?"

"Well, good food for one. You see, we have fresh meat. Alligator to be specific. And fresh vegetables. We have raised gardens with the tastiest treats! A restful night's sleep to go along with it. And medical attention…"

"Which brings us to you!" Again, a direct comment from Frieda.

"Ah, yes. You." Dr. Fred chuckled, "Well now, you see Mr. Kirk. We need to be certain that you aren't bringing…well…anything into us that we don't want. If you know what I mean."

"I know what you mean. I can assure you. I'm clean."

Frieda responded with a hint of sarcasm, "I'm afraid your word isn't good enough."

"Yes, well you see, Mr. Kirk, we do have the ability to provide a simple blood test. It will take about twenty-four hours for the results to come back, but they are quite reliable. Moreso than most. We may have only meager equipment, and our resources here are somewhat inadequate in contrast to what we had to work with in Georgia obviously." Dr. Fred spoke proudly, pointing into the air, "But, we are doctors and can tell if you are infected or not! We have perfected a test. Much better than those old, expired at-home type tests. Much more like a lab test."

"You want to poke me with a needle?"

"Well, yes. That's the only way we can be sure. It's quite sanitary." Dr. Fred said with enthusiasm, "And, in the meantime, you are welcome to come in and partake of our hospitalities. We'd obviously restrict your movement somewhat around the compound until your results are received. I'm sure you understand?"

"Yeah, I get it."

"Well then, are you agreeable?" Dr. Frieda inquired, still with a snarky tone to her voice.

With a bit of caution in his response, "Yeah, okay. I'll play along."

"Splendid!" Dr. Fred blurted, "Please, come this way!"

Kirk began to follow. Before entering the gate, he glanced towards the land bridge and spied a couple of men messing around on the water's edge. One had a bucket and the other a long pole. They'd just exited the gate near the land bridge. Before losing sight of them it appeared to Kirk that they were chumming the waters with a bucket of some type of bloody mess, possibly trying to catch the evening's dinner as he spied an alligator swimming towards them, obviously interested in their bait.

The entourage led Kirk into the visitor's center with the two armed sentries remaining outside at the doors. He followed Doctor Fred and Frieda inside the building. As Kirk took a look around, he could tell that at one time the building held a great deal of beauty and information. Some of the posters about the former wildlife refuge were still intact and hanging on the walls and in a kiosk. The various television monitors that once provided visitors with live-action information about the area were now centrally located in front of the welcome center's counter, each displaying a different location of the marsh and surrounding area on live security camera footage. Seated at the visitor's reception desk was another sentry watching the cameras.

"Solar?" Kirk inquired as his head turned around to take in as much information as he could.

Doctor Fred responded, "Some. We also have a generator and are attempting to complete a wind farm, freeing us from the need for fossil fuels. Which, as I'm sure you know, is nearly impossible to come by these days."

"Then how do you power your generator?"

"Biofuel. From what we grow…"

"*Ahem!*" Frieda interrupted and warned her other half by loudly clearing her throat that he was disclosing more information than she wished him to.

Kirk was led straight through the building. He laughed to himself as he compared his gracious hosts to characters from DVD movies he had onboard and enjoyed. Comparing Dr. Fred to Frankenstein's character from George Romero's *Day of the Dead*. And Dr. Frieda to Beula Ballbreaker from *Porky's*.

They exited the center and stood at the entrance to the interior of the compound. Kirk viewed a large area full of activity. He saw many people walking throughout and glancing in his direction. The area was well-wooded, and he couldn't see an end in either direction as far as where the fencing stretched to. The area resembled a campground, with many large tents that appeared to have been, and still were, the colonists living quarters. There was also an abundance of campers and tag-along camping trailers set up, apparently as housing units as well. Lastly, it appeared they'd been attempting to create far more permanent housing in the form of constructing several raised yurts.

Through the tree, Kirk saw that the gardens were located in a clearing straight ahead. Again, it appeared that many were tending to the fresh food source. The gardens themselves appeared to be constructed of rows of raised beds, plus a large greenhouse.

"We're attempting to get every resident set up in their own permanent structure." Dr. Fred continued, "Hence the construction you see," pointing to the yurts. "Of course, building materials are scarce and we avoid the mainland as much as possible. When we do find ourselves required to venture out, it's usually a targeted journey to an area where we believe a hospital or a university once stood in an effort to see what's left for us to take advantage of, if anything. We do have a small sawmill, but the trees around here don't make the best lumber."

"I bet." It was a busy little village, Kirk thought. And, not necessarily a cult-type situation, as everyone was independently dressed in whatever they preferred, or fit into. Kirk didn't notice anyone carrying weaponry inside the walls. He did notice, though, that everyone was masked and had on their signature sunglasses. "Is there a problem with light sensitivity?" He inquired, a bit sarcastically.

"What? Oh…*heh, heh*…" Dr. Fred seemed nervous in his response, "No, no. It's just the sunlight. They get used to wearing them all of the time. Oh, and the masks. Yes, of course…well, everyone was alerted to your presence. And again, we can't be too careful. You'll notice them all wearing the face protection until after your test results are returned."

Dr. Frieda extended her arm, "If you please."

Kirk looked in the direction she was motioning, it was toward one of the longer, larger 5th wheel travel-trailers.

"Ah, yes." Dr. Fred prompted, "That's our little medical

center and lab. If you would, please. That's where we'll take your test and make certain that you're…well, safe."

Kirk allowed himself to be led to the trailer. He noticed that he seemed to be the anomaly of the day, as the residents of the colony just couldn't keep their sunglassed eyes from looking in his direction. Dr. Fred opened the trailer's door and followed Kirk inside. But, not before receiving another 'look' from Frieda before she scurried away on other business, her notebook held tightly under her arm.

Inside the trailer, it resembled a small medical office and chemist's laboratory. The pop-outs on the camping trailer were attached to two larger yurts and the walls opened up to make it appear as one large, open laboratory. Kirk noticed several people in lab coats, masks, and of course, sunglasses. His facial expression, if they could have seen it behind his own mask, was puzzling in response to the wearing of sunglasses inside the building. Possibly, he thought, they were being overcautious as it had been rumored throughout the years that the virus was believed to be transmissible through the eyes. But why not wear clear goggles while indoors, if this were to be the case? He held his questioning on the matter until a more appropriate time.

Dr. Fred motioned for Kirk to sit at a station with one of the lab workers. Kirk held up his short sleeve and he watched carefully as the younger-looking female removed a fresh needle from its packaging, and an alcohol wipe.

"Be gentle." Kirk half-heartedly joked.

"Oh, she will," Dr. Fred responded as he pulled up a chair in front of Kirk. "We're quite careful. Our resident students are very good and well-trained. Although, they don't get many 'live' volunteers. *Heh, heh*…you're a treat for them!"

"Students?"

"Yes, of course. We're a teaching community. Or perhaps 'learning' is the better terminology. We're all learning to live again. Adapting to our environment, and our circumstances."

Kirk winced as the needle was inserted, and the 'student' retrieved the first vial. He attempted to ignore the pain, "So, tell me, Doc, why do the pirates leave you alone?"

Dr. Fred pretended to act surprised, "Pirates? Oh, yes, them. Well, we pose no threat. We've held…*errr*…meetings with them and have an agreement of sorts."

"Agreement?"

"*Heh, heh*…Yes, agreement. You see, we're able to provide medical attention when they…well, you know. They seem to enjoy fighting amongst themselves quite a bit. Quite immature, but it does allow our community a bit of peace as they leave us to our business. And, possibly we receive some type of protection as well."

Kirk wasn't buying it. *"Bullshit,"* he thought. Pirates are pirates. They take what isn't theirs, and this place seemed to have things to take. But who was he to argue? As long as they weren't planning an attack while he was visiting, he didn't really care.

Kirk winced again when the student shoved another vial into the tube that was inserted into his arm, and she obtained a second sample.

"Hey Doc, how much of my lifeblood do you need?"

"Just enough, don't worry. Anyway," the doctor continued, "while we're waiting for them to analyze the sample and make certain that you're safe, you'll be provided all the basic necessities." He spoke jovially again, "A warm shower, soap, and even a toothbrush. A decent meal. Which, I'll have to ask that you enjoy the company of just yourself. You know…just until it's safe for us to be around you unmasked. You'll be provided with your own tent and a cot with clean sheets."

"Doc, I appreciate that you're going to let me know whether or not I'm healthy and allow me to mingle, but I'm not planning on stay…"

"Oh, I know!" The doctor cut him off, "You're quite free to go anytime. But, please, accept our hospitality tonight. And tomorrow, I'll personally show you around.

You'll have the ability to see up close everything that what we have to offer here. You never know! You just might decide to stay a while!"

Kirk smiled, not that the doc could see, and agreed. "Okay, Doc. I'm looking forward to seeing your little campground. And I appreciate all the effort."

"Splendid!"

The young lady completed her task and put pressure on Kirk's arm with a cotton ball. "I'm sorry, I don't have a Band-Aid."

"No worries." As Kirk bent his aching arm and held pressure on the wad of cotton that was staining red. She truly hadn't been that good at taking his blood.

The girl looked closer at Kirk's shoulder. "How did this happen?" Referring to his recent gunshot wound.

"It's a wild world out there, kid. Not everyone is as nice as you." Kirk smiled a fake smile, forgetting that she couldn't see it anyway with his face mask in place.

As he stood back up, Kirk couldn't help but let his mind wander to what Maude had told him about others that wandered into this area of the Albemarle Sound but hadn't returned. Had they all discovered this place and decided to stay? Possibly, but he needed to keep his guard up.

Chapter 9
SNEAKING AROUND

A clean tent was provided to Kirk by his hosts. Inside he found a cot, a small bureau, and a kerosine lamp with a partial box of matches beside it. On a small bench sat a clean towel, face cloth, and flip-flop footwear. Another clean face mask was also provided. A travel-sized toothbrush, toothpaste, and bar of soap sat next to the towel. A couple of old books and magazines had also been left for his reading pleasure. Lastly, a clean cotton robe had been left on the cot for him.

"Nice little hotel room," Kirk said out loud as he rotated his head and checked his surroundings. At the front of the tent there was a screened-in section and an old lawn chair sat in the center. Kirk had been requested, that if he preferred to sit outside the tent, he put his face mask on. Otherwise, he could remove it while inside the tent or while sitting in the screened porch.

At around 5:30 p.m. a voice was overheard announcing that Kirk's dinner had been prepared and was ready for him. He poked his head out to the screened section and saw Dr. Fred along with another younger-looking boy holding a tray.

"If you don't mind, we'll leave your tray on your chair here," the doctor stated. "I hope your accommodations are to your liking?"

"Yes, quite nice, thank you." Kirk forced a polite tone, remaining suspicious of the entire setup. It was all too cozy and convenient.

The boy, masked and darkened glasses, placed the tray on Kirk's lawn chair as the doctor continued, "I believe you'll enjoy it. Our chef does a fine job with alligator, deep fried, of course. There are hot potatoes straight from our gardens along with other steamed vegetables. I don't believe you've had anything like that in a while, Mr. Kirk?"

"No, you are correct in that assumption. Again, thank you."

"Do you mind polite conversation while you eat?"

"Not at all." In fact, Kirk preferred this as he had questions that needed answers. Whether they were the truth or not.

"Please bring our visitor here a glass of wine. And I'll take my tray and a beverage as well," the doctor directed the boy, who scurried away to do as he was told. Dr. Fred turned back to Kirk, "Please, feel free to remove your mask while we eat. As you can see, the others are all in the dining hall. I'll just keep a distance from you, please don't be offended."

Dr. Fred grabbed a nearby lawn chair and dragged it to the screen porch, keeping a safe distance. He sat while Kirk looked his meal over. It appeared safe enough. Hell, if they were going to poison him it may as well be during a last, tasty meal, he thought. He removed his face mask and dug into his dinner. His expression told the doctor that his palate was quite satisfied. The alligator tasted amazing. It had been deep-fried perfectly, and the meat was tender and juicy.

The young boy arrived again with the doctor's tray and a small folding table to place it on. A second kitchen helper carried their drinks. Dr. Fred removed his mask and revealed his aging face. He had a childlike grin, and demeanor to match, with several days of facial hair growth surrounding his mouth. "So, tell me Kirk, how long have you been on the high seas?"

"Since day one, after the fallout," he managed to get the words out past his full mouth. "I watched it all unfold and saw the world slowly go mad. By the time the bombs came, I had already made my plans to get off the mainland. When they hit, I launched the boat." Kirk looked up and felt a bit better to see another person eating. Although, he was smart enough to realize that he still could be in the midst of being poisoned, but highly doubted it.

"What did you do before that? Before the virus, I mean?" The doctor now speaking with his mouth full.

"Police officer in New England. A small Maine town."

"Respectable. And, remarkable in your ability to survive. We could use that around here."

Kirk was savoring the meal, as it was indeed delicious. He attempted to not be rude, however, it was difficult to speak with his mouth full. "Is that what you look for when visitors arrive? Strong people willing to do a day's work?"

"That's certainly preferred." As the doctor shoveled another bite, "Although not always the type we get."

"So, what happens to the rest?"

Doctor Fred sat back and chewed, "Well, to be honest, we try not to turn anyone away. Unless, of course, their test results aren't to our satisfaction. The truth is, we need strong ones if we're going to survive and thrive here. So, we do our best to educate and accommodate people where their abilities suit them, and us." The doctor savored a taste of wine, holding his glass up first as if to toast Kirk. "Another truth…there aren't many 'weak' ones out there.
Anyone still *alive* most likely has strengths and something to provide."

Kirk held his glass up to return the gesture, "True. But, what about those from the mainland?"

The doc motioned to Kirk with his glass, "Ah, yes. Now, those are truly the undesirable ones. Luckily, not many from inland appear, but there are those occasions. And really, if they're not infected, they also have the strength and a strong will."

"But the ones that don't?"

"Do you mean the ones that show up already infected?"

"Yes."

The doctor hung his head and gazed into his wineglass, swirling the spiked fruit juice around the rim. "Would you think less of us if I said that we offer to end their suffering right then and there?"

"No, I probably wouldn't. In fact, I'd probably do the same."

The doctor smiled a weak smile, "Well then, now you know what we do with them. Of course, they have the choice to simply walk away the same way that they came in. We're not savages. And, they are humanely disposed of, if they so choose to be relieved of their burden."

"Of course, I wasn't hinting…"

The doctor waved his hand at Kirk, reflecting that he understood, and no offense was taken.

"What about people like me? You need to know that it's highly unlikely that I'll remain here after tomorrow. Not that you don't have a good thing going here…"

"…Understood. We can't force you to stay. We can only offer, and hope."

The two continued their meal and casual conversation. The doctor only provided half of the answers that Kirk had questions to. And Kirk only believed half of what the doctor had to say. They completed their meals while enjoying a bit more small talk.

Finally, the doctor groaned while standing back up. He picked up his tray and tiny folding table and turned to his guest. "Please, leave your tray where it is, and I'll have one of the kitchen staff retrieve it later once you're comfortable in your tent. If you prefer to sit outside here for a while, please have your mask on. You're fine if you wish to sit inside the screen porch. Not that there's a difference, it's for the comfort of our residents. I'm sure you understand. I have some other business to tend to so I may not have the pleasure of your company again until morning. I wish you a good evening."

"Understood. Same to you, Doc."

♦ ♦ ♦

That evening Kirk sat in the outside air, inside the screened porch, and watched as the colony's residence trickled back from wherever the dining hall was located, and they performed their evening chores. Everyone continued to wear face protection and sunglasses. Funny, Kirk puzzled in thought, he hadn't been provided or offered any eyewear.

Residents were overly polite. As they'd pass by Kirk's tent, they'd make an effort to say hello. Several even asked his name and carried on short conversations before moving on to their tasks. Although nobody asked any questions about him specifically. Where he was from? Where was he going? Etcetera, etcetera. It was always something about the weather or how good the garden crops were. Mostly touting the place itself, rather than details about him. Kirk found this to be a bit strange. Wouldn't they want to know more about the *stranger* within their midst? They all seemed overly trusting, and very odd to Kirk.

At 7:00 p.m. another errand boy arrived. He explained to Kirk that there was a set of showers that he was to escort the visitor to. He reminded Kirk that he had a robe and flip-flops inside his tent. The lad explained that Kirk's clothing would be cleaned, be ready again for him by morning, and waiting for him in his lawn chair. After changing, Kirk was escorted to the showers where he thoroughly enjoyed a hot water cleansing before being led back to his tent for the remainder of the evening.

On the way back Kirk had spied the two wind turbines that the doctor had mentioned poking above the cypress trees on the northern side of the compound. And, as dusk arrived, a series of spotlights lining the fencing as well as many that were sporadically mounted inside the compound came to life and dimly lit the area. And, as Kirk sat inside his porch and the evening sun set entirely, he noticed a strange occurrence take place.

Almost as if it had been on cue, and Kirk felt that possibly it had been, everyone removed their sunglasses at once. For the remainder of the evening and until the last person had seemingly retired for the night and disappeared from the compound, their sunglasses remained off. He thought that it certainly wasn't strange that people took off their sunglasses in the evening, but all at once?

By 11:00 p.m. that night Kirk was going stir crazy. The compound was empty, and he wasn't accustomed to just sitting idle in a tent. At least when he was on the boat it was his to move around on and watch movies or something to keep his mind occupied. Or even lately watching the mutt acting playful and stupid. Here, he felt like a prisoner. He knew that they were being careful by requesting that he remain in the tent until his 'test' results came back. But he still couldn't take it. He also wasn't pleased that all he was given to wear was a robe, held together with only a waist tie and basically allowing his goodies to be exposed in the breeze when he stood or sat.

He wasn't certain whether or not he was being watched, or if so, how closely. They'd done their best to make him feel as comfortable as possible. So, were they just as comfortable leaving him to be for the night believing that he wouldn't leave the tent? Either way, by 11:30 he'd had enough and needed to get out.

Kirk decided that he'd attempt to find the laundry room and retrieve his own clothes. In the event they were watching him, he decided that rather than sneak out the front, he'd lift the tent in the rear and duck underneath. Lights were still lit in the compound and along the fence, but they were low enough, and there was enough ground cover, that Kirk felt he could get around unnoticed. Even though he was currently wearing a bright, white bathrobe.

He ducked underneath and out the back. He meandered through the trees and brush, and around the scattered tents and campers in the general direction he'd watched the errand boy go earlier that evening. He saw no one else wandering the compound and very few lights glowing from inside any of the structures other than the visitor's center and the structure that housed the medical lab that he'd been inside.

He located the dining hall, a rather large tent. Behind that he discovered the laundry building, an actual small stick building. Nothing seemed locked and he easily made his way inside. It was dark, but he didn't feel like alerting anyone to his presence by turning the solar-powered lights on. He pawed through the stacks of clean clothing until he found what he believed to be his and wiggled into them. When he exited back into the low light of the compound, he discovered that instead of his own clothing, he was wearing a pair of women's XXXL jean shorts that, when Kirk turned his body, he found that they had the words 'JUICY' embroidered on the ass end. He'd also grabbed a loud, Hawaiian, short-sleeved shirt that was 'faded' bright orange and one size too small. It didn't extend below his waist or cover the 'juicy' part.

"Shit!"

It was too late now, he thought. At least in the morning, his clothes would be laid out and he could make a change then. For now, he had to put up with what he'd grabbed as he was anxious to continue with his snooping. He was remaining confident that the security cameras were primarily located outside of the fencing, seeing that so far no one seemed to be coming for him. He continued to crouch and duck as he crept through the compound.

Nearing the visitor's center, which Kirk had seen very little of the massive building when the doctor escorted him through it, he decided to scope it out further. He also wanted to check out the vehicles parked near the gate by the land bridge at the far end of the building, so he began there. There were close to a dozen vehicles, many appearing to be in disrepair or parted out. While quietly looking around he discovered only two vehicles that appeared as if they may have any life left in them, and had keys.

While he was looking over the vehicles, and through the other natural noises of the swamp and the humming of the lights at the fencing, Kirk heard scratching coming from inside the building behind him. Both bewildered and a bit curious, Kirk edged his way to the outside wall where the noises were coming from. Pressing his ear against the wall, he discovered that the sounds were coming from the opposite side. He looked the building wall up and down, noticing that on this side the windows had been boarded over. The scratching noise was coming from his eye level right in front of him, just on the other side of where he was standing.

He whispered, "Rats? It can't be."

Kirk pressed his ear up against the outer wall again and thought he heard the faint sounds of voices, along with the scratching. He also felt that whoever was causing the noises was about to breach the outer wall. Kirk gently tapped the wall twice with his knuckles and waited. The scratching ceased, and moments later two taps were returned from the opposite side.

Kirk frowned and gave the wall a befuddled look. He then tapped two more times, a bit harder, and in doing so he poked a hole the size of his fist straight through the wall.

"Dammit!"

"Who's there?" A male voice emitted from the hole in the wall.

"Me! Who's that?" Kirk whispered loudly.

"Are you the one they brought in today?"

"Who wants to know?"

"Don't believe anything they're telling you!" The voice whispered loudly before an eye appeared in the darkness of the room behind as Kirk squinted and gazed through the hole, "They're lying to you!"

"Who are you?" Kirk whispered directly. "And keep your voice down!"

"We're the same as you. We came here after following the transmission, just like you did, I'm guessing. That's what led you here, right?"

"Maybe. Who are you?" Kirk tried to see through the opening. "Are you trying to dig out of there?"

"Yes."

"Okay, then. Give it up! What's going on here?"

"They're lying to you! They bring us here under false pretenses! They told you they're testing you for the virus, didn't they? They're all wearing masks and want you to do the same until tomorrow, don't they?! They're wearing sunglasses too, aren't they?"

"Okay, yes to all. Now, what's up?" Kirk looked around behind into the dimly lit area to make certain nobody had noticed him lurking around or talking to a wall. He then directed himself back to the hole, trying to see inside the room without getting too close. All he could see was the eye looking back.

"They've got it! They've all got the virus!"

Kirk reared his head back from the wall, and his eyes widened.

"Think about it! They're not protecting themselves from you! It's all a ruse! They want you to believe they're protecting themselves! They also don't want you to see their eyes!"

"How can they all be infected? They don't show signs of fever! They're functioning! The infected can't function?!"

"Doctor Frankenstein and his sister worked for the CDC before all this happened! They were the top epidemiologists in charge of finding a cure before…"

"His sister?! He said partner…"

The loud whispering continued from the person on the other side of the wall, "They're lying about everything! That med lab?! They took your blood, didn't they?! Just like they did with us! They need to test it to see if it has the gene!"

"The what?"

"They need to know if your blood type has the gene

they're looking for. They discovered a gene that lessens the symptoms of the virus. It's not a cure! It just controls the fever so they can continue to function as normal!"

"Bullshit! When did they discover that? What gene? What blood type?!"

"I don't know, but they found it! We don't know when! But they did! Maybe part of the research they started from before! They need the blood to function! They need our blood! If they find that we're the correct type and have the gene, they take it! Otherwise..!"

"Keep your voice down!" Kirk whispered loudly.

"Sorry. They're like vampires. They need their blood transfused regularly. As near as we've been able to determine, about every four to five months for each of them before the fever begins to show signs of increasing again."

"So, you all have the right blood type? How many are in there with you?"

"There's fifteen of us right now. And we don't know who has the correct blood type and who doesn't. And no, we don't all have it. They won't tell us which do, and which don't. But I can tell you, the ones that don't aren't kept long if we don't cooperate! A lot that didn't have it, but still agreed to cooperate are wandering around out there with you and living among them. The ones that don't play by their rules and don't have the correct gene? They're disposed of!"

The lightbulbs in Kirk's head were beginning to turn on. "Yeah, he mentioned that they 'dispose' of infected ones. What do they have in here, some type of crematorium or something?"

"Hell no! They feed them to the alligators!"

Those lightbulbs in Kirk's brain now glowed brightly. A sudden wave of nausea overtook Kirk and this time it wasn't from the motion of the ocean. "Are you shitting me?!"

"No, don't eat the alligator, whatever you do!"

A female voice from within the room echoed through the hole and interrupted, "Stop talking to him and get us the hell out of here! It took long enough to make that hole! They're going to catch us!"

Kirk, feeling quite ill, continued, "So, the sunglasses thing..?"

"They don't want you to see their eyes. You'd know for sure that they're infected if you could see their eyes!"

Kirk's mind was racing and becoming clearer at the same time. This is exactly why the pirates leave the colony alone, he thought. They know the truth. They leave these assholes alone because they don't want to catch the virus, not because of any *agreement*.

Kirk looked around in the darkness before speaking to the hole again, "There can't be many with the gene…or even the correct blood type."

"There isn't."

"So, if you have it? I mean the gene? Are you immune?"

"We don't know. It could be that you're a carrier. Or, maybe immune. We don't know."

The female voice rang out again, "Shut up and get us out of here!"

The male voice turned away and responded back to her, "Cool it! He'll help us! He can go inside and get us out from the other side now! Forget this stupid hole!" The man turned back to the wall, "Look, none of us asked for this. We did the same thing that you did. We came looking for a safe haven and instead, we fell in with these ghouls! Come morning, or maybe the next day, they're going to put you right in here with us regardless of whether you're what they need or not! They're just waiting for results to know if you have what they want. Either way, you're going to be imprisoned!"

"Yeah, I'm beginning to figure that out." Kirk's stomach was still turning at the thought of what his dinner ate before he devoured it.

"You need to get out of here, tonight! And, please, let us out before you go! You can sneak inside and unlock the door! There's only one guard at the welcome station where they brought you in! There must be a set of keys with him!"

"And if there isn't? What if the only set is with the doctor or Mrs. Frankenstein?"

"There's got to be! It's the guard that throws us scraps and keeps up alive. Well, alive enough! He must have a key!"

"Okay, okay. Stay where you are…" Kirk shook his head, "Sorry…I meant hang tight. And give me a few minutes. This might take some time."

"Okay, thanks! Hurry!"

Kirk snuck around to the front of the building between the visitor's center and the fence where he figured he'd be less likely to be seen. He crept along the front of the building towards the entrance, remaining low. He saw that the area near the front entrance emitted more light from the open doors and lights coming from inside. Not feeling like sneaking through the front entrance only to be caught by the guard, Kirk decided to remain back along the fence and find another way in.

The building itself was fairly large with many windows that were both covered and some exposed. Most of them didn't have glass anymore, and some looked as if they had been replaced by wooden shutters constructed by the colony's residents.

Kirk tiptoed up to one of the darker windows on the ground level where the shutters appeared unsecured. He stood and looked inside, seeing very little in the darkness other than it appeared to have been used as an office at one time.

Kirk gently opened the shutters, boosted himself up, and crawled through the opening, landing on the floor behind an old desk. He got back to his knees and saw that the office, with light illuminating from the lobby and reception area through a door that wasn't there anymore, appeared otherwise unused. He snuck up to the doorway and slowly peered around the frame. He saw the lobby that he'd been brought into earlier, and he spotted the sentry seated behind the welcome counter. The man appeared to be dozing with his chair tilted back, feet up on the counter, and arms folded across his chest. The lobby itself was massive and open to a second story and skylight directly above the space where the public once congregated. In the center of the room was a long, spiral set of stairs leading to the upper second level, and a walkway that went along a set of rooms on the back side, and on both ends.

Kirk stayed low and crept out into the hallway and along the back wall until he was close enough to the rear of the welcome desk that he could get a view of the video surveillance monitors. With most still in operation he could see that they all had IR capability, and he spied a variety of locations that they were monitoring. They showed views from the front gate of this building all the way out of the marsh, and even parts of the I-64 bridge and the bridge keeper's gatehouse where it appeared the sentries and airboats were based, and where his boat had been parked. Kirk squinted and looked hard at these particular monitors. He thought to himself, was it possible that the bridge is intact to the gatehouse? He also looked hard to see if maybe he could spot his boat on the video, but he didn't immediately see it.

A door opened on the upper level and Kirk quickly ducked behind an old kiosk, peeking around the side and looking up. Emerging from one of the second-floor rooms was Frieda Alverez. She had on her white lab coat, however, the front was splotch-stained dark red in blood on the upper bosom, and it splattered outward speckling the entire coat. She had latex gloves on her hands that were also drenched dark red, in which she was carrying what looked like rubber tubing, also dripping with fresh blood. She held the tubing in one hand and held her other hand underneath it all to poorly catch the droppings before they hit the floor, which they still managed to find as it dripped from her hands. She also wasn't wearing a face mask or the sunglasses. She exited one door only to scurry to an adjacent door and enter that room, with the door closing itself behind her.

Kirk looked back to the sentry. The activity above hadn't seemed to rattle him. He still remained reclined and fast asleep, a baseball cap down over his eyes to hide any remaining light. Kirk peered down the hallway and believed that in the darkness at the end, he'd spotted the room where the captives were being held. He glanced back to the sentry, knowing that either on the counter or his belt there had to be a weapon.

He also thought to himself how complacent these idiots were. Well, why not? They had a good story and up to now had managed to dupe who knows how many that stumbled upon their secret, with fifteen in storage at the moment. He was also still in disbelief that anyone had managed to 'control' the virus. Although, he wasn't certain that controlling it was any better than the alternative. It was bad enough that you could get infected by a creature that was easily recognizable. Now, they're walking and talking…and making decisions! Not to mention, the guy talking through the peephole was correct, they're pretty much vampires. Taking the lives of healthy people to keep themselves from dying through the use of their blood. It was all too much!

Kirk startled again and ducked back when Frieda emerged once more. This time wearing fresh gloves and carrying clean supplies. It looked like more tubing sealed in plastic, and some hypodermic needles packaged in the same manner. Her coat hadn't changed, still covered in blood as if she'd been shot in the tits by a high-power rifle. With or without a mask, the woman wasn't any more attractive than Bertle had been, he thought, and she was just as mean. Kirk peeked as Frieda went back into the room she'd originally emerged from and let the door close behind her.

As he crouched, Kirk's mind was still racing. He debated whether or not to let those people out of that room. Chances of there being any more than possibly one of them having the correct gene and blood type were slim to none, and all of them were probably infected with the virus to some degree by now. They might make a good diversion, though. Anyway, his first priority was to himself right now, and how to get himself off this island and back to his boat, which probably wasn't where he'd left it at this point. He also thought about the mutt and hoped it hadn't become alligator bait.

Kirk looked around as if that was going to help him clear his mind and come up with a plan. He decided that his best chance might just be to take a hostage. And, he thought, the most valuable hostage might just be Frieda Alverez herself.

Chapter 10
MAKING HIS GETAWAY

Kirk crept slowly and quietly from the kiosk over to the welcome counter. He glanced up to make certain the door on the upper floor remained closed, and then over to the sleeping sentry to make certain he hadn't stirred. He made his way to the end of the long welcome counter and ducked down. Peering around the aging laminated woodwork, he saw that the sentry had a holster on his belt that contained a semi auto.

Peering back up to the second-floor landing, Kirk began to creep to the backside of the dozing guard. He glanced up at the monitors. No human activity, just an alligator on one of the cameras swimming into view somewhere in the swamp. Kirk's stomach went queasy again at the sight. It caused him to frown and shake his head.

When he reached the back of the chair where the guard was reclining, he looked on the guard's belt for anything he could use to take the guy out that wouldn't make noise. He saw that a multi-tool was secured in its sheath by Velcro on the opposite side of the gun. He knew that there was no chance of slipping that out and using it without making noise. Kirk quickly glanced around the desk and spotted, among other useless items, an old rusty letter opener. It had a nice long blade and a stainless-steel handle. Perfect.

He gingerly reached up and took hold of the makeshift weapon. He knew that he needed to be quick and swift, not wanting Frankenstein's bride…*errr* sister…or anyone else that might be in that room to hear anything.

Kirk crouched back behind the chair. The sentry's neck, with his head resting forward, was nicely exposed to him. Kirk extended his arm back, aimed straight for the jugular, and swung. He plunged the knife deep into the guard's neck, leaving the blade where it landed, and yanked his arm back. Kirk quickly shuffled backward, not wanting to get any more blood on himself than need be seeing that everyone here was infected by the virus.

The blade had hit its mark, deep. The guard's heart pumped the blood out of his body, and it spurted out from all sides of the blade. His shoulders became drenched in the thick liquid as he briefly came back to life, and his eyes opened wide. One hand made a pathetic attempt to grab the handle where it was sticking out of his neck before both of his limbs fell limp to either side of the chair. His head fell to the side opposite of the blade, and his baseball cap dropped to the floor. He never made a peep as the life quickly drained from his body, along with his infected and thickening life fluid as it splashed down onto the baseball cap and pooled on the floor beneath his chair.

When his neck stopped draining, Kirk slid back up to the body and looked into the guard's eyes. They were bloodshot and dilated. This guy certainly did have the virus. Carefully, Kirk slid the semi-auto out of the holster, removing the Hawaiian shirt he was wearing and using it to wipe the remaining blood from the weapon. Kirk was now just down to the flip-flops and 'juicy' cutoffs.

Kirk crawled to the stairs and began his ascent up to the second level. Staying low, he pointed the gun at the room that Frieda was inside. However, hoping she wouldn't emerge as he didn't want to alert others with any loud yelling, or a gunshot.

He made it to the landing and skulked to the room she'd obtained the supplies from. Carefully, he opened the door, making certain it wasn't going to make a creaking noise, and he peeked inside. The room that once was an office area was now a disheveled storage space being used for medical and other supplies that the colony had collected over time. Anything and everything surgical that the 'doctors' and their cohorts had stolen, scrounged, or traded was inside here. Kirk slid inside the room and managed to quickly nose-around, locating a pair of scrub pants and a lab jacket, and a box of latex gloves. He put the clothing on along with a pair of gloves, and he pocketed another pair. He also grabbed a face mask and donned it, pocketing an extra one with the gloves.

Kirk slid back out into the walkway, checking first to make certain the coast remained clear. He made his way to the adjacent door and stood close to the frame. With caution, he slowly reached down, turned the handle, and cracked the door. Peeking through the sliver of an opening that he'd created, he was immediately sickened at the sight and smell.

Frieda was back to him and yet unaware of his presence. She was standing next to a metal hospital bed that was tilted forward with no mattress or linens. Strapped to the metal at a slight forward angle and facing Kirk was a woman. She was nude, average in size, although quite emaciated. She was intubated to provide air, however, its primary purpose seemed to be more to prevent her from making any noise. She had a feeding tube inserted into her upper chest, force-feeding nourishment down into her stomach. An IV extending to her left bicep was feeding liquids into her brachial artery. Two more IVs extending from both of her forearms fed her own blood down to large glass pickle jars that were sitting on the floor. Two more IVs in her femoral arteries on both sides of her inner thighs fed her life liquid into the same two jars. The tubing appeared to be driven straight through her skin rather than by a needle and surgically taped to her body. Dried blood stained her skin while fresh liquid trickled past the tubing and down her limbs where each tube was stuck into her veins.

A ventricular assisting device was crudely mounted to her sides and laying on her chest. It seemed to be pumping out her blood at intervals into the tubing and down to the bottles, prompted by some type of laptop computer sitting on a stand near the gurney and connected to the heart-pumping machine. It was obviously programmed by the 'doctors' to pump at intervals by some design they had created and programmed. There was also another IV hanging from a pole that held a blood-red liquid. The tubing from this IV extended into her jugular. Kirk's immediate belief was this was probably blood plasma from other infected colony residents that matched her blood type, or not, that was being transfused back into her body to keep her alive while her fresh blood, with the gene type that they required, was being pumped back out.

Kirk quickly determined that these morbid assholes had developed a system that allowed them to mix tainted blood with healthy, making certain their victims lasted as long as possible, and kept pumping out the life juice they needed to keep their own 'alive' for a longer period of time. It was also even possible that the immune system in these people's bodies was taking the infected blood and somehow naturally recycling it into fresh, healthy blood.

Kirk, somewhat in shock at what he was viewing, had frozen in place long enough to watch Frieda pull the tubing from the woman's jugular. Even though she held a hand over the hole in the woman's flesh, she didn't flinch when the powerful vein spurted and stained the doctor's jacket even more than it had been. Frieda even had a cruel and evil grin on her ugly face. Ultimately, she let go entirely and blood squirted and poured out of the woman as she writhed in agony against her restraints. Frieda grabbed clean tubing from a rolling instrument cart beside her and shoved one end into the gaping hole in the woman's neck, taping it off around her neck and head with gauze and medical tape. She then poked the other end into another, new bottle of tainted plasma and replaced the empty one on the IV stand, tossing that one into a nearby open trash container that was full of empty, dripping IV containers. It was apparent her aim wasn't always on, as many other filthy used bags were strewn around the trash can, which was also covered in blood.

Once the procedure was complete, she gave the new bag of plasma a good squeeze and forced the infected liquid into the woman's veins. It oozed from the incision and bubbled through the gauze, staining it as the liquid dribbled down the woman's neck and body. The poor woman spasmed and choked up blood and phlegm into her intubation tube. Her coughing caused the bloody mess to travel through the short tube and spurt out of the open end and splash back down on her face.

The 'doctor' then picked up a nearby suction device and pathetically suctioned out the tubing and ran it around her neck. Kirk watched as blood, puss, and other fluids traveled up the cloudy suction tube into a container mounted on the wall behind the woman's head. It squirted thick, reddish fluid into a jar as if the woman was experiencing a liposuction procedure. Kirk's stomach was turning in knots at the entire, grotesque sight.

Kirk hadn't realized that in his state of shock and disbelief that he was involuntarily pushing the door open wider. He looked to his left and now within his view was an entire row of several hospital gurneys stretching the length of the room. Each one held a helpless victim the same as the woman that Frieda was working on, all lined up and strapped down to their own metal deathbeds. Each with bloody, encrusted tubing protruding from their bodies. He looked to the very far right where he saw what appeared to be one of the colony's residents laying on another bed. This woman appeared to be the receiver of a transfusion with one IV tube extending from what Kirk felt was a modified kidney machine. It seemed that it was cycling the fresh blood into the infected woman's veins. A second IV on her opposite arm appeared to be sending her own infected blood back into the jury-rigged machine to be combined with the new blood to create a longer-lasting concoction. Kirk remained mesmerized by the sights he was seeing.

"What in the hell are you doing in here?!!!" The loud, angry, and surprised voice coming from the 'doctor', which startled Kirk back to reality. He swung the door open wide and lifted the loaded pistol, pointing it at Frieda.

"Don't move! Don't you dare move!"

"I asked you what you're doing in here?! Why are you out of your tent?!" The doctor appeared far more agitated by Kirk's presence than to be overly concerned with the gun that was pointed at her head.

"I said don't move!" Kirk couldn't help but glance around the room again, stunned by the gruesome sight now in his full view. All of the victims lay in pain with bloody tubing protruding from their bodies, and thick, red liquid dripping into jars lined up on the floor. Bodies and bedsheets, if any, all stained deep red. Each healthy victim was writhing in pain against their restraints, unable to cry out due to the tubing that had been shoved down their throats. Most were coughing up blood and bile as it bubbled in and around the intubation tubes and spit out from the ends.

The only person lying down that even hinted at comfort or sterility was the infected woman that was receiving her transfusion that would keep her infection in check. The odor in the room was of something worse than death. It all severely sickened Kirk. He let the door go and held an arm up to his masked mouth, keeping the other hand with the gun pointed straight at the doctor.

"You sick bastards!"

"Guard..!"

"Your guard is dead! You're going to be right behind him if you don't shut up right now and do what I tell you!

Let me see your hands, now!"

The doctor lowered her tone but still spoke with arrogance. And, still with the grin on her face, "I can't raise my hands. If I don't finish securing this tube in her neck, she'll bleed out and die."

"That's better than what you've been putting her through, you sick bitch!" Kirk motioned with the hand that was covering his mask, "Dying is far more humane than what you're doing to all of these people!" He squinted, "And, to think that it could be me lying there if I hadn't bothered to snoop around! And would have been if I hadn't! You're all just a bunch of liars! Taking life from healthy people who may be immune and giving it to your infected group!"

"Ha! Immune? They're not immune! They're carriers!"

"Oh, really?! Not immune? Then how are they keeping your merry group of *assholes* alive?! You should all be walking around like every other ghoul! Bumping into trees and carrying a fever of about a hundred and ten! Isn't that right, Doc?"

"Who told you that?! Who have you been talking to?!"

"The poor shmucks that you've got locked up downstairs, all waiting for their test results just like me! Now, get your hands up where I can see them and step away from that gurney!"

Frieda's evil grin widened. She raised one eyebrow as she stared at Kirk and responded calmly, "Fine." She stepped away from the woman on the bed, purposely pulling the tubing from her neck. The medical tape and gauze tore, and the plastic tubing popped from the jugular vein it had been shoved into. Blood spurted from the wound, striking Frieda's lab coat and adding to the collage of stains that already existed. Kirk's eyes widened as Frieda put her hands palm up in front of her, chuckling as she did so. The squirting stream of blood from the woman's neck quickly turned to a trickle as the life drained from her body. Her head dropped sideways, and her eyes became fixed and dilated. Her suffering had come to an end.

Kirk responded with disdain and sarcasm, yelling, "Do you think that was funny?!" Frieda simply gazed at Kirk and burped out a smug laugh. Kirk yelled out again, "Well, then! You're going to think this is hilarious!"

Kirk turned the gun towards the infected woman who'd been receiving her transfusion. She'd been awake and alert, quietly watching what was going on. Her eyes bulged as she lifted her IV-tubed arms in defense as Kirk pulled the trigger. Half of the woman's face ripped from her skull and blew backward into her pillow. Pieces of skull tore through the fabric and pelted the metal bedframe, ricocheting to the wall behind her. Brain matter exploded in all directions, covering the equipment surrounding her bed. When the remainder of the woman's head came to a rest after bouncing backward, it tilted to the side and any remaining blood, fluids, and brain fell to the floor beneath her. One eye that remained on her unrecognizable face stared straight ahead in her state of instant death.

"*Nooo!*" Frieda screamed out. Snapping her head back to Kirk, she seethed with anger, "You son-of-a-bitch! Do you know what it took to keep her alive?! What it takes to keep them all alive?!"

"Yeah, it takes bleeding all these other healthy ones dry! It takes putting them in a locked room downstairs to wait to die, too! Just like you were going to do to me!" Kirk stepped entirely into the room and allowed the door close behind him, keeping the gun pointed at Frieda. "Listen up! First, I'm not wasting the bullets in this gun! These are for you and your followers if any of you try to get in my way! So, you're going to take care of the rest of these people. Right now and humanely!" Kirk took the other face mask from his pocket and tossed it to the doctor. "You're going to put this on! I don't want anything that you've got getting inside of me! You get one, I get one!"

Frieda smirked, "Screw you."

"Oh, okay. If that's how you want to play it."

Kirk pointed the weapon and touched off a round. The bullet pierced Frieda's left shoulder. Blood, bone fragments, and flesh exited her lab coat and sprayed the window behind her, shattering any glass that remained and splintering the wooden shutters that had been closed, causing them to violently swing open and slam against the outer wall.

Frieda winced, doubled over, and grabbed her bleeding shoulder with her already soaked, latex-gloved hand. *"Dammit! You asshole!"*

"It hurts, doesn't it?! In fact, I happen to know that it does!" Kirk now became the arrogant one, "Now, I figure that if this gun was loaded, I've got about twelve or thirteen more rounds left! So, unless you want to take a chance and do something *really* stupid, don't make me use another one on you! Get your *fat ass* moving! I'm sure we've woken up the camp with these gunshots, so time is limited!"

Kirk looked around the room and, among the other miscellaneous medical equipment, he noticed a glass cabinet containing various vials of medicines. He also noticed a desk and bookshelves in a corner that was overflowing with paperwork, textbooks, and notebooks. He motioned to the cabinet, "Do you have something in there that will take care of the rest of these people?"

"Yes," spoken with animosity, along with her deeply embedded scowl as she kept a hold of her aching, bleeding shoulder.

Kirk motioned with the gun while sliding over to the corner where the desk was located. "Then, get to it!"

"It would be faster if I just pulled the tubes," she remarked in a snarky tone.

Kirk felt defeated. He knew that she was correct, and it would be quicker to simply allow the others to bleed out. And, it wasn't as if they weren't in agony already. Reluctantly, he shook his head and motioned again with the gun, her signal to go ahead and do it.

Frieda's detestable grin and frown remained as she approached each bed and began to yank tubes from each person's jugular, using her one good arm. She seemed to almost enjoy the task as she made her way from one to the next. With every tube she violently yanked out, blood spurted to the floor and quickly diminished, ending the life of each victim that had lain suffering. The sound of the initial surge of blood from each tube pulled and splashing onto the floor, and the brief coughing of their last, mucous-filled breath through their tubes sickened Kirk even more. As he kept an eye on Frieda while thumbing through the paperwork on the desk, he dry-heaved each time a tube was yanked out without regard for the poor soul that had been attached to it.

When Frieda was done with the last person, she pulled off her blood-soaked latex gloves in view of Kirk. When each one snapped from her fingers it flicked blood into the air and sprayed on the doctor's face, staining the paper mask she'd been ordered to put on. She never flinched and kept her evil smirk going underneath her mask with one eyebrow raised the entire time.

Kirk picked up one of the binders and waved it. "Hmmm, this one looks familiar. Isn't this the one you were carrying around earlier? The one with all your secrets in it, perhaps? The one that you keep tight when you're strolling around this hell-forsaken campground?!" He could tell by the look in her infected eyes that he'd struck a nerve. "Possibly the secret of how you turn healthy blood into a life-prolonging concoction for your infected friends?"

Frieda's unseen smirk turned into a scowl, "You put that down! That's none of your business! That's years of hard work and research that you're screwing with! It's of no use to you!"

"*Ahhh*, touchy, touchy." Kirk was now the sarcastic, snarky one as he quickly wrapped a roll of gauze in a cross-shape around the notebook, tying the gauze to the beltloop on his shorts and around his waist, never once taking the gun off his target as he did so. He secured the notebook to his hip and freed his hands of the burden, "I'm guessing this is something very valuable. And, something that I'm certain you'd need once I leave! Just so that you ghouls can carry on your twisted procedures and keep your followers walking upright and functioning. Isn't that correct, Doctor Moreau?"

Frieda snapped, and, with her hand back over her aching bullet wound, "Screw you! And, you're not going anywhere, so it doesn't really matter! Now, put that notebook back down!"

Kirk ignored her demand and motioned with the gun. Frieda, covered in blood from head to toe, some of it hers but most from the victims now lying dead in the room, began to walk toward the door. She slipped momentarily in the puddles of hemoglobin as she rounded a gurney, however, she managed to remain on her short, stocky feet. As she passed by Kirk, he stuck the barrel of the gun into her backside as they exited the room and descended the stairwell. At the bottom of the steps, she stopped and looked over at the dead guard.

Kirk gave her an extra jab with the barrel to prompt her to continue toward the front door near the gate to the swamp.

Kirk wasn't surprised to find that arriving outside were Doctor Fred and several of the residents. Two of the colonists, each standing to either side of Dr. Fred, were armed with rifles. They formed in a half circle, blocking Kirk and his hostage from going left or right along the fence, or out through the gate to the wharf. Not surprisingly to Kirk, nobody had their masks or sunglasses on.

"What's going on here?!" Dr. Fred called out. "What's the meaning of this?!"

"Isn't it obvious, you dunce?!" His sister, with her hand clutching her still throbbing arm, yelled back angrily, "This idiot decided to wander around and poke his nose where it didn't belong! I told you before that it was a stupid idea to leave them unguarded! But *noooo!* You said it would make them trust us!" She yelled louder, "Look where that's gotten us, you idiot! He's gone and killed all of our precious subjects upstairs and murdered one of the residents! And he shot me!" Spoken as if people couldn't tell already. And, with the amount of blood on her lab coat, they probably wouldn't have known before she announced it.

"Precious, my ass!" Kirk yelled out. "Nice of you ghouls to disclose to the visitors what's really going on around here!" He motioned to the group blocking his way to the path to his right towards the vehicles. "You! Move over next to Frankenstein there near the dock or this bitch gets it!" He moved the barrel of the gun to the side of Frieda's head while taking her wounded shoulder in his grip in his other hand. He gave a good squeeze to her wounded arm.

"Ouch! *Goddamit!* Take it easy!"

"Shut up, fatass!"

Fred pleaded, his arms outstretched, "Please! Don't hurt her! She's the only one that can complete the process!"

"Well, there's some brotherly love for you!" Kirk's suspicions had been correct in that Frieda was his ticket out, and the brains behind their operation. Not to mention the notebook itself. "Whatsa matter, Doc? Not a fast learner like your sister, here? Does she run the whole show?!"

"It takes both of us. She developed the blood recycling procedure. We need her to make it work!"

"He's got the notebook!" Frieda blurted out. "Don't let him get away!"

Kirk thumped the woman in the side of her head with the butt of the pistol. "Shut up, bitch!"

The others moved as directed while Kirk kept the barrel against Frieda's head, and also kept reminding her to behave by squeezing her arm each time she tugged against him, causing her shooting pains. He crouched behind her and began to pull her along as he backed his way along the pathway between the building and the fence, glancing behind himself every few seconds to make certain that nobody was attempting to ambush him from his backside. They were heading toward the vehicles parked near the road bridge at the end of the building. The others slowly followed at a safe distance with Dr. Fred leading them.

Kirk continued to direct his comments to Dr. Fred. "Nice little setup you got going! A real friendly bunch, aren't you?! How about you tell one of those idiots next to you to go release the people you're holding captive in this building!"

Frieda cried out, "No! Don't do it! We need them!"

Kirk jammed the barrel into her temple deeper and gave a good squeeze to her bicep.

"Ahhhhhhh! Goddamitt!"

He looked back to see Dr. Fred, who gave the heads up to the guard next to him. The colonist disappeared back inside the building as Kirk and his unwilling captive continued to creep backward, and the group slowly moved along with them. When Kirk backed himself to the corner of the building and up against one of the vehicles, he saw the guard re-emerge from the front entrance. Behind him were the fifteen golden tickets. Each appeared emaciated and disheveled, and a couple looked to Kirk to be quite ill and being assisted by the others. The one that he'd apparently been holding the conversation with through the hole was leading the small group just behind the guard. He stopped and assessed what was taking place at the end of the building, waving to Kirk.

Kirk waved back, a signal for his group to make their way to the land bridge. The former hostages passed by Dr. Fred and the others, and cautiously approached Kirk, keeping themselves out of any line of sight in the event any bullets began flying between Kirk and the guards.

Kirk commanded the leader, "Get your group out of here! Run!"

"Some of us can't run. Why can't we…"

"Just get your asses out of here! I hate to say it, but don't wait for anyone slower than yourself! This place is full of the infected and I can't do any more for you! I'm leaving too! Now go!"

The group took off on foot, some far more agile than others. They apparently hadn't realized that Kirk had done this all for a reason and that he had an ulterior motive. Among the captives were obviously those with the correct gene in their blood, and the colonists needed them if they were to stay alive. Or, at the very least keep their infection under control. They needed the blood as much as they needed the doctors to recycle and administer it. Kirk now had up to fifteen more targets of prey for these predators to chase through the swamp other than himself. Although, he realized that he'd be their focus. If not for Frieda, then for the secrets contained in the notebook currently attached to his hip.

Kirk said quietly, yet sternly to his captive, "Which one of these jalopies still works? And don't lie to me! You have plenty of more fat places that I can put a bullet into!"

Seething, Frieda responded while still holding her aching arm that Kirk kept squeezing, "That one over there!" She motioned her head to a pickup truck just behind the vehicle they were standing up against.

"Wait!" Dr. Fred cried out. "You don't have to do this! You can stay with us!" He struggled for an excuse, "…You're…you're safe! We tested you…you're immune! You can stay with us…help us!"

"Bullshit, you *asshole!* You're lying! And, even if you weren't, I'm only worth the blood that's in my veins to you! Now, stay back! I'm warning you all!" Kirk dragged Frieda to the truck and began to get in, keeping a tight grip on her arm.

"No, wait!" Dr. Fred continued his pathetic pleading, "You must listen to me! You must..!"

"Hey, Juicy!" One of the guards yelled out, cutting the doctor off. "Go ahead and run! We're coming for you!"

Kirk ignored the words and directed his comments to Dr. Fred, yelling out, "I'll leave your savior here at the bridge when I get there. Don't follow us, and don't radio your cohorts out there on those airboats, either! Or you'll find a dead fat woman when you get there!"

Kirk backed himself into the truck and dragged Frieda inside with him. "You're driving! And you better go really fast and do exactly as I say or these idiots won't see you or your notebook ever again!"

The angry doctor had now lost all use of her injured arm, which was still in Kirk's clutches. She had to reach across with her left hand to start the truck. Kirk was truly surprised that it even started. Frieda shifted into drive and they began to exit the gate and cross over the land bridge. At first, Frieda was obviously going slower than Kirk wanted her to.

"Faster!" Kirk looked back to make certain nobody had jumped into another vehicle and attempted to follow them, still holding the gun to her head. He saw the group assemble at the gate as the two disappeared down the winding road into the swamp. He turned back forward, "And, don't even think about clipping anyone running up this road thinking you'll come back later for the blood they're carrying!"

Frieda turned her head and screamed in Kirk's face through her mask, "Do you want to get out of here or not?! If they're in my way, they're getting run over! I don't give one rat-shit about any of them. You shouldn't, either!"

A wide-eyed Kirk, staring straight into Frieda's infected eyes, reached over and pointed down, touching off a round straight through the fleshy fat at the bottom of her left inner thigh. The sound of the shot rang through the cab of the truck. The bullet tore through her flesh, continued through the seat, and straight out through the bottom of the truck.

"Owwweeefuck!"

"I'm sorry, did you say something?!"

Frieda screamed again in pain, tearfully crying at the same time, *"Jeesus Kriste!* Will you *please* stop shooting me?!"

"Keep your mouth shut and we'll see!"

The truck sped and swerved, weaving through the trees and underbrush, and dodging the captives who were trying to put distance between themselves and the colony. They even struck a ten-foot alligator that had been laying in the dark, weather-battered roadway. Violently driving over the animal and nearly crashing the truck in the process, Kirk had seen that in its powerful jaws had been one of the captives, the 'leader' that he'd been talking to earlier. At first glance it appeared as if the alligator had attempted to swallow him whole as only his upper body was visible from the animal's mouth and the man appeared to be frantically attempting to pull himself back out. At second glance Kirk saw that his lower torso from his stomach down, along with the severed entrails, were laying in the road. The alligator had cut the man in half before taking his upper body in its jaws. While only half of a person now, and with his last bit of life, he was beating the animal on its snout in an effort to save what was left of himself. He'd survived the colony only to ultimately become a meal for one of the swamp's own creatures. He looked up at the truck's headlights with wide eyes and blood pouring from his mouth as the truck plowed over the animal, also ending the man's suffering in the process.

Kirk continued to jam the gun into Frieda's right side and kept an eye behind them. At one point he briefly searched the cab of the truck, locating a partial roll of duct tape in the glove box. With the gun still on his driver, he tore the notebook away from his hip and held it between his knees. He unwrapped the gauze, replacing it entirely with duct tape. He wrapped the tape tightly around and around until it was gone from the roll.

"What are you doing *that* for?!"

"Shut up and drive!"

Daybreak was arriving and the sun was cresting the horizon as they continued for over five miles. Approaching the outskirts of the swamp, and approaching the river ahead, Kirk could see the bridge in the light of dawn. Several hundred yards onto the bridge was the old gatehouse. Beyond that the bridge ended, damaged, with a space several hundred feet in length before the other end of the tattered bridge continued over the river to the next broken section.

Kirk smiled when he spied floating in the water at the end of the bridge near the gatehouse the two airboats, and next to those was Kirk's sailboat, still floating and anchored.

"When we get out on that bridge you don't slow down until I tell you to!"

"Are you crazy?! We're doing fifty now!" Frieda pointed with her useless right arm, causing herself to wince. "That bridge ends just past the gatehouse!"

"Just drive!"

Kirk could see the four guards standing near the gatehouse. They'd obviously been alerted, which came as no surprise. They had their guns ready, but Kirk knew they'd been told who was driving and not to take the chance of shooting their precious life-giver.

When Frieda made the swing in the road onto the bridge, they were still doing nearly fifty miles per hour. The truck went into a wheelspin and skidded sideways out onto the bridge. Frieda straightened it out, however, she began to ease on the throttle again. Kirk noticed and slammed his foot down onto hers, grabbing the wheel with his free hand and holding the truck straight toward the gatehouse. As they raced towards it, the four in the road were forced to take evasive actions to avoid being hit. Three of them managed to leap off the bridge into the water, while one wasn't so lucky. One of the men was struck broadside as he attempted to jump out of the way. His hip was immediately shattered as his body flew into the air ahead of the truck and into the gatehouse. The remainder of his bones fragmented as he went straight through the old wooden structure. The gatehouse exploded from the force, and chunks of wood and glass went flying off the end of the bridge. Along with them, the guard himself. His body, which had been torn apart from the impact of the truck and building, continued to sail out over the water before making a splash and skipping on the surface before coming to a lifeless, floating rest.

Kirk kept his foot planted as the truck left the broken

end of the bridge and sailed out over the ocean.

"Shhhiiiiiit!"

These were Frieda's last words before Kirk braced himself with one hand on the dashboard and kicked the passenger door open wide. He also pulled the trigger one more time. The bullet penetrated Frieda's throat, much like the tubing she had jammed into her victims' jugulars. The bullet tore through her neck and exited, taking with it the woman's flesh and blood before impacting the driver's window, causing it to burst into tiny pieces.

As the truck struck the surface of the water Kirk held his breath and launched himself out, hitting the surface hard and rolling beneath the waves. He kept his wits and as quickly as he could, regained control and swam, surfacing next to one of the airboats. Taking hold of the side and lifting himself, he flopped down onto the bottom of the boat. Squatting and peering over the rail he spotted two of the three sentries still alive and bobbing in the water, knowing the third was still on the opposite side of the bridge.

The two that were treading water on his side snapped their heads to the sound of Kirk's voice. "Hey! You better hurry up! Your leader is trapped in that truck!" Kirk pointed and they instinctively looked in the direction of the sinking vehicle. The cab was just going down and the color of deep red bubbled and plumed at the surface as the truck sank deeper into the river. A female guard who was closest to the wreckage began to swim for the truck.

Kirk called out to the other guard who was further away, "Hey, stupid! You probably should be more worried about that thing swimming behind you!"

The guard turned his head just in time to see a ten-footer with its eyes just above the surface about twenty feet away and closing. The sentry began to swim frantically towards the bridge as the alligator neared, diving under and out of sight before it reached him. The next thing Kirk heard as he darted across to the bow of the airboat was the high-pitched shrieking as the creature came up underneath the guard with its jaws wide open, clamping down on his lower torso, and plunging its teeth into his flesh. The man frantically splashed on the surface as the gator began to cut him in half, and it went into its death roll.

Kirk stopped and looked back as he grabbed a rope on the bow of the airboat. He saw the female guard's feet as she dove down to the pickup truck, believing she was going to help save the doctor. He stood and looked across the end of the bridge and still didn't see the third guard anywhere yet. He turned back and leaped with the rope in hand, landing on the port side of his sailing vessel. Moving quickly, he ran along the gunwale. On his way past his cockpit, he reached in and slammed the toggle switch to the anchor, and it began to raise. When he reached the stern, he jumped down into the dinghy and tied the rope from the airboat to the bow. From where he was now, he could see the third guard at the head of the bridge trying to climb back up one of the mounting posts to the remnants of the gatehouse. Kirk could see that he still had his automatic rifle, but it was swung around his neck and shoulders so he could use both arms on the rungs that were mounted to the post.

Kirk ripped off the wet facemask that was hanging under his chin and tossed it aside. He shook himself out of the dripping lab coat and let it drop too. He was now back to simply being 'juicy'. Leaping back to the stern of his vessel he reached into a compartment under one of the floorboards. Luckily for him, he thought, these fools apparently hadn't been given the orders to clean out his vessel yet, and they hadn't done any major looting on their own. Most likely that had been on their busy agendas to complete today or tomorrow after the colonists had planned to lock Kirk up with the others. Kirk had figured out that part of their strategy was to make their visitors 'trust' them. If he'd asked to see his boat and belongings before being taken captive, it was likely that they would have actually been shown to him, fully intact. However, he also realized it may have been just dumb luck, too, that his boat hadn't been scrounged and scuttled yet.

From the hidden compartment, Kirk produced a loaded 30/06 with a 50mm scope. He wrapped the sling around his arm and took aim, waiting for the guard's head to crest the bridge.

It was too late for the man once he'd climbed up and his face appeared in Kirk's sights. The sentry looked towards the sailboat when Kirk yelled out, "Hey!" Kirk had the crosshairs right on the guy's nose when he pulled the trigger. He watched through the tiny telescope as the back of the guard's head blew out, sending his grey matter and chunks of skull into the air in a circular pattern, similar to watching fireworks explode in a night sky. He lowered the gun after watching the guard fall from the post and out of sight to the water below.

After picking up the empty shell and tucking the rifle back into its hiding place, he started back and stopped at the bulkhead and darted into his cockpit. This time as he glanced down into his cabin's stairwell and noticed a furry face looking back up at him. Smiling, "I was hoping you'd still be hanging around." Kirk's voice caused the mutt to tilt his head, wag, and raise a paw. "Wait there a few more minutes for me, okay?"

As Kirk cranked on the wheel and turned the rudder, he also activated the diesel engine. He had no time to waste, he thought, and he planned to raise the sails after putting some distance between himself and his would-be captors. But, for now, he needed to burn some of his valuable fuel. As the boat came around and pointed in a direction out of the bay, Kirk throttled slowly forward. He crawled out of the cockpit and darted to the stern, leaping back down into his dinghy. He reached over the side and scooped up the duct-taped notebook that was floating on the surface and drifting away from where the truck had gone under.

It was at this point that he also noticed the female guard still in the water. She'd discovered that Dr. Frieda was dead in the truck and resurfaced, and she'd been swimming towards the bridge. She'd stopped and turned around, bobbing in the murky water and having a bit of difficulty as her automatic rifle was also slung around her neck. She'd kept a hold of it after jumping from the bridge and it was now weighing her down.

Kirk leaned over the side of his pontoon again as if he were going to help her out of the water. She even smiled briefly as Kirk's sailboat slowly motored past and his arm extended out. Her smile dissipated quickly when Kirk grabbed her rifle sling and the gun caught her chin hard, dragging her body face-up for a few feet before the heavy weapon scraped across her face and the bolt catch caught her nose. As the saltwater muffled her screaming, her nose tore off to the point that it was merely a dangling chunk of flesh. Kirk left her drifting and bleeding in the river, holding her face and chumming the waters for the next alligator to easily find her.

Kirk dropped both the gun and notebook in his pontoon, and he jumped back to the stern, dragging himself into the sailing vessel. He performed a somersault on the floorboards and landed back on his feet. He dove into the cockpit and slammed the throttle forward. The vessel motored past the end of the bridge and out into the bay. Finally, he hoisted the mainsail and the jib and caught the wind as he looked back at the wagon train he'd formed behind. His sailboat dragged the dinghy, which was dragging the big airboat behind it.

He returned to his tiny wheelhouse and glanced back down the cabin stairs. "C'mon, you can come up now." The mutt scurried up the stairs, bounced out, and hopped to the stern. Looking out over the waters, he barked vigorously. A final warning to those left behind to not screw with the two ever again.

♦ ♦ ♦

As Kirk set his course south and out of Albemarle Sound he contemplated turning back towards Nag's Head and finding Maude to alert her to what had occurred. In afterthought, he decided against doing this. Knowing Maude, he thought, she was probably somehow already aware of what had occurred. And he was certain that going forward she'd warn others to stay away, as he should have heeded her words too.

After inspecting his vessel, he determined that the only things he found missing were a few food items that the guards had taken throughout the night, and possibly they located some extra shells for the weapons they were carrying. He could live with that. He returned to the open air from his cabin with some clothes in hand, and he dropped the jean shorts to the deck. After getting dressed in much more appropriate attire he grabbed a hammer and some tacks. He picked the jean shorts back up and leaned out over the stern of his vessel. He then proceeded to tack the shorts to the rear of the boat. From that point on, he was now sailing on the 'Juicy Rotten Banana.'

Kirk continued his southerly direction along the Outer Banks toward Pamlico Sound. He was in hopes to soon be back in the open Atlantic somewhere around Cape Hatteras, and far away from the colony on the Alligator River.

Chapter 11
HAPPY HOUR

"That's where we're headed," Kirk was speaking to the mutt as if he could understand. Both were in his main cabin below deck, with the mutt standing on a counter. Kirk had laid out a map and was pointing to a location off the coast of Georgia, somewhere near Blackbeard Island. Kirk was plotting a course for "Happy Hour."

He'd already had it in his head to make this a stop along his journey to the Keys even before Maude had mentioned it. Appropriately named, "Happy Hour" was a safe haven for all those seafarers who were seeking a temporary fix, who had something of value to trade, and who could also play by the rules.

A nautical mile or so offshore, Happy Hour was a derelict floating oil platform. Damaged and set adrift after the bombings, it was salvaged by a group of survivors who turned into a stationary, floating mini Las Vegas. Anyone willing to behave themselves, excluding anyone being affiliated with pirates, could enjoy a variety of luxuries from a good meal and drink, to gambling, to a night with your preference of partner.

Kirk felt that whoever the owners and proprietors were, they surely had some sort of professional background. They dealt strictly in trade and ran a safe, clean oasis for those that had the goods that they wanted or valued. In fact, the more Kirk thought about what Maude had told him, the more he felt that Happy Hour might possibly have ties to the mainland and whatever was brewing there.

The rules were simple; if you had a good to trade and were willing to abide, you anchored a safe distance away from the platform, within sight, and sent a radio request to the rig. An armed escort would then motor out to meet you. If approved, you were made to take a SARs-CfR-5 rapid test. Whether reliable or not, a chance both parties had to take, if you tested negative you were brought to the rig for your evening, or night, of choice. The derelict rig was set up with real feed animals such as live chickens and even cattle, a full casino to enjoy, and private sleeping quarters with company if you preferred. They had a greenhouse and a small refinery where they created corn-ethanol fuel and could supply a small amount at a high price. Or, you could simply enjoy a good night's rest in the 'hotel', complete with a 'happy ending' to your evening. The value of your meal and any 'company' depended on what you had for trade. Male or female, you could score anything from what looked like a top-scale Hollywood model, right down to something that more resembled Bertle.

The facility itself was known to treat its 'employees' well and kept them safe. No harming of the girls, or guys, in any way. Respect is key, there's absolutely no fighting allowed or tolerated, or you immediately got thrown off the rig and had to fend for yourself in the open ocean. And chances are that you weren't going to survive the swim back to your own vessel. They 'employed' and housed hundreds. Even Kirk had been offered a position as a 'bouncer' in return for food and hospitality after making several successful visits. Appreciative of the offer, he was far too much of a nomad and had politely turned down their offer as he preferred his solitude on the open ocean.

Not surprising was that a few of the pirate clans had, in

fact, attempted a takeover of the rig on more than one occasion. No doubt with it being the largest 'bounty' on the ocean, they'd felt it was worth going after. But, seeing that the rig was rumored to be very heavily armed, and, from the state of operations today, chances were that those 'pirate ships' were now sitting on the bottom of the ocean beneath the platform, along with their crew.

Kirk continued his conversation with the dog, "That airboat should provide me with a decent, landlubber's meal instead of fish. Plus, a bit of company for the night." He petted the mutt on its head, "Other than you." The dog panted and wagged. "If you're good though, I'll bring something back for you." The mutt simply lifted a paw as if he'd been requested to 'shake'.

Over the next couple of days, Kirk sailed steadily toward his destination. During which time he spent reloading empty shells and cleaning up the guns he'd acquired recently, especially the full auto that had ripped off the sentry's nose. It had turned out to be an AK-47 in decent shape. Kirk already had plenty of weaponry onboard, so he figured that this one might also possibly come in handy as trade. There aren't too many that would turn down a firearm these days, regardless of how well stocked they were.

The weather hadn't exactly been desirable, as a small storm had been heading towards him and blowing north up the East Coast. Kirk encountered a squall just below the Carolinas and he'd decided to sail straight through it. Many hours were spent hunched over the rail, and not due to fishing efforts.

By day three the skies had cleared, and Kirk was nearing the Happy Hour rig. He spent the morning landing a small swordfish and he and the mutt had a good breakfast, plus it added some fresh meat to the chest freezer. By mid-morning they were in sight of the rig and within radio distance on the short-wave citizen's band.

Kirk radioed on their frequency and received his usual response instructing him to anchor in place and wait for their arrival. Within minutes a small vessel arrived that looked as if it may at one time have belonged to a police department or the coast guard. There was high-caliber weaponry on turrets mounted to the bow and stern, and several armed and muscular men, and women were aboard.

One of the men on deck that was holding an M-16 called out, "Ahoy, Rotten Banana! *Errr…Juicy, Rotten Banana?!* It's Good to see you again!" The boat drifted alongside, and the two vessels tied off together. The same man stepped onto Kirk's sailboat. "What's your pleasure at Happy Hour during this trip?"

Kirk kept his hands well within sight for the man to see, "I was hoping for a good meal and possibly some company tonight."

"What do you have to trade?"

Kirk pointed, "That airboat back there. And, an automatic rifle, an AK." Kirk pointed to the weapon he'd placed on deck, however, made no attempt to pick it up.

The man looked over the bounty and Kirk could tell by his expression and nodding that he was impressed. Without words, he signaled with a nod to one of the others on his boat. Another Happy Hour employee, a woman, exited their cockpit and boarded the Banana. She had a rapid test kit in hand and motioned for Kirk to take a seat on his deck.

Kirk knew the drill and he allowed a swab of his nose to be taken. He worried a bit during the wait. With all that had occurred lately, he was skeptical that he was still 'healthy' and free of the virus. While waiting, the woman scratched the mutt behind its ears as the dog was seated right beside Kirk.

"You don't see too many of these nowadays."

"Yeah. He's a good, little companion."

"The dog will need to stay here," came from the man with the M-16.

"Understood."

Still scratching the mutt, who was thoroughly enjoying the attention, she glanced at the test kit. "He's clean."

The gunman signaled to others on his boat, and they proceeded to secure the trade items, taking the weapon and tying the airboat to their vessel. Kirk gave the mutt a last pat on the head before boarding his escort.

The rig itself never ceased to impress Kirk. It was massive and must've been a handful to anchor and set up, possibly taking more than a year to do so and plenty of manpower and supplies. The interior space, obviously modified from the original construction, was clean and well-guarded. People were polite, but you also knew they meant business. No rabble-rousing and no drinking yourself to excess in the bar or making a fool of yourself anywhere else. No harming the staff and you only received what was given to you, determined in advance by what you had to trade. No extras, and you left when you were told to leave.

Laid out on the large deck of the floating village there was the small animal barn, the greenhouse, and a nicer-than-you'd expect 'restaurant' and bar, plus the small casino area. All on the first level. On the second were the guest sleeping and pleasure areas, and on the third the employee quarters and other office space. Underneath the platform, at the water's surface where a grated platform once was they now stored all the 'trade' items, plus Kirk figured they probably had an armory and also their own watercraft stored there. That was just a 'guess', of course. On the old drill towers were a series of crow's nests where the lookouts were stationed.

In the casino, there was nothing to win, just the pleasure of playing the games themselves. Poker chips were the bet, with no valuables, and no side betting. For your meal, you ate what they brought you, as they were also limited to what they had available on any given day. For your 'company', other than your preference, you also had to deal with what was offered based on what you brought to barter with. If you needed fuel or supplies, it all reduced the value of your trade, and you dealt the hand that was provided, so to speak. Haggling over the deal or complaining were not options.

As for your presentation, the customers too were expected to be clean and polite. Upon his arrival, Kirk was taken to a shower area, as were all 'guests'. After cleaning up, including oral sanitation, Kirk was provided with a change of clothes for the stay, and he was expected to change back into his own upon exiting. Once he was satisfactorily dressed and smelling better, Kirk was allowed inside the main structure. He was wearing a pair of black dress pants and a clean and crisp dress shirt, and nice shoes. The rig certainly treated 'guests' well, and they expected the same courtesy in return.

Apparently, his trade offer had been a good one. Kirk was provided a decent meal that consisted of fried chicken, a vegetable, and even a beverage of choice. Kirk chose a nice red wine. He was provided a stack of poker chips and tokens and was told he could play in the casino until they were gone, or until the casino closed at 1:00 a.m. He opted for blackjack and enjoyed a complimentary beverage and even a tasty cigar. Later that evening in his room he was visited by a better-than-average-looking companion, and he enjoyed a night of conversation and debauchery, all much to his satisfaction.

The following day Kirk was escorted back to the changing rooms. His clothing had been laundered and he was provided a ride back to his vessel by the same crew that had picked him up the previous day. Before disembarking their boat for his, the woman who'd tested him for the infection handed over a small bag. Inside he discovered five cans of real dog food, gourmet-style, and a few dog bones. Kirk smiled, tipped his head, and jumped back over to his sailboat.

Kirk wasted no time in rewarding the mutt for the poop it had left on the deck overnight with a nice can of beef and gravy.

Chapter 12
THE DERELICT VESSEL

Setting his course for the Keys, Kirk didn't know exactly what he was going to do once he arrived there. Other than turning around and going back, which he'd done many times before, he hadn't made a plan as of yet. Rounding the horn of Key West wasn't something he was planning on doing, as the weather in the Gulf of Mexico had become far more unpredictable in recent years. The pirate activity there was also rumored to be worse than it was on the East Coast. The furthest he'd ever sailed was Miami, and even the activity there was more than what he preferred.

Anywhere he went was a gamble. It was a 50/50 split as to whether he'd find treasure or trouble. Most times Kirk discovered nothing to be left other than the walkers, and maybe a few small items that he could use, like the spices he'd been searching for to flavor up his meals.

Kirk also left cashés in various locations. He could only carry so much on the boat, so when he came across something that he might need later on, either for his own use or in trade, he'd stash it on land. He'd then mark a waypoint on his GPS as to where it was. He had several stashes along the East Coast just onshore. Sometimes he'd hide his items inside the wall of an abandoned building, or possibly underground if he could locate something watertight to bury it in. He had replacement electronic navigational equipment, canned foods, weapons, and other small items hidden in several locations. He was also fairly certain that others were doing the same. Up to this point he hadn't stashed any shiny valuables that he'd located, tossing many aside for someone else to find. But, after speaking to Maude, he felt maybe he'd better start if he were to be lucky enough to find any more.

As he sailed towards the area of Jacksonville on a bright, sunny, and warm morning he continued to think about the next destination. Kirk knew that at some point, someday, he'd need to brave the Gulf of Mexico. Either that or he was going to have to go further east to the Bahamas. And that, he thought, was a real gamble. Or at least an idea that made him nervous. Maybe it was the thought of history repeating itself and the whole, "Pirates of the Caribbean," thing. Whatever it was, the concept didn't exactly thrill him.

"Shit, I don't know," he said to himself, overheard by the mutt who was enjoying the ocean breeze, seated just outside of the cockpit's open window. Kirk looked over his map again. "Let's try Key Largo. I haven't been there, yet." He looked back up at the mutt, "There's a lot of canals we can check out. Most should allow the sailboat to fit. Or we can just park this and zip around on the dinghy. What do you think?"

The dog didn't respond, other than to tip its head.

"Key Largo it is, then."

◆ ◆ ◆

That afternoon Kirk was doing some fishing. He was enjoying the weather, the calm seas, and the fact that his stomach wasn't rolling. So far, he'd managed to hook two groupers and a redfish. The mutt had been chasing a couple of seagulls all morning long that had managed to make their way out to the boat and would tease the dog as he darted from the bow to the stern and back.

Kirk was re-baiting his line when he looked to the distance and thought he saw something, a faint spot on the horizon. "What in the hell is that?" At the same time that he uttered the words, he heard his radar ping in the cockpit. He grabbed his binoculars and glassed the water. Far off in the distance, he spied a vessel. Kirk jumped down into the cockpit and checked his equipment. The radar showed an anomaly off to his southeast. It wasn't moving fast. In fact, it was barely moving at all.

Kirk's mind began racing, as it always had when a boat was spotted nearby. He glassed it again. It wasn't a junk boat, he determined. It's too far out and, according to the radar, too big. It looked larger than his boat. Almost the size of a tug. Pirates, maybe? Probably not. They move quickly when they realize that they're in sight of someone and usually are in pairs at the very least. He looked down at the equipment again. The vessel was coming from the southeast, the open ocean. And it was barely moving as if only at a drift.

Kirk turned his sails to purposely lose the wind and he remained at a drift himself, keeping an eye on the anomaly both on radar and with the binoculars. It just wasn't moving and certainly not getting any closer. Kirk was already scanning the channels on both the VHF and citizen's bands. Nothing could be heard.

He adjusted the sail again and turned the rudder, cautiously pointing his boat towards the other vessel. Holding still, he watched to see if the other boat was going to turn or start toward him when they realized he was pointing right at them. After several minutes it appeared to Kirk that it was just continuing its drift. He also saw no other vessels in the area and nothing on the sonar.

"I don't think it's an ambush." Kirk scanned the seas before lowering his binoculars and looking down at the mutt, remarking calmly, "We're probably going to regret this."

Kirk turned the sails again, picking up a bit of wind, and began to creep towards the other vessel while keeping a watchful eye. As he began to close the gap, Kirk noticed that the other vessel was a sailing ship. However, the sails were tattered and flapping effortlessly in the breeze. He saw no life on the deck of the large three-mast schooner. But it also looked to have good-sized interior cabin space so the life could be taking refuge below decks. The style of the sailing vessel resembled something possibly built in Asia or Taiwan. Kirk was fairly certain at that point that the vessel had been disabled for some time and was simply drifting. Maybe they'd weathered a bad storm and the crew had felt that they weren't going to make it, and had abandoned ship. He kept his guard up, though, as he continued to approach slowly. He didn't want to get himself into a situation where the pirates had parked this tub and were just waiting for someone to do exactly what he was doing.

Kirk glanced at the mutt again, "Curiosity kills cats. Let's hope it likes dogs better and doesn't do the same to us."

He was on high alert as he neared the vessel. Turning out to be much larger than Kirk's boat, he wasn't going to have the ability to see the deck once he tied off, nor would he have the ability to see if someone were to sneak up from the cabins and out onto the deck. This didn't give him a warm and fuzzy feeling. Already with his 9mm tucked in his belt, Kirk armed himself with an additional Remington sawed-off containing six slugs in the tube and one ready in the chamber. He'd found this particular weapon hidden away in an abandoned bar in Martha's Vineyard a couple of years ago. He had it tucked into a quiver on his back so he could keep his hands as free as possible.

Kirk pulled up to the port side. The multi-colored, old wooden craft's paint was cracked and faded, and there was no visible name on the stern of the vessel. He tied off to a cleat that was mounted on the side. He couldn't see inside any of the few cabin windows, as they were too dirty and grimy. With his head being about a foot below its gunwale when standing, he was going to need to put up a boarding ladder. He unfolded a metal ladder that he had on deck and gingerly placed the hooks over the vessel's rail.

As he reached up and grabbed the rail, placing a foot on the first rung, he looked back at the mutt. "If I don't come back, promise you'll date others." He was attempting to calm his own nerves with a bit of levity. The mutt just tilted its head in response.

Kirk crouched as he stepped off his vessel and onto the ladder. He carefully pulled himself up, stretched his neck, and got his first peek at its deck. There was little to view as the rear third of the boat was all cabin area. Along the gunwales was a walkway to the bow. The cabins and wheelhouse extended the length of the vessel, with the narrow walkway rounding the bow in a horseshoe fashion. There wasn't a lot of room even if someone had been on the deck unless they were walking above the cabin, and there didn't appear to be anyone up there. Halfway between the bow and stern was the standup doorway to the wheelhouse on either side. There wasn't much in the way of nautical equipment on the deck. No life preservers and no ropes other than the tattered ends of what once held the sails up. Stretching his neck further, Kirk could now see into the boat's wheelhouse through the open doorway. He saw no crew.

Slowly and as quietly as possible in the gentle bobbing of the ladder from waves created by the breeze, he climbed up and put a leg over the rail. He stepped down and crouched, looking the situation over and removing the 9mm from his belt. He had no idea what, or who may be waiting on the starboard side. It was also evident that the access to the interior cabins was from the wheelhouse. The doors to the wheelhouse were open on both sides and Kirk confirmed by peeking in that it was empty. He stayed low and snuck to the bow and rounded the walkway to the starboard side. Still no signs of life. Satisfied that at least the deck area was clear, he stood up.

Entering the wheelhouse, he attempted to locate anything that would provide information about the vessel and where it had originated from. There was very little to be found and all he saw were the compass and a sexton. No other navigational equipment, no radio, no radar. Not that these items had necessarily been stolen, indicated by the fact that there were no torn wires dangling anywhere, but possibly they'd been removed in advance of their journey. Whoever set sail with this vessel was putting a lot of faith in the sun, the moon, and the stars. All of the wheelhouse windows were missing, and it was apparent that the boat had seen a few storms on its journey, as much of the area appeared water damaged.

Kirk turned around and saw that the stairs leading down to the cabins below deck were open at the top and had a closed door at the bottom. There was another closed door in the wheelhouse just to the left side of the stairs that provided access to the upper deck cabin space, possibly an upper-level 'captains' berth at the stern end.

"Okay," Kirk began to whisper to himself out loud. "Best case scenario, the boat is empty of people and loaded with treasure." He looked down and frowned, "Worst case scenario, there's nothing of value on board and someone's hiding somewhere, or possibly there are some infected ones on board." Kirk attempted to rule out the last choice in his mind, thinking it was unlikely that anyone that had been onboard had started out with the virus and had infected an entire crew during the journey. But, without knowing how long the vessel had been drifting, it was still a possibility.

Kirk stood thinking and thinking. And, thinking even more. He played the scenarios in his mind as he looked the doorway to the captain's berth up and down. He continued his conversation with himself, "I can handle a couple of infected ones if there's something to be found." Kirk was either attempting to talk himself into it, or out of it. He crept down the stairs and pressed an ear against the door. Over the sounds of the two boats now gently bumping into each other, he thought he may have heard movement coming from inside. But he just wasn't certain.

Like an idiot, Kirk gently tapped the door, knowing good and well that it was a bad idea. As if someone on the other side would tap back. He then recalled how this turned out at the colony and quickly regretted his decision.

Nothing immediately occurred and Kirk began to doubt whether the boat had any occupants left. He stood at the base of the short stairwell and looked around the cramped area. He glanced back up to the cockpit. Squinting, he felt that he noticed something. Something behind the wheel in the cabinet space underneath. A short piece of wood? Kirk puzzled a moment. Something that possibly blew in during a storm? Maybe, but, in the middle of the ocean?

Kirk's head turned back to the door when he thought again that he heard a noise. He pressed his ear against it once more. Footsteps, maybe? Not exactly on the immediate other side of the door, he thought, but possibly further back in the cabin space. He glanced back up, that piece of wood was getting the better of his curiosity. He had to check it out.

Ascending the short stairwell, when he got to the top, he heard a *"Thump"* against the door below. And then nothing. He turned back, reached down, and removed the piece of wood. It was maybe a foot long and looked as if it had come from the deck of this very boat. There was scribbling on it. It was faded and looked like it was written with a black Sharpie pen. It wasn't in English.

"Thump!"

Kirk looked down the stairwell, then back to the wood as he continued to squint and attempted to read the words. They were faded as if written a long time ago. Not all of the words were legible. Either, due to the weather-beating the piece of wood had taken, or how long the boat had been floating on the ocean. Probably both. What he could make out was the following, written in the language of the person who'd written it;

"Preduprezhdeniye! Ne otkryvayte... dveri kabiny! Moy... zarazilsya! YA ne mogu vzyat' ni....! YA vzyal spasatel'nuyu shlyupku i ostavil ikh zdes' umirat'! ...Prostite menya!..."

"Thump!"

Kirk knew that there was an infected person in the cabin space below, and that door could remain closed as far as he was concerned. He disregarded the noise and returned his focus to the piece of wood. Kirk couldn't make heads or tails of the words. He only knew they weren't in English. He glanced down at the door again, certain that there was at least one infected person behind it. He was nearing the point that he was about to abandon this ship rather than have to dispatch any infected people, let alone get into a tight space with them in the cabin area. The problem was; his curiosity was still eating at him.

Kirk attempted to sound out the words, but he just couldn't. He could only tell that there were exclamation points in the writing, a sign of warning, no doubt.

"Thump, THUMP!"

"Give it your best shot, I ain't opening that door," Kirk remarked casually, as he knew that the infected had no real strength to display. And it was apparent that this boat had been out here a long time so whoever was in the cabin area had probably been infected with the virus for a long time and was far gone.

"THUMP…THUMP!!"

Kirk frowned and made *that* expression. That look which expressed the fact that a lightbulb had just turned on inside Kirk's head again.

He looked back at the writing. It wasn't in English. He frantically looked around for anything else that provide him an idea of the origin of the boat. A survival ring, an emblem, anything. He went to the starboard side and looked all over, hoping to find something with writing on it. There he found, still tied to the side of the wheelhouse cabin near the bow, a survival ring faded orange and white. He turned it around and on the other side, away from the weather, was the faded name of the vessel. Among the words, Kirk recognized one of them; "Rossiya."

"Oh, shit!"

The moment that Kirk uttered the expletive, the door to the lower cabin area flew open. Five of the infected crowded the stairs and began to fumble their way up. Almost unrecognizable as to whether to be men or women, one thing was certain, they were angry.

"Shit! Russian biters!" Kirk dropped the piece of wood and found that his other hand was also empty. He looked into the wheelhouse and discovered he'd inadvertently, without thinking, set his 9mm down by the wheel.

The first creature crested the stairs and stumbled into the wheelhouse. Its clothing, a sleeveless shirt and cargo shorts, were tattered and stained with dried blood and other crusted body fluids. Its deeply recessed and wrinkled face was a grayish color. Its eyes, recessed in their sockets and fogged over, were seeping infectious body fluids that were streaming down its face. The same was oozing from its nose, ears, and mouth. The creature was thin, and its skin clung tightly to its bones. It appeared to have been male, only recognizable from the hairstyle of its greasy, dirty short strands. It turned its head towards Kirk, who was just outside of the forward window near the bow.

Kirk had only heard tell of the infected ones from Russia and the rumors about how vicious they could be due to the government's experiments on them. Now, he knew it to be true. The creature stood a moment, staring at Kirk. Its teeth inside its skeletal face clenched, and its hands with their long, bony fingers outstretched as if it wanted to grab something and rip it apart. The four others behind it on the stairs began pushing against it. Kirk knew that it was going to make a move soon. He pulled the shotgun from the quiver and backed up against the starboard rail. He wanted to get a shot straight at the creature, hoping to force it back against the others. Kirk knew that he was on the wrong side of the boat, and he needed to get around the bow to the port side where his vessel was.

He took a step to the side and pointed his gun through the front wheelhouse window opening. Unfortunately, he hadn't been quick enough and the creature moved towards the door on the starboard side, exposing the next one behind it. Very much looking like the first, Kirk didn't hesitate or choose targets.

He pulled the trigger, and the slug went straight through the thin, rotting skin of the creature in its upper chest. The round exited and penetrated the skull of the one behind it that was standing one step down. The slug traveled through both and splintered the woodwork in the stairwell behind them. Infected blood and puss sprayed on the bulkhead's ceiling above them. Both creatures dropped, blocking the other ones behind momentarily as they were all knocked down. The other two behind that hadn't been hit frantically began to crawl over the bodies.

Now standing at the corner of the bow and starboard side, Kirk looked back to the one that had exited onto the deck on his side. It was apparent that these creatures had poor vision, as it stood and looked in all directions. The direct sunlight after being below decks for so long probably wasn't helping it to see.

Kirk's attention turned when the door to the captain's berth flew open. It was immediately apparent to Kirk that the 'captain' hadn't made it off the vessel either. This creature too, possibly female, was as grotesque as the others. Long since infected, its eyes weren't quite as cloudy as the other four, and it seemed to have better vision as it glared directly at Kirk through the broken-out wheelhouse windows. It looked at him only for a moment and then darted out of the wheelhouse door to the port side.

Kirk looked back to the stairwell when he saw the one with the hole in its upper torso clumsily getting back up, with another right behind it now having crawled over the body of the creature on the stairs that had been shot in the head.

Kirk flashed a brief, puzzling expression as he noticed that his shotgun blast had created a gaping hole straight through the creature's decaying body and he spied the fourth one looking back through it as it too crawled over the only one that wasn't getting back up.

He sarcastically remarked out loud while racking the next round into the chamber, "Oh, this is just great!" Kirk raised the shotgun back up and pointed at the face of the one with the hole in its chest.

This time the creature's head exploded entirely, sending chunks of rotting flesh and bone all over the wheelhouse. It splashed over the other, unphased creatures behind it as its body dropped straight down at the top of the stairwell.

Racking the next round, and out of the corner of his eye and through the front window opening, Kirk spotted the one to his right approaching quickly as it passed by the wheelhouse windows on the starboard side. Kirk quickly swung the shotgun and pulled the trigger.

His shot went through the front window opening and out through one of the starboard windows. Unfortunately, it hadn't been a good shot and it struck the creature in its right shoulder. The slug severed its arm entirely and it flew out over the ocean. Deep, thickened, red fluid drained from the opening that was left in its shoulder and oozed onto the boat's wooden rail, and down the side of the boat. The shot did, however, stop the creature momentarily and caused its body to turn toward the ocean as it watched, as best it could, its own arm land in the water. Kirk took advantage of the creature's hesitation, racked the next round, and took better aim.

The next slug struck its target at the back of the creature's head. Its face exploded and its entire body flopped over the rail and into the ocean below.

Kirk's head turned back to now see three of the infected

crammed into the space at the top of the stairs. He also noticed the 'captain' on the port side going past the windows in his direction. He racked the next round into the chamber and aimed to the port side.

This time his shot went through the front and impacted the frame of the window on the port side before hitting the creature in its neck. Chunks of wood flew outward as the weather-beaten frame slowed the round, however, it still penetrated and lodged in the creature's throat. The slug severed its spinal cord and its head slumped to one side. Thick puss and deep, reddish fluid drained from the wound, but it continued to remain upright with its head flopping against its chest. Still apparently with the ability to maneuver, it continued to walk clumsily toward the bow.

"Dammit!"

This creature was moving slower so Kirk redirected his attention to the three left in the wheelhouse. They'd stopped moving at the top of the stairs only for a fraction of a second before one went right to the port, and one darted left to starboard. The third lunged straight forward at the helm and Kirk instinctively reared his body backward against the rail at the bow. The boat's wheel and dashboard stopped the creature as its arms reached for Kirk through the front window opening. Kirk swung the gun back up and pulled the trigger.

"Click!"

"Shit!" Kirk quickly racked the next round. He then decided to disregard the one that was caught on the wheel in front of him and he looked for the others. Floppy-head was slowly tripping towards the bow, slowing the one behind it on the port side. The one to starboard was nearing the bow to Kirk's right. He turned and aimed, waiting for it to round the corner.

The creature emerged at the bow. Appearing to have 'forgotten' that it was after Kirk, it stopped and gazed out over the water.

"Nice attention span you guys have!" Kirk yelled out as

he decided to save a shell and he ran up to it, kicking the creature in its side and sending it over the rail and splashing into the ocean.

When Kirk turned back and came in view of the front windows again, he found himself nearly staring at his own gun. The creature at the helm had picked up his 9mm and was pointing it aimlessly left and right. Kirk's eyes widened when it pointed at him. He quickly dropped down to the deck as the creature pulled the trigger. The bullet flew out over Kirk, over the bow, and landed somewhere in the ocean.

"*Sonofabitch!* It would figure that you *assholes* were taught how to use weapons!"

The next round shot by the creature traveled through the boat's dashboard and out the front of the cockpit's wall just above Kirk's head, causing Kirk to flinch and raise his arms to protect himself. Without putting any thought into it, Kirk foolishly raised the shotgun with one hand, reaching over and pointing the barrel into the window opening, and he blindly pulled the trigger.

The force of the blast from the one-handed shot rocketed the gun backward, and his hand struck the bow hard. His fingers let go and the shotgun hit the rail and flew out into the water. He pulled his hand back and held it tightly to his chest as the pain shot through it.

"*Fuck!*"

Kirk hadn't hit his target, as the next shot from the creature put another hole in the front of the wheelhouse and the bullet lodged in the bow's woodwork near Kirk's feet.

Kirk's shotgun blast had managed, quite unexpectantly, to hit dangle-head in the left arm with his reckless shot, severing the creature's limb at the elbow and straight through its ribcage from left to right. Full of holes, it was still slowly moving forward with the other infected 'biter' still trying to get around it.

Kirk turned over onto his knees, his hand still shooting pains through it. He backed up a bit and stuck his head up just enough to see inside the front window from the corner. The creature was still reaching and pulling the trigger, not truly pointing the weapon anywhere other than down where it 'believed' its target to be. Another round traveled through the front of the boat, this one further away from Kirk.

Kirk thought to himself that he truly didn't want to wrestle with the creature over his gun, and he also didn't want to be that close to one. He was also unaware, even though they didn't look it, just how strong these things were. Not to mention, these things were rumored to bite fairly hard. Additionally, his hand really ached. Still holding it, he looked down at his hand and flexed his fingers. It hurt like hell, but they didn't appear to be broken.

He stretched his back and looked over the rail, thinking that maybe he should just jump into the ocean and try to swim back to his boat and leave this mess behind, seeing that his escape was being blocked by a gun-wielding zombie and two others on the port side where his boat was. When he peeked over, he was dismayed to see a swarm of tiger sharks swarming and feeding on the creature that had gone overboard and was bobbing in the water, having been chumming the area by not only it but also by the blood and flesh of the armless, headless one he'd just sent into the ocean. He slumped back down to the deck, defeated. "This day couldn't get any worse."

Kirk startled when another hole appeared in the bow near Kirk's feet as his own gun rang out again.

"Goddamit!"

As if things truly couldn't have gotten any worse, Kirk saw bobblehead begin to round the corner at the other end of the bow. It was moving very slowly and didn't seem to have the other one on its tail anymore. Kirk's mind raced briefly. He uttered *"Crap!"* as he sprang up, hoping that it hadn't jumped down to his boat. He stood at the corner of the bow and the starboard side, using the corner woodwork to hide himself from the 'shooter' while he peeked into the cockpit from the front starboard window.

He spied that the biter had apparently given up trying to get around bobblehead and was now making its way back through the wheelhouse, entering the doorway on the port side. He also saw that the shooter was now crawling up onto the dashboard and attempting to exit through one of the front windows. Kirk spun his body around and saw the creature's hand, with his gun, poking out through the front window opening. Without hesitation this time, he turned around again and reached down, tearing off a loose piece of the wooden rail just as the other creature was emerging from the doorway on the starboard side. Holding the wood in both hands he spun again and lunged, striking the forearm of the creature who had his gun. Kirk heard a loud *"Crack!"* as the zombie's wrist easily broke and Kirk's gun dropped to the deck. In the same swift motion he dropped to his knees and picked the gun up. He pointed up at bobblehead and pulled the trigger.

Pain shot through Kirk's hand as the bullet struck its mark. The shot traveled through its dangling head and continued through its chest. Kirk didn't bother to watch it drop before standing back up and pointing into the window opening, placing the barrel up against the head of the creature that was attempting to crawl out of the window, and he pulled the trigger.

This bullet traveled straight through, spraying blood, puss, and brain matter all over the compass mounted next to the boat's wheel, which also shattered when the bullet impacted that. The creature dropped limp, its eyes remaining open and clouded over.

He spun back around only to have the last creature from the starboard side grab onto his arm. Unfortunately for Kirk, it was the arm that was holding the gun. The infected one locked-on with both bony hands and attempted to bite Kirk on his forearm. Kirk yanked his hand away and with his other hand, he tried to push the creature's head back. He grabbed the infected forehead, and his thumb penetrated its eye socket. When he pushed back, the thin skin on the creature's face tore off, exposing the skull beneath it. Kirk's hand slipped away, and he saw that half of its face was hanging from its cheek with infected muscle, veins, and thick blood now exposed to the air. It all began to slowly drool down its skull.

"Yuck!"

Kirk back peddled and put a couple of feet between himself and the creature. He raised the gun back up and fired, taking out the other side of its head. The bullet ripped through the bone and sent chunks of its skull out into the ocean. The creature's upper torso turned sideways from the bullet's impact, and its 'dead' body dropped to the bow.

Kirk switched hands with the gun and shook his aching hand in the air, *"Jeesus!"* He slowed his breathing and looked out over the port rail down to his vessel and saw the mutt sitting on the roof of his cockpit cabin. Kirk frowned and called out, "I told you this was a bad idea!" The dog simply raised a paw and waved.

Kirk regained control of his adrenaline and looked the situation over. There were bodies everywhere, and infected ones at that. He stepped over them, climbed back down to his boat, and went down into his kitchen area with the mutt on his tail. Kirk cleaned up in the sink and wrapped his aching hand in gauze while popping a couple of painkillers. Or rather, what he believed to be painkillers.

"What do you think? Let the boat go?" Kirk truly hated to walk away from a potential score, or an adventure. Even the ones that nearly killed him. He kept speaking to the mutt while taping his hand, "That was a lot of work. What if something's aboard?" He turned to the dog, who stood and began wagging its tail frantically. "It looked like a shithole of a boat to me. But…" He got up and walked to the other side of his berth and opened a footlocker he'd scavenged at one time or another somewhere on the mainland. Inside was a pile of weapons, including several more sawed-offs. He grabbed one of the shotguns and held it up, racking a round into the chamber with his one good hand. "…I gotta see what's on it!"

Kirk didn't bother to reload his 9mm. Rather, he grabbed a loaded .357 from the locker and tucked that into his belt. He put a face mask on, knowing that he was going into the lower cabin area of the boat where the air was certain to be stale, and he even put on latex gloves. He always kept an ample supply of both, and they were fairly easy to find on the mainland.

Climbing back up and over the rail, Kirk decided to check out the upper cabin first. He gingerly opened the door wide with the barrel of the shotgun and peeked inside. It was typical; a bunk, desk, cabinets, and chairs, all in disarray and dirty. Some clothing and empty food containers were strewn about. A few books and papers, all in Russian. Dried blood and other bodily fluids stained much of the furnishings. There was one weapon, an AK, on the floor. Quite possibly the 'captain', or whoever had ended up here, had secured the other infected in the lower deck and had written the note on the piece of wood. However, hadn't quite made it off the boat before succumbing to the infection themselves. Kirk tossed the AK onto the port walkway and began to step over the bodies and down the stairs. First making certain that all the ones in the wheelhouse were, in fact, entirely dead.

He stepped down and emerged into a small kitchen space, with bunks to either side and what looked like a bathroom area in the back. It too was filthy, disheveled, and dark. Everything was broken and covered in blood, both damp and dry. The smell was awful, even through his mask. He squinted at the stench of the infected air, not to mention the body fluids and feces. Kirk didn't see anything while scanning the area, and he didn't feel like remaining in there too long.

He turned around at the base of the stairs and found that the bow area seemed to be an enclosed storage area of some sort, or possibly another bunk room. The door was closed.

He remarked out loud, in a sarcastic voice, "Oh, great."

This time Kirk decided to just simply knock on the door. If he were to hear anything at that point, he'd probably just bolt out of there and be on his way. He knocked, loudly, and stood back with his shotgun ready. Nothing was heard. He crept back to the door and listened, also hearing no sounds. Taking a step back, he pointed at the door with his gun, reared back, and kicked it square in the center. Sending it flying open, he took a stance and hoped that nothing was going to jump out at him.

With nothing, and nobody leaping out, he cautiously stepped inside the small, dark storage area and looked at the doorframe as he did so. It had been locked, as indicated by the fact that the frame had splintered from the force of his method of entry. This space smelled no better than the one he'd just stepped from, although, this one also had the stench of rotting food. Shelves lined each side and were mostly empty. Obviously, any canned food items had been used up on their failed journey to wherever they'd been going. It appeared they'd also used up any sanitary supplies as well, as empty boxes were also lying about. Kirk was looking for any hint of who, or why they'd been on the ocean to begin with. Had they been destined for a location in the Eastern Europe area, or were they trying to get to America?

He located a couple of boxes of ammunition, but no further weaponry. There were also several empty boxes of vodka and one that was still full. Kirk decided not to take any of the vodka. Not immediately noticing anything else of interest, he was about to give up the search. He was also second-guessing his decision to risk his life and had fought for little-to-no reward.

Taking another step and a deck board under his feet creaked, more than the normal creaking of any boat's decking. In fact, the board nearly gave way under Kirk's feet. He knelt, tugged at the board, and wiggled a short piece of planking free. It was too dark in the storage area to immediately see what, if anything, was underneath. Kirk looked around and found a rag. He began wiping dirt, grime, and possibly what he believed to be dried blood from a porthole window to allow more sunlight to pass through, hoping he could get a look under the deck board. He cleaned two windows, one on the port and one on the starboard. The dank room lit up and Kirk looked around. The new light confirmed that there wasn't much of anything to salvage.

He looked down and noticed the light was now illuminating the floor. He squinted as he saw a glimmer coming from something solid just below the deck boards. Curious, he knelt back down and easily pulled another board free. *"Holy shit!"* His eyes widened when he discovered beneath it, shining in the light, were several gold bars.

Kirk lifted one out. It was heavy, very heavy. The bar was several inches long and at least two inches thick. He turned it in his hands and looked it over. It was crudely constructed, as if a novice had melted down someone's precious gold jewelry and made the bar from it. The edges were a bit jagged as if the casting had been hastily created. Kirk reached back into the space and removed one that appeared to be made of silver. It was of the same shape and dimensions, and just as heavy.

"Damn, maybe Maude was right. Maybe something is going on," he whispered as his mind created several scenarios for the situation he was in. Was it possible that there is a form of government again on the mainland? Were countries talking to each other again? Were these Russians heading to America to trade? Or, perhaps to buy some type of safety for themselves? Maybe they hadn't been destined for America in the first place.

Kirk continued his thoughts; Maybe there really is somewhere safe. Somewhere else. And these assholes were trying to buy their way to it. There were simply too many possibilities, and Kirk didn't understand any of them. Nor did he care at that moment.

Kirk gathered up the bars, counting twelve in total. Eight

gold and four silver. His mind was contemplating just what their expected use was, or even why he was taking them. But that's what you do when you find bars of gold, he thought. You take the booty and don't ask questions. There was nobody to ask, anyway.

◆ ◆ ◆

Back on his boat, Kirk untied from the vessel and let it drift away. It might have had some trade value, but it was a mess that he didn't feel like cleaning up. Plus, he had twelve bars of gold, what need was there for the boat? He laughed to himself at the thought.

He stashed the bounty in one of his 'hides', and then jumped into the ocean with some soap to wash off most of the smell. He also took a longer-than-usual shower in his fresh water to wash off the saltwater. His new reverse osmosis machine was working well and creating plenty of clean, fresh water.

With his hand still aching and freshly taped up, he and the mutt enjoyed an evening meal of redfish. Over the next two days, he slowly inched his way toward the Keys on calm seas. He was in no hurry to get there, as he had nothing to do once he arrived other than the usual scrounging in places he hadn't been to, and then planning his return trip north again. He also wanted his aching hand to heal up. Lately, he thought, between his shoulder and hand his luck hadn't been so good. So, for the next few days to pass the time he and the mutt would continue to fish, and Kirk would do some reloading of ammunition and watch movies.

And, luckily for him, the calm seas meant a calm stomach.

Chapter 13
PIRATES

"This is not good." Kirk lowered his binoculars and remarked to the mutt as they both stood on the stern. The seas were choppy this day, and Kirk had noticed two anomalies on his radar approaching from the northeast. He couldn't make out what they were yet, as they were still quite a distance away. But he was more than a bit concerned as to what they may be.

Kirk looked down at the mutt, "Let's not wait and see who our guests are. We better put the sails into the wind and put some distance between us and them."

Kirk looked up to the sky at the cloud cover. It didn't look good. The ocean wasn't impressing him either, as the swell was picking up in the wind and the seas were running around two feet. Kirk felt the queasiness stirring in his gut again. The wind would, however, work to his advantage and he adjusted the sails.

They were just inside the Keys now and quickly approaching Key Largo, not more than an hour or so away. Kirk hoped the vessels on his radar were simply other scavengers like him. Unlikely, though, he thought. Scavengers and general residents of the oceans like him were not typically found traveling in pairs.

Kirk trimmed the sails in an attempt to pick up more speed. While juggling between checking his radar and looking back through his binoculars, he saw that the vessels were steadily closing the distance. This wasn't a good sign.

He could also just make out the size of the two vessels now. Through his binoculars, he determined that they appeared to resemble commercial crab-type fishing boats. Both were at least 100 feet long, Kirk estimated. Each with at least one working, and possibly two powerful diesel engines.

"Shit!"

As he glassed the boats, Kirk finally spotted the colors that both vessels were flying. Cliché or not, pirates historically were pirates. Kirk spotted the raggedy black and white skull and crossbones waving in the wind on tattered flags.

Kirk lowered his binoculars and called out to the mutt, "They're definitely pirates!" He raised the glasses again and kept talking, "Well, we have three choices. One; stop now, do some talking and let them take what they want. And possibly, we die. Two; we stop, die first, and then they take our stuff anyway. Three; try to outrun them…and possibly die in the process."

Kirk had encountered pirates in the past. And he'd outrun them as well. The one time that he'd stopped and attempted to talk his way out of trouble resulted in him losing everything and being set adrift in his dinghy. Plus, he'd worked too hard for what he had on the Banana now, and he wasn't willing to give any of it up without a fight. It didn't take him long to decide that the only option he was willing to take was to try and outrun them.

"We're going for it." Kirk motioned with his head, "You get down below. It may get rough up here." The mutt did as it was told and scurried down the ladder to Kirk's bunk.

Kirk looked down at his radar, and then back again. The boats were well within his eyesight now. Kirk jumped on deck and worked the sails, gaining as much of the wind as he could, and he picked up speed. Ocean water from the chop was splashing over the deck and soaking Kirk as he steered from the deck's wheel and looked back again. Even though these were pirates, and were prone to stealing anything they wanted, he hoped that their weaponry was limited to hand-held automatic weapons. And, that he could stay enough ahead of them to remain out of their effective range. He also hoped that they didn't have smaller, fast vessels waiting to be launched. He glassed them again and didn't see any smaller watercraft, such as jet skis heading his way, so he was in hope that the only thing he needed to do was stay ahead of the limits of their diesel engines. He knew that the size of their vessels would somewhat restrict their speed.

Kirk also knew that they now realized that he was running. And, that they were certainly going to chase him. Kirk looked back again and saw his dinghy bouncing on the waves. He knew that if he cut it loose, he'd gain more speed, but he was stubborn. These things are hard to come by, he thought, as he shook his head and watched it flop behind him in his wake and on the waves.

Kirk ducked back into his cockpit and checked his maps. He thought, and hoped, that he could make Key Largo before they caught up with him. He quickly flipped through the maps and found a detailed map of the city itself. He discovered a canal at Ocean Cay that led to several other smaller canals. He felt if he could make it there, he could duck into the narrow canals where he felt they couldn't give chase due to the size of their vessels.

Kirk's heart was pounding and his adrenaline was running high as he set a long tac for Ocean Kay. He was also beginning to feel very nauseous. The fast movement on the wavy ocean was getting to him, and the adrenaline wasn't quelling his queasy stomach. He hopped back out on deck, glassing the vessels again.

Through the binoculars he saw both vessels racing towards him, the distance having been closed even more now. He also saw thick, black smoke starting to pour out from one of the boats. Kirk smiled, only briefly, before doubling over and puking on deck.

He quickly regained composure and looked back again. The dark cloud of smoke was billowing from the boat now. He jumped back into his cockpit and checked the radar. One of the vessels was slowing.

"One of them blew an engine!" He called down to the mutt. "Serves them right for burning shitty, homemade diesel and chasing us! One down and one to go!"

Unfortunately for Kirk, the remaining boat was still going strong and didn't appear to stop or turn to go back for their cohorts. The deep sea-style fishing vessel was at full throttle, cresting and crashing through waves as it shortened the gap between them and Kirk.

Kirk looked at his navigational equipment. His nerves were building, and his stomach still turning badly. He looked out to the shoreline, which was well within his view and very close. He yelled back down to the mutt as if talking to a deckhand, "Not much further! We just need to hold out a little longer!" Kirk checked his navigational equipment again. "Only a couple more minutes!"

Waves broke over the bow and splashed through the windows into his cockpit as Kirk stepped out and looked back again, quickly realizing that his vessel just didn't have the speed that the pirates did, as again their boat was quickly closing the gap. Kirk also thought he saw a 'flash' and a puff of smoke come from the bow of their vessel. A moment later and he heard the delayed, *"Boom!"*

Kirk saw the flaming ball approaching. There was a splash in the water just behind his sailboat that just missed the dinghy. Kirk's eyes went wide, "Jeesus! It can't be!" He glassed their bow and spotted the black, cast iron gun mounted on their bow. *"Holy shit!* They have a cannon! A real, *fucking* cannon!" It appeared to Kirk to be a small caliber cannon. Not the typical ones from pirate ships of long past, but it was operational. And, certainly powerful enough to disable any boats they were chasing rather than simply destroying them, which is probably what the pirates were going for, Kirk surmised. They were also obviously either heating or soaking the shots so they'd ignite during launching.

"Jeesus!"

Just then Kirk saw a second flash and another puff of smoke. As the *"Boom"* was heard, the flaming shot ripped through the gunwale on the port side of Kirk's sailboat. Wood and fiberglass fragments flew into the air as the solid burning stone traveled straight through the sailboat and plummeted into the sea. Kirk's eyes grew even wider at the sight of his precious Banana breaking apart.

"Shit!"

Luckily, the splashing of the waves prevented any fire from starting where the destruction was left by the cannonball.

As they continued to draw closer, Kirk now spied that they had at least two of the ancient, boat-killing devices mounted to their bow. And, he hoped there weren't anymore. He also knew that it would take them a minute or two to reload their archaic weapons.

He looked down at both his maps and equipment, and then back up at the shoreline again. He was nearing the turn at Ocean Kay. He was truly hoping that it wasn't blocked by anything, or simply not there anymore. Kirk turned the wheel and rudder just a bit, bringing himself even closer to the shoreline. Dangerously close, where he hoped they wouldn't have the ability to follow. Kirk was honestly scared now, drenched in a combination of his own sweat and the ocean spray still splashing over the bow from each wave he crested, and trough that he landed in.

Looking up again, Ocean Kay was in his sight. Or, at least what he believed to be the Ocean Kay peninsula. Hell, he thought, any canal will do right now! Kirk continued to surge his boat through the waves, keeping the sails tight and hoping for the best. Making the turn into the canal was going to be tricky at this speed and with the action of the waves. It required a 180-degree turn at the head of the canal. It was going to be tough to keep the boat from capsizing.

Kirk heard another echo in the distance. His head snapped back, and he stretched it outside of the cockpit just as more fragments exploded and flew from the stern. Shaking his head he jumped back on deck, ran back, and bent over the rail to see a jagged hole in his boat to his right, just above the water line. It went through the stern and exited the port side. Fire was now burning the edges of the impacted area where the cannonball had hit.

"Dammit! Their aim is getting better!"

He stood back up and looked to the shoreline. It was time, now or never! Kirk grabbed the jib, pulled hard, and ducked as the mainsail boom swung swiftly over the cockpit. He grabbed the wheel on deck and spun it hard. The boat turned sharply and listed, raising the starboard side and nearly exposing the keel as the port rails touched the water just as the second cannon went off again.

Kirk held tight as this shot ripped through the starboard hull. It would have struck above the water line, but with the boat listing hard into the turn and exposing the hull, it landed low. It had created a clean hole about two inches in diameter.

Kirk strained at the wheel, holding tight. His eyes nearly closed and the veins on his forehead popped out as his boat completed the 180-degree turn, ending up pointing north at the mouth of the canal. When the boat straightened out again up righted, Kirk found himself pointing at the bottlenecked channel at Ocean Kay.

He started the diesel engine and throttled hard, having lost the wind in the turn and he needed to put some distance between himself and the mouth of the canal. He also knew that if he continued straight, parallel to the ocean, he'd still be exposed to the pirates. The Ocean Kay peninsula and boulevard wasn't very wide. There was only one single road traveling the length of the peninsula that once had million-dollar homes lining each side. Hopefully, the shells of what was left, plus the overgrown vegetation, would be enough to make it difficult for them to spot him before he had a chance to duck down one of the narrower channels.

Kirk also knew that with the sailboat upright again, he was now taking on water. Luckily for him, though, the splashing of the waves and the turn had put the fire out on the stern.

Kirk soon discovered that the wind on the open ocean had all but diminished inland, and the waters were much calmer in the canal. From the maps he'd studied, he knew there were several channels to his left leading inland towards the Overseas Highway, the road that once led all the tourists to Key West. He also knew there were other canals off those, and he wanted to put as much distance, cover, and obstacles between himself and the pirates. He knew that they couldn't chase him into the canals, but they could launch a smaller vessel if they had any. The fact that they hadn't launched one yet was a good sign, but they could also probably get at least two more shots off before he'd have the ability to duck out of sight down the maze of canals, he thought.

Kirk headed straight up the channel, knowing that the pirates had also turned, and were tracking him from the ocean side of the peninsula as close to the shore as they dared to be. He acted quickly, wanting them to believe that on their next shot that they'd hit him. He also really didn't want them to hit him!

Kirk grabbed a can of gasoline from his supply. He hated to, as this stuff was like the gold he'd discovered, but he had no choice. He also activated the pumps to keep the vessel afloat as he was most certainly taking on water.

He looked at his surroundings as he moved swiftly up the channel. What was once a wealthy community of luxury waterfront houses and condos along both sides of the man-made canals were now replaced with wind and water-damaged buildings. Most were now just the rotting framework of what once stood. Palm trees were either overgrown or fallen down. Neatly trimmed lawns were now patches of tall weeds and scrub. In the canal itself were deteriorating boat lifts and both partially, and fully-submerged luxury yachts scattered in the water. Kirk had to maneuver around everything, including the area where the beautiful rock walls that once lined the canals had fallen apart and crumbled into the saltwater, creating an additional obstacle for him to work around.

Additionally, as he looked around, he now saw that the once wealthy summer and year-round residents had been replaced by dozens of walkers aimlessly wandering about.

Kirk heard the next shot from the distance. He helplessly watched as the flaming ball arced over Ocean Kay and it landed just ahead of him, slamming into the decaying cement and stone barrier of the canal just above the water line. Shards of rock and stone blew outward and peppered Kirk's sailboat, landing chunks of stone and pebbles on the deck that he shielded himself from with his arms.

He knew that he had to move fast now. He quickly dropped his sails. As they landed on deck he looked around and found that just off his stern in the narrow channel was a semi-submerged sailing vessel that he was just now passing. The once multi-million-dollar sailing yacht was now a dead relic, with more than two-thirds submerged beneath the water line at a 45-degree angle. With little to no other choices, it was close enough to resembling his own boat and would have to do. Kirk swiftly reached over with the gas can and drenched the deck of the vessel that was still visible, swinging back and forth, making certain to saturate as much of it as he could. He then tied a rope to the vessel and gave plenty of slack, tossing loose rope into the water. Throttling up his engine, he slowly began to move away from it.

Kirk jumped down into his berth and flipped open another footlocker. He grabbed one of the several Molotov cocktails that he kept at the ready, just in case of a close encounter and he needed one. He quickly petted the head of the mutt, who was sitting on his bunk with his tail frantically wagging, and then ran back up on deck.

The sound echoed again from a distance just as the shot came crashing through the house that was onshore adjacent to Kirk's boat. The dry, wooden construction exploded and fragmented. Splintered boards and shards flew at Kirk, causing him to duck and cover to avoid being hit in the face by the projectiles. The impact of the flaming ball striking the woodwork acted like a match on a striker, and the remainder of the building began to burn. The cannonball itself had continued, slowed by the impact, but still found Kirk's boat as it crashed straight through the cockpit. It blew out windows and damaged his radar equipment. Sparks and glass flew as it exited and splashed into the canal.

"Goddammit!"

Kirk wasted no time in lighting the cocktail, tossing it back onto the submerged boat. The saturated deck erupted in a ball of fire as Kirk gave his boat a little more throttle, dragging the derelict vessel to the center of the channel. He not only wanted the pirates to believe they'd hit their target, but he also wanted to block any smaller boats that would come looking. Additionally, he wanted them to believe that there was nothing left to scavenge or salvage.

Kirk managed to drag the boat just enough to block the canal. He then grabbed two more cocktails, lit the saturated cloth on each, and tossed them. He was hoping to make it appear as if his fuel resources were exploding. He also reluctantly cut his dinghy loose and shoved it towards another nearly fully submerged boat nearby, hoping it wouldn't drift towards the fire and also make it appear that it once was part of the burning wreckage. He was in hopes to come back for it later.

Not willing to wait and see what happens, he cut the line to the burning boat and began motoring his way up the canal, taking the first opportunity to turn onto another watery avenue and disappear. Hoping desperately that these bozos were busy watching the smoke from the fire and not his masts, and didn't have adequate equipment, or smaller boats, to track him. Just in case, once out of the site of the burning wreckage he slowed to a crawl and turned off all of his remaining electronic equipment. When he drifted into a spot in between two other derelict vessels just a short way down from where he'd left the wreckage, he tucked in against the canal's cement wall and sat silently. The only noise now in the area where he stopped was the pumps that were putting out water from his disabled vessel.

Kirk went below deck to check the damage. He had a good amount of seawater accumulating in his boat. The pumps were doing their job, but he still had the issue of the reason why he was sinking. He put on some goggles, grabbed a light, and gently eased himself into the water. He wasn't happy about it, being that he was now in the Florida Keys and alligators were probably lurking. He discovered the shot that had struck the starboard hull had gone straight through, creating two clean holes. The cannonball that hit the stern and exited the starboard side was still just above the water line, but still threatening to let water in if the boat sank any deeper. Luckily, the fire that had ignited the stern had put itself out, although, there was still damage from that impact as well. This, plus the destruction to his tiny wheelhouse made for one badly damaged sailing vessel.

Kirk climbed back into his boat, dripping with seawater and sweating from the hot, Florida Key's sunlight. He looked to the mutt who was waiting patiently for him to return.

"We're in a bit of a pickle."

Chapter 14
OLD JACK

Kirk spent the next hour diving down under his boat and shoving fabric into the holes to slow the leaks. He didn't stay down for more than seconds at a time just so he could keep an eye on the canal. He wanted to be certain the pirates weren't coming, and also to avoid any other wildlife that might threaten his safety. He also patched the upper damage as best he could with any materials that he had on the boat that would work for a temporary fix, all the while watching the black smoke in the distance from the fire he'd started slowly dissipate into the air above until it had finally burned out.

"We need to drydock and find the right stuff to put her back together properly," he mentioned to the mutt. "I mean real stuff. Fiberglass, fillers, and maybe even paint. Plus, a new radar, or at least something that will suffice until we can locate one of our hides that has one in it." Kirk wiped his sweating brow. "Ain't going to be easy. That kinda stuff is really difficult to come by nowadays." He looked around, seeing nothing but decaying concrete, hollowed-out buildings, and a few walkers above wandering on the dry cement landmass above him. "Not to mention, I don't know how in hell we're going to drydock this tub." He continued to survey his surroundings. "We've never been here. I don't know who, or what is lurking on dry land, or where the nearest boat yard was."

The mutt continually responded by wagging its tail.

Kirk threw the remaining fabric down, tired and defeated. He looked down at the mutt, "I'm hungry and thirsty. How about you?"

As he said this his head snapped up, having heard a noise. But, not coming from the direction of where he'd started the fire. This noise was coming from up the channel where he hadn't been, however, had planned on heading sooner or later.

"...*Chug, chug, chug...*"

Kirk looked to the next bend in the canal, not far away from where they sat, and determined the sound was coming from around the 90-degree turn ahead.

"What in the hell is that?"

The noise became a little louder, "...*Chug, chug, chug...*"

Kirk scooped up the dog and ducked down in his cockpit. He grabbed his 9mm pistol and peered out of the open windows.

"...*Chug, chug, chug..!*"

Kirk spied blackish smoke wafting in the air above the channel wall and between the buildings that was slowly approaching the bend. He frowned and was puzzled about what it might be. He also prepared himself. Some sort of vessel was approaching. Probably a local that had seen the fire and was now curious. He continued to peek and checked to make certain that he'd remembered to reload the pistol.

The pointed bow of a vessel came into view at the bend. Its long, old, wooden bow was faded red and white. Ancient, thick, braided, and fraying ropes were wrapped around the hull, acting as a bumper. As it came into view and rounded the bend Kirk saw that it wasn't a tall vessel, but it was long, maybe thirty feet. It was a square stern and fully open, with a seat in the rear and one single occupant holding a long, wooden rudder.

"*…Chug, chug, chug…*"

In the center of the boat was a large, barrel-shaped steam engine with a tall, rusty chimney pipe. The grayish, black smoke poured out of it as it chugged along slowly.

Whoever it was, they didn't mind announcing themselves as the old combustion engine was loud and put up a good plume of smoke. Kirk began to stand from where he was peeking behind the wheel, however, he kept his guard up. He squinted to make out that the man in the rear steering the boat appeared quite old. He was wearing appropriate attire for the keys; a faded short-sleeved shirt, raggedy cut-offs, and probably had on sandals. His white beard that nearly touched the bottom of the boat matched his long stringy hair and thick white mustache.

When the boat finally made the turn and was approaching, Kirk cautiously began to step out onto his deck, with his gun ready in hand just in case.

The old man spotted Kirk and he stood, with a bit of difficulty, as if he'd been sitting for a very long time. He raised his hands and waved, "Hey there!" As he neared, the old man spotted Kirk's gun, "Hey! Ho! Don't worry about me! I'm not here to make trouble!" A big smile was beneath his thick beard.

Kirk approached the rail, still keeping an eye on the area as the boat drew closer. Kirk didn't get a feeling of dread, or warning, but he did remain cautious.

As the old timer closed the steam valve and disengaged the piston and gears, he drifted up to Kirk's disabled vessel. Kirk looked at the faded name on the side of his bow. He squinted to make it out. It read, "African Queen." Kirk allowed himself to smile and chuckle.

"*Heh, heh…*" The old man leaned down and with difficulty, grabbed an old, frayed rope. "I just wanted to see what all the commotion was about. I saw the smoke and fire over the palm trees." The old man grunted as he tossed his rope to Kirk.

Kirk caught it, obliged, and tied the old man's boat to his. "The African Queen? Cute. Nice replica, old man. Did you do the artwork?"

"Replica? *Heh, heh.*" The old man sat back down, flopping his bony ass onto the old, wooden bench seat. He looked back up, "Do you know of the Queen?"

"Yeah, I've seen the movie. Old Humphrey Bogart flick, right?" Kirk was more at ease now. He stepped up on the rail and down into the old man's boat, taking a seat on a side bench. He did keep his gun in his hand, though.

"Yep, sure was." He patted the old, wooden rail, "The old Queen has a metal frame and wooden hull. They don't make them like this anymore."

"And that steam engine. Nice touch. I'm impressed. Who mounted that for you? Was it your own handiwork?"

The old man puzzled, "What do you mean? John Huston, I think. He named her, too, from what I've read."

Kirk disregarded the comment. Not that he knew who this guy's friends were. He continued, "Anyway, I had a run-in with your pirate buddies out there."

"They're not my friends!" The old man blurted. "They're a pain in the ass! There's no need of acting the way they do! It's tough enough these days without them dirty bastards trying to steal anything they can." With a deep breath, he managed to calm himself, "Anyway, the names Jack. But you can call me Old Jack."

Chuckling in his response, "Kirk. Nice to meet you, Old Jack. You live around here?"

"Yep. Just around the bend in the old hotel. Got it all to myself. Not too many living people left. None that's worth a spit, anyway."

"Amen to that."

"Looks like you had some trouble there."

Kirk turned to look at his damaged boat. "Yeah, it's not good. Six holes and a bit of fire damage. Plus, my radar and a few more cosmetic issues. She's going to sink if I don't get some supplies. I need to find a boatyard nearby and see if I can drydock her somehow. I'm not sure how I'm going to do it."

When Kirk turned back, Old Jack had an equally ancient six-shooter in his hands.

"Whoa, old man!" Kirk's eyes bulged and he put his hands up, "I don't want any trouble!"

Old Jack chuckled, *"Heh, heh.* Don't worry there, young feller. I just can't stand those things getting too close to me."

Old Jack raised his gun, aiming past Kirk. He used his other hand to steady the gun. Kirk looked up to his left and saw standing on the edge of the outcropping of stones above, a walker. The skinny, wrinkled, and deeply infected zombie stood, swaying, and seemingly looking down at the two. Half of its jaw was missing, now only displaying an upper jaw and tongue dangling from where the mandible once was. It was drooling thick mucus and blood that was oozing down the front of itself.

The shot startled Kirk, and he jumped in his seat as he watched the back of the ghoul's head blow out, spraying its infected body fluids from its skull to the air around it, and it dropped over backward.

"I hate them damn things!" Old Jack muttered as he opened the barrel of his gun and loaded a fresh round from his shirt pocket.

"Nice shot, old man." Kirk turned back and forced his nerves to calm. "You don't enjoy their company, I take it."

"Goddam nuisance is all they are!" The old man put his pistol back down on his seat. "So, young fella. We need to see about getting your boat fixed up for you." Old Jack squinted and read, "The….*Rotten Banana?*"

"I didn't name it. Yeah, I don't hold out much hope of that. She'll probably sink before I find a place to fix her. Let alone the materials she'll require to do the job correctly." Kirk sighed, "I just hate the thought of starting over. There aren't many vessels left that can be put together. Let alone the supplies and equipment they require. Been there, done that."

"Lost a few, have you?"

"It's rough out there. Too many fools like the ones that just chased me into here. How do you make it, old man?"

Old Jack reached into a small, dirty ice chest on the floor of the boat and pulled out a bottle of water. He reached across and offered it up. Kirk obviously had a look of concern, and the old man recognized it. *"Heh, heh*...go ahead. It's clean. Just water. And I ain't got nuthin'. Hell, if I did, I'd be dead by now. Or walking around like them things."

Hesitantly, Kirk accepted the offering. Old Jack removed a second bottle, removed the cap, and took a sip. The not-so-cold water spilled down his beard. Kirk removed his cap and drank. What the hell, he thought. If it was safe enough for this old man, it was safe enough for him. The water wasn't cool at all, but it was refreshing.

The mutt began to whine, standing at the rails and looking down. Kirk looked up, and then back at Old Jack. "Do you mind?"

"Naw, go ahead. Give him some."

Kirk stood up and grabbed the mutt, lifting him down into Old Jack's boat. The old man handed over a tin cup and Kirk poured some water into it. The mutt enjoyed the thirst quencher, laying down on the aged decking and lapping it up.

"Well, I just fish, mostly." Old Jack continued, "There's plenty to catch. I don't go out in the open sea too much. As you can see, that can be a bit dangerous. I've had plenty of years to build up a little supply of things. Food, water, whatnot."

"You come from around here?"

"Heh, heh, no. Just ended up here. We all ended up somewhere, just like you just ended up here too." Old Jack took another sip and smiled. "How have you survived so long?"

Kirk didn't mind telling his story, as he had no secrets to hide. He spent the next several minutes providing Old Jack with a brief history of life as Kirk had seen it since the virus, and since deciding that the open ocean was his home now. The old man seemed thoroughly impressed and attentive to Kirk's story.

After Kirk was done, Old Jack commented, "You've certainly seen and done it all, it sure sounds. It isn't easy living out there, but, it seems you've done well for yourself. Now, young fella', we need to see about your boat."

"I told you, old man, I don't have the materials or the resources to fix it."

Old Jack just chuckled at Kirk's comment while looking up to the left past his guest. His grin turned to a frown and again he reached for his pistol. Kirk turned and looked back. On the opposite side of the canal wandering up to the edge of the concrete in front of what was once a beautiful, expensive cape was another walker. This one appeared female. Her ragged, faded, and stained sundress was in tatters and blowing in the breeze, along with her long, once-blonde stringy hair. After gazing down, she turned and began to lumber along the edge, almost realizing that if she hadn't, she'd have fallen into the canal. The direction she turned was towards the two men as if she'd realized they were there. Kirk continued to stare while Old Jack pulled the trigger.

The ghoul tilted sideways but remained upright as Kirk watched the blood and infectious fluids eject from her shoulder. The bullet had entered and exited, taking with it chunks of her skin, rotting muscles, and fragile bones.

"You missed," Kirk mentioned quite nonchalantly as he continued to watch the creature meander along the edge of the canal.

"Damned arthritis!" Old Jack exclaimed, again holding his shaking hand with his other and aiming again.

This bullet struck the creature just above her left breast. Thick, red blood oozed from the hole the bullet had created and added to the dried fluids caked on her already-encrusted sundress.

"Damn!"

Kirk turned back to see that Old Jack's arms were tiring. "You're wasting your ammo. I'll take care of this one." Kirk turned again, raised his 9mm, and squeezed the trigger.

The woman's head snapped backward as the round entered her temple and exited the top of her head. Blood sprayed outward, having followed the exiting round. When she tilted her head back forward blood and greenish, infected brain fluid drained down her face from the hole in her forehead. She teetered momentarily at the canal's edge before falling forward and splashing into the water.

The two watched as she floated for a moment before a twelve-foot alligator emerged, mouth open, and grabbed her body between its jaws. As it surged out of the water, it flopped over in midair and landed again, taking her lifeless body beneath the surface. It splashed salt water onto the two men, and the mutt, and caused a wake that rocked Old Jack's boat.

"Jeesus!" Kirk's mind flashed back to when he'd dove under his boat to check the damage. Mental note to himself; don't do that again.

"Goddam gators! They're a nuisance too!" Old Jack muttered.

"Yeah, I'm not partial to them either." Kirk turned back, tucking his 9mm into his belt and continuing their conversation. "So, old man, what did you do before? What was your trade?"

"Well," he replied, "I was in Georgia as I recall. Believe it or not, I was a pretty smart guy." He pointed and winked, "Edumacated! I was working for the Center for Disease Control on this whole infection thing. Had a bunch of people working for me, too!"

Old Jack lifted his water bottle and extended his arm. Kirk obliged, extended his, and 'clinked' the old man's bottle in a 'cheers' fashion, both taking a sip when they sat back.

Old Jack motioned with his bottle towards Kirk, "I'll tell

you something. The truth is, we nearly had this thing beat. That is until them damn Ruskies decided to go off on their own and screw it all up." Old Jack leaned back against the boat, reclining on his bench seat. "We were working with them on a cure, believe it or not. And then, they commenced to fidget with the formulas and created something that turned them things mean instead of working towards a cure. And then, of course, they realized they'd screwed up. The bombs came next and ruined everything."

Old Jack sat up again, "We were close, too. So close. And then, it all went to hell…and here we are now."

Kirk nearly whispered, staring at the floor of the boat, "Yeah, well, there's no more room in hell now." He thought for a moment and then perked back up, "The CDC, you say?"

"Yep. Like I said, you don't have to believe me, but it's true. We had a big lab that we were working out of there. My division was put together to specifically work on a cure for the infection. Like I said, we were close, too. If the world hadn't fallen apart like it did, we would have cured it!" Old Jack took another sip of water and then motioned with the bottle behind Kirk's left shoulder. "Would you mind?"

Kirk turned to discover that yet another walker had wandered to the edge of the stonework and was standing, swaying, and staring down at the two.

Kirk turned back, smiling, and chuckled. "You really don't like them things, do you?"

"No, I don't. They get in the way of doing things. They ain't worth a damn once they're too far gone." He leaned down and refilled the mutt's cup, which the dog happily slurped down to the last drop. Old Jack groaned as he sat back up, "If you can't cure them, kill them!" He motioned again and said calmly, "If you don't mind."

Kirk obliged his host and took the 9mm back in hand. He stood, aimed, and pulled the trigger, taking this one square between its eyes. This creature had been a little larger than the others. When the back of its head blew out from the force, and the fluids spurted out of the hole above its nose, it wobbled a moment before dropping backward and out of sight.

"Thank you."

"Don't mention it," Kirk responded before sitting back down. This time just setting his gun down beside him in wait for the next walker to show up.

Old Jack stood, with difficulty. "Okay! Time to show you something! Let's hook up to your boat there and drag it up the canal a bit closer to my place."

Kirk's look of surprise was apparent. "What? Where?"

The old man limped past Kirk to open the boiler and reengage the gears. "Back to the wharf." He pointed to the sailboat, "You need to get that out of the water before it sinks if you ever want to fix her up. Those pumps won't last forever."

Kirk was still a bit stunned and confused at the old man's offer to assist. He stood, his puzzled expression remaining as he pointed towards the mainland. "You have a way of getting that out of the water at the end of this canal?"

Old Jack just chuckled and kept on. He was about to crank up the boiler and open the steam port and he motioned for Kirk to move the ropes and tie off to his bow. "No need to waste your gas. I have plenty of coal and this old tub has some power to her still."

Kirk interrupted, "Wait a minute, old man. You said that you worked for the CDC in Georgia just before everything went to shit."

Old Jack sat back down on the bench across from Kirk and rested his bones. "Yep, sure was. We had a good team. The best. In fact, I had this one gal that was right there!" Old Jack squinted and smiled, "Right on the edge of a cure that we felt would work. And then…kaboom! We got word that the Russians had sent their bombs into the air all over the place. Soon after that, sirens started going off and everybody ran for cover. All the testing equipment was destroyed in the mayhem. It was every man for themselves after that. There was no going back."

Kirk rubbed his chin and gave Old Jack a look. "I don't suppose you remember what her name was, do you? The one that you said was so close to the cure?"

Old Jack puzzled over the question. "Her name? Well, let me see." He looked up to the sky as if the answer were written across it. "Hmmm…Freida. Frieda something. Freida…Albatross, Alberta, Alveena…"

"Alverez?"

Old Jack smiled and pointed, "Yeah, that's it. Frieda Alverez. She's the one. Smart gal. Meaner than a wet cat, but smart. She and her brother both worked for me. She was the brains though. I tell you, she was close to that cure!"

Kirk hung his head and muttered, "Sonofabitch, small world."

"You say something?"

"Wait here, old man." Kirk got up and hopped back over to his boat while Old Jack stared, throwing a confused look Kirk's way through his facial hair. Kirk hopped down into his cabin and returned moments later with a duct-taped notebook in hand. He jumped back down and handed it to Old Jack, and then sat back down.

"What's this?"

"You tell me. Take a look inside." Kirk opened a pocketknife, reached over, and sliced the duct tape so Old Jack could open the binder.

Old Jack limped back to his seat at the stern and rested his bones again. He retrieved a pair of scratchy reading glasses that he had setting nearby and perched them on the bridge of his nose. Opening the notebook, he gazed at the pages, taking his time. With each page that he scanned and turned his old eyes grew wider. Kirk sat quietly as he could tell that Old Jack seemed to be quite intrigued at whatever was hand-written on the pages. After flipping about a quarter of the way through, Jack looked up and smiled, inquiring with enthusiasm, "Where did you get this?"

"From Frieda Alverez."

"Where is she?!"

"She's gone."

Old Jack's expression turned sad, but only momentarily. He perked up again, poking the notebook with one finger. "Do you know what you have here?!"

"I was hoping that you knew."

Still poking the pages, "This is it! This is the cure!" He flipped through a few more pages, scanning the information. He looked back up at Kirk and took his glasses off, poking the pages with them. "At least the beginning! Maybe the whole thing!"

"I'm glad you're enjoying it, old man. What good does that do anyone now? Even if the secrets to a cure were in those pages somewhere, who's going to ever know how to use them? There are no labs anymore. No equipment, no real doctors…"

Old Jack slammed the notebook shut with a wide, toothy grin on his face. Standing up, he handed the book back to Kirk. "C'mon! We need to get going. I have something to show you. Put that someplace safe. No, wait! Keep it right where it is, in your hands!"

Kirk smiled and shook his head. He undid the ropes and tied off to his bow. He had to set the notebook down and noticed that Old Jack was keeping a close eye on it. For some strange reason, Kirk didn't feel threatened by the old man, nor overly worried about where he was being led to. Not that he wasn't being cautious, he'd been duped before. He just felt a bit more at ease around Old Jack.

Jack fired the boiler back up and engaged the pistons. The antique steam engine ran hot, but she certainly had some power as he'd said. It towed Kirk's boat easily, and Old Jack carefully maneuvered the two vessels up the canal and into the turn. There was certainly no speed to the antique steam engine, but she could pull a sinking sailboat.

As they weaved and meandered around sunken boats and other debris, and after a couple more turns, they made their way further inland towards the Overseas Highway. The steam engine was loud and smoked a great deal. Kirk had to raise his voice to carry on a conversation with the old man as they slowly made their way up the canals.

"Hey, old man! Is it true that some people are immune to the virus? Like, they can't catch it and all?"

Old Jack responded over the "chug, chug, chugging" of the engine from his seat at the tiller. "Who told you that? Was it Frieda?!"

"Her brother! He swore that some…some people have a gene in their blood…!"

"Well, let me ask you this? How close have you been to the infected since this all began?!"

"Too close!"

"Close enough to catch it?! Ever felt like you should've caught it?! Ever felt sick?!"

"Yes…and no, not once!"

"Well, then. There's your answer! You just might be one of them! There's more than you think out there that might be, too. Some can be completely immune. Some can just be a carrier, too!"

"Did all your research prove that?!"

"Yes, it did!"

Kirk could see the end of the channel ahead. It squared off at a wall of cement. Off to the left side was a long, old, wooden wharf. Old Jack steered towards it and docked near the end. Kirk noticed that from a sidewalk at the top of the canal, there was a stairwell leading down to the wharf. On the left side of the canal, there appeared an old restaurant and hotel that was once in operation. Another large hotel sat to the right side. Just ahead at the end of the canal was a parking area, and then the Overseas Highway. This, and all the buildings had to have been something to see at one time, Kirk thought as he looked around. Now, they were all just derelicts. Empty buildings and empty parking lots.

Old Jack shut the boiler down while Kirk tied off Jack's boat and lifted the mutt, setting him on the dock. He hopped out and tied his boat to the wharf as well. He then boarded and checked to make certain all the pumps were still in operation, going below to check the damage. Water was coming in faster than it was going out and threatening his engines and lower deck space. When he came back up, Old Jack was waiting on the dock, kneeling, and petting the mutt. The notebook was tucked under one arm. He looked up at Kirk, "How's the boat holding up?"

"She isn't going to stay afloat much longer," Kirk remarked in a defeated voice.

"Well, c'mon, then!" Old Jack stood with Kirk's help. The old man handed the notebook back to Kirk and started up the stairs, turning back and pointing to the Banana. "She'll be safe there next to my boat. Nobody's gonna' mess with it."

As Kirk followed, he stopped when he saw an old, faded marquee poster hanging on the cement near the stairs. It appeared to be part of an old collage of framed photos, with a few still hanging on the wall. Kirk looked it over, the pictures seemed to be of Old Jack's boat. The marquee was an advertisement, with photos and a description of the very boat that Jack was operating. Kirk read a bit of the information and looked over the photos. His eyes widened and he called out to Jack, pointing at the old man's boat. "That's the African Queen?! The real African Queen?! Isn't it?!"

Old Jack was making his way up the stairs and didn't bother to stop. "I told you it was!"

"*The African Queen?!* I was just riding in the boat that Bogart sat in?! The very same boat from that old movie?!"

Old Jack finally stopped and looked back down. "Whatsa matter? You didn't believe me? I told you it was." Old Jack sighed, "They brought that thing over from Africa in the 1960s. Long after the movie had been made. It ended up here around 1980-something. It was used to take tourists around the canals until…well, you know…"

Kirk was still excited, turning around and motioning to the boat with both hands. "My ass was sitting in the same spot that Bogart's was!"

"Don't forget about Hepburn! Her ass was nicer than his! C'mon! It ain't that special! Let's go!" Old Jack continued up the stairs.

"Not special?!" Kirk began to follow, picking up the mutt and carrying him up the stairs with the notebook still tucked under an arm. "That's probably the only historical monument left in America that someone hasn't stolen, traded, or destroyed! And I was sitting on it!"

"Yeah, yeah…"

At the top of the stairs at the mouth of the parking lot, the two men stood. Old Jack checked the area, it was mostly desolate. A few walkers could be seen meandering in the distance.

Kirk set the mutt down and looked around. The parking lot and roadway were littered with junked vehicles. Tall vegetation grew in the wide cracks of the old tar roads and all over the lot. Palm leaves, both fresh and dead, were covering everything and blowing in the breeze. Buildings were decaying and falling apart. An old gas station sat directly across the street. The gas pumps were tilted sideways and the sign from the garage had fallen down long ago. Even though the road hadn't seen traffic for many years, it still gave Kirk an eerie feeling as he looked the area over.

"That's my place." Old Jack pointed to the hotel to their left. It was a long building, extending the length of the canal to the first bend, and three stories high with what appeared to have been the old restaurant on the far end. Entirely boarded up, no open windows still existed. The siding was weather damaged, and it didn't appear that it would take too many more storms before the entire building was to come down. The only thing that made the building stand out was the chain link fencing that had been put up near the edge of the parking area. It surrounded Jack's hotel, the parking area, and the next hotel on their right. Obviously, it was to keep any walkers out.

"You did a lot of work on that fence." Kirk mentioned as he followed Old Jack to the doors of 'his' hotel. They too were covered over, preventing anyone from seeing inside. Kirk looked over the building and the fact that all the windows had been covered over some time in the past. "Got it all set up for hurricanes I see."

"Yeah. That's one reason we keep it this way."

"We?"

Old Jack sighed and turned to Kirk. "I'm going to trust you and show you something, okay? Only because you trusted me enough to show me that notebook," poking the duct-taped book that Kirk was carrying.

Kirk shook his head, "Okay, old man. Whatever you say."

Old Jack pulled open the doors to the hotel. The bright lights illuminated from within, even through the sunlight of the clear Florida day. Old Jack stepped aside, and Kirk peeked in. It resembled a large laboratory. As if several conference room walls just beyond the lobby had been taken out to form a massive space. It was modern with clean furnishings, cabinets, sinks, workstations, and all the necessary equipment to perform research and development. Kirk even saw computer stations that were in operation. There was obviously a source of power somewhere, most likely solar. Kirk also saw people, maybe 50 or so. All dressed in white lab coats, they all seemed to be working on something important. Either at lab stations or at the computers. It was a massive working scientific laboratory and medical facility. Kirk felt that beyond the massive laboratory area had to be living, kitchen, and recreation space, too. Plus, wherever they'd hidden the power generators and supplies. Kirk also suspected they had a hidden armory somewhere as well.

Old Jack was holding the door open for Kirk. "You don't have to go in if you don't want to. I'm not here to force you into anything. But I'm hoping that you will."

Just as Old Jack said this a younger man, maybe in his

30s, approached the two. He was clean-cut, had coke-bottle glasses, and had on a clean lab coat. He was carrying a second coat. Old Jack stepped inside the door while Kirk held it open. The young lad held up the coat and Old Jack slid his arms into it.

"We wish you wouldn't take off like that, Doctor Morgan. It isn't safe." The geeky young man looked Kirk up and down, "Who's this?!" He directed his comments back to Old Jack, "Doctor, we can't be letting just anyone inside! We can't trust others! You shouldn't have brought this man here! *Who is this?!*"

Old Jack turned around and adjusted the coat to his shoulders, and he spoke directly, "Who's running this place?! You or me?!"

Sheepishly, "You are, Doctor Morgan." Others in the massive space, who had overheard and now noticed the stranger and his dog at the door, had now stopped what they were doing to observe.

"Then don't ask! Now, go tell Johnson and Davenport to meet me across the way!"

"Yes, Doctor Morgan." The young man gave Kirk a 'look', and then one to the dog before turning around to go complete the task he'd been given.

Old Jack stepped back outside, leading Kirk, and let the doors close. "I'm sorry about that. They're a bit overprotective of me."

Kirk formed a wide, somewhat deviant smile, "You old fooler, you! You smart, old fool! You're still working on a cure in there, aren't you?!"

"What else is there to do nowadays?"

Kirk's smirk remained. His enthusiasm was like a child with a new toy, "I can't believe it! How long have you been here? I mean doing this? How long?"

"Oh, hell. I've forgotten now how many years it's been. Too many." Old Jack began to walk across towards the adjacent hotel. Kirk and the mutt were right beside him. Kirk continued to be in awe of what he'd just seen.

"How close are you? I mean, it looks like you have all the equipment to solve this! Those people, are they all doctors? Students?"

"Some. Some are doctors, and some scientists." Old Jack stopped and turned around. He sighed, "The truth is, we had to go somewhere when everything happened. A few of us wound up here and we began to rebuild. Others came later. And yes, we are a teaching facility." He reached up and placed a hand on Kirk's shoulder, "Kirk, we're looking to finish what we began all those years ago. It hasn't been easy. Everyone that I'd worked with was gone. I had to find new people…and teach them. It's been a long, tedious process." The doctor removed his hand and pointed, "That notebook holds the key. It has all the secrets that we lost when we were forced to run. Plus, whatever else she may have figured out over time." Jack turned and began walking again. "Now, c'mon. I have something else to show you."

Kirk was still smiling as they approached the adjacent hotel. It was also all boarded up too, and a locked chain was holding the front double doors shut. Old Jack dug into his pants pocket, removed a key, and worked it into the lock. The chains dropped to the ground and he opened the doors.

The two men plus the mutt stepped into another large, open space. Old Jack activated the lights and Kirk heard a "whirring" as if a generator had turned on. The space reminded Kirk of a large garage, as it appeared that many of the rooms on both the first and second levels had been gutted out to form the working area. Kirk stepped inside and was instantly in awe once more. He saw a huge electronic boat lift. It had a heavy steel frame with wheels, and it was apparent that it could straddle the canal. On the wall facing the canal they'd built a large rolling door to allow the lift access to the channel. In the middle of the space were various size watercraft all mounted on smaller, mobile boat lifts and neatly arranged. There were also several vehicles parked in a row, also quite obviously operational. Along one wall was a row of benches with neatly arranged tools. On another wall were dozens of shelves full of what appeared to be cataloged vehicle and watercraft parts.

On the far left, mounted up on wooden posts was a beautiful sailing vessel. It was of wooden construction, and a deep marine varnish shined on its hull. A three-masted vessel, the masts were down to allow it to fit in the space. It was a little larger than Kirk's boat and obviously had been well taken care of. Kirk gazed and wandered up to it, placing his hand on the smooth surface. He smiled and turned to Old Jack, "This was yours, wasn't it?"

"Yes," the old man simply replied as two other men joined them in the massive garage area that in appearance from the outside looked like an old, dilapidated hotel. The two younger men were both fit and wearing street clothes. Old Jack turned and addressed one of them. "Take the lift outside and pick up the sailboat that's parked behind the Queen. Be careful with it. Shut down the pumps, drain the water out of her, and take down the masts. But be quick about it and get it inside here! It requires repairing that I want you two to get on right away!

"Yes, Doctor Morgan!"

"And upriver you'll find a floating pontoon. Bring it back here and get it inside the garage too."

"Yes, Doctor Morgan!"

Kirk patted the hull of Jack's vessel and returned to speak with him while watching the two younger men hurriedly start to prepare the big boat lift to be moved outside. "Okay, I get it. You obviously have the materials to fix my boat. But what do you want in return? Guns? Ammo? Gold bars? The dog? What?"

Old Jack chuckled and knelt to pet the mutt. "Heavens, no. We have protection and supplies already." He stood back up, once more assisted by Kirk. "Look at what we have here. It would be foolish not to have the means to protect it all. We lost everything once. We can't afford to lose it all again. It's taken us years to build this place and to keep it secret from others. We have means that you couldn't even begin to understand here. Things that I'd like to show you."

"Well, then, what? I wasn't kidding about the gold, Jack."

The doctor laughed out loud. "Gold? What would we need with that?"

Kirk frowned and looked at the ground, mumbling, "I don't know. Just something I heard once."

Old Jack put a hand on Kirk's shoulder again. "Tell me, Kirk, is Frieda Alverez truly dead?"

Kirk raised his head and spoke softly, "She wasn't really alive when I met her if you know what I mean. I ran into them, both of them. It wasn't good, Jack."

"What do you mean?"

"They didn't have the setup that you have here. They'd both gone mad and created more of a cult-type situation rather than any type of laboratory or medical facility. Plus, they were…well…doing things to others. They did have the infection under control, I'll give them that. But it wasn't good, and it certainly wasn't a cure. Maybe if they'd had a setup like yours…it wasn't good."

Old Jack nodded, "Understood." He let go of Kirk and held the lapels of his lab coat, smiling, "Well, then, my friend. The price is that notebook. It holds the key, Kirk. If what you're saying is true, then her secrets are in those notes somewhere! That is our *gold*, Kirk! But that's only half of what I want."

"What are you talking about, old man?" Kirk had an intriguing look of concern on his face as he asked the question.

"How long have you really been out there, Kirk? On the ocean, I mean. How long?"

"Years."

"Then, stay with us!" Old Jack had a gleam in his eye as he spoke, "Please! Stay here! We can use a man like you! Working right alongside us. Plus, I meant it when I said that you just may be immune!" Old Jack poked Kirk's shoulder, "You may be holding part of the answers right there in your veins! You're a survivor, Kirk! We need that! I have so many here that can perform the science, but not nearly enough that can help protect it all! I want you for that!"

Kirk sighed, "Old man, you can have the notebook. It means nothing to me. Hell, you can even have as many pints of my blood as I can spare to give to you. But I can't stay. I'm too used to being on the move, on the water. There's nothing on land for me anymore…"

Kirk startled when the two men rolled open the bay doors that faced the canal and began to move the lift outside. The sunlight shined through the bay on Kirk and Old Jack. They began to wander together toward the doors, the mutt on their heels.

"Believe it or not, Jack," Kirk pointed towards the bay as he spoke, "it's safer out there."

"Ah, well, yes. Maybe." Old Jack spoke with a heavy sigh of his own, "I can't make you stay. But you're more than welcome. At least until your boat is repaired properly. But just remember, like I said, we could use a man like you. You obviously know how to find things. And you're obviously quite clever when it comes to keeping yourself safe." They arrived at the bay doors and looked out together, down to Kirk's sailboat and the Queen as the doctor continued, "We watched you with those pirates, Kirk. I told you, we have means here that would amaze you. We also have plenty of room. Very nice accommodations, if I do say so. Food, water, all the necessities. And obviously medicines…"

Kirk was distracted away from what Jack was saying when a very attractive, 40-ish-year-old lady in an open lab coat and a casual, knee-high dress underneath walked into the space from the parking lot. Her long, auburn hair, green eyes, tall, shapely build, and long legs down to her high-heel shoes immediately stole Kirk's attention. He barely heard what the old man was saying as Old Jack basically spoke to the canal, believing that Kirk was listening.

"…And of course, the highway…only one way in, one way out. Quite easy to protect ourselves…"

"Uncle Jack?"

The doctor, who'd been lost in his thoughts in an attempt to convince Kirk was startled back to reality, and he turned to the woman. "Hmmm, what? Oh, yes, my dear."

"They need you in the lab. Jackson has discovered something again…or, as usual, thinks he has. And he needs your input."

"Yes, of course."

The woman smiled wide when she knelt down to pet the mutt, who certainly didn't mind the attention. Its tail wagged frantically as she scratched the fur under his collar. "Hello, there cutie! Awe, such a sweet little guy!"

Kirk looked over her head to Old Jack and mouthed the words enthusiastically with a smile, and without saying them out loud, *"Who's that?"*

As if they had been voiced, Old Jack replied, "Hmmm? Oh, yes. Dorothy, my dear, I'd like you to meet Mr. Kirk."

Dorothy smiled up at Kirk. "Hi there. I heard about you. I heard that you fooled those foolish pirates and have something of value that my uncle has been looking for. Something very valuable."

Kirk smiled back, however, and gave her a puzzling look as if to ask how she knew all this.

"Word travels fast around here. Anyway…" Dorothy looked down at the dog, scratching both sides of its head, "Who's this cute, little guy? What's his name?"

Kirk fumbled his words, "Ummmm…I, ah. Well, actually, he doesn't have one yet."

Dorothy stood up. "Well, then. We'll need to work on that. Everyone deserves a name." She knelt back down to the dog and her cleavage didn't go unnoticed by Kirk, who was trying hard not to stare, but the truth was he was mesmerized by her natural beauty. Old Jack noticed Kirk and simply smiled.

Dorothy took the mutt's fuzzy jowls in her hands again. "Maybe Toto. That's a good name, now, isn't it?" She turned to look up at her uncle before standing back up.

"You'd better hurry before Jackson mixes the wrong chemicals together and starts a fire or something."

"Yes, of course. I'll be right along."

Dorothy stood. "See you later," she remarked to Kirk, giving him a wink and a wave as she turned to leave.

Kirk, mesmerized by her pirate's smile and with a dumb, childish grin on his face, involuntarily raised a hand and remarked softly, "Yeah, see you later." He took a step or two in her direction as she exited the front door. After she disappeared out into the parking lot and the door slowly closed, he stood staring at the empty space for a moment. Old Jack stood behind at the bay, still smiling to himself.

While staring at the closed door, hoping she'd come back for anything, Kirk inquired, "How long did you say it would take to fix my boat?"

Old Jack rocked on his heels with his hands tucked in his coat pockets. With a smirk remaining beneath his facial hair, he responded softly, but with delight, "Oh, a while…"

Kirk turned back, the same dumb smile still on his face as he strolled over to Jack.

Old Jack turned to look out at the bay. Gazing up at the clear blue sky, his smile turned down when his attention was redirected, and he spotted another one lumbering in his direction along the old sidewalk of the canal. Kirk noticed it too, sticking his neck out and peering out the bay doors.

Turning back to Kirk, Old Jack smiled again as he removed a hand from his pocket and motioned, "I don't suppose you'd mind..?"

The End..?

MOVIE NEWS
EXCLUSIVE

QUEEN CRUISES AGAIN!

The iconic vessel the African Queen is located in Key Largo Florida. Made famous in the 1951 movie of the same name starring Humphrey Bogart and Katherine Hepburn she still remains a timeless classic. This famous steamboat is available for daily canal cruises in the Port Largo Canal area and also for private events.

The African Queen was built in Lytham, England in 1912 for service in Africa for the East Africa British Railways company. She was used to shuttle cargo, missionaries and hunting parties across the Victoria Nile and Lake Albert which was located on the border between the Belgian Congo and Uganda. In 1951 she starred in the famous movie directed by John Huston. Afterwards she remained in service in Africa until 1968 when she was brought to the United States working in San Francisco, Oregan and Florida. She has been the pride and joy of Key Largo since 1982, where she is registered as a National Historic site and in 2012 celebrated her centennial year.

ABOUT THE AUTHOR

David Wilson was born on Halloween day in Bangor, Maine in the late 1960s. His life has been spent living in Maine to this day. Having retired from a long career in public safety, when he made the decision to become an author it only made sense to him that along with his memoir and Maine humor novels, that he also pencil a book in the genre of horror as well.

There's No More Room in Hell, a story of a man surviving on his own after a global pandemic that spirals out of control, is David's second novel in the horror genre. His first being the psychological horror/thriller about a man that ends up in hell after being execute for crimes he committed entitled, *Last Stop, Ground Floor.*

* 9 7 9 8 2 1 8 2 6 3 2 5 6 *